SILVERFALL

(RAVEN CURSED BOOK 2)

MCKENZIE HUNTER

McKenzie Hunter

Silverfall

© 2019, McKenzie Hunter

McKenzieHunter@McKenzieHunter.com

ISBN: 978-1-946457-05-9

ACKNOWLEDGMENT

Each time I finish a book, I reflect on how many people directly and indirectly helped me and I'm always humbled by it. I'm forever grateful to my friends and family for their encouragement, support, and making sure I leave my writing cave (also known as my office). Thank you to my beta readers: Robyn Mather, Sherrie Simpson Clark, and Stacey Mann, who gave so freely of their time and offered incredible constructive feedback. Elizabeth Bracker, my PA, no words will adequately express how much I appreciate you and your gift of making authoring much easier. I can't thank you enough. To my author friends: Annette Marie and Bilinda Sheehan, I'm grateful for all the help you provide and being there when I need you.

Meredith Tenant and Therin Knite, I appreciate your hard work and dedication to helping me improve my stories. They are better because of you. Thank you Orina, for my beautiful cover. I love it.

If it weren't for my readers, I wouldn't be able to do this for a living. I am grateful that you chose to follow Erin through her adventure. You're the best. 😊

CHAPTER 1

The empty bottle of white wine that I dropped in the garbage clinked loudly against the bottle of whisky I finished a couple hours before. It joined the bottle of red wine I'd started that morning at a time I considered acceptable for day drinking.

"That didn't help," I muttered after filling my water bottle and taking a drink. My body was in desperate need of hydration. Nearly twenty-four hours of drinking wasn't a good thing and it didn't help the problem.

"I need to find out if they're my birth parents." Just saying it aloud felt wrong. This had to be a bad dream.

My parents might not be my birth parents.

It shouldn't have been a surprise and yet it was. The signs were there, and I had ignored them. My parents'—or rather my mother's—magic never mirrored mine. I never expected it from my dad; he's human. But my mother was a half-mage. Half death mage. Half Raven Cursed. There should have been some similarities.

I recalled her look of sorrow and helplessness during the years I spent struggling to control my magic. I assumed it was because she couldn't help her daughter manage her magic the way she had. My father's look was simply one of bleak sympathy. But what if what I was seeing was regret for adopting me? I shuddered at the thought but quickly pushed it aside. No, they didn't regret taking me in as their daughter.

It felt like it had been more than twenty-four hours since Mephisto told me he suspected that I was the daughter of Malific, a god of chaos and destruction. Malific was stuck in the Veil while her army remained cursed and forced to live outside the Veil. They'd made it their sole purpose to remove the curse, return to the Veil, and release Malific from the prison she was deservedly confined to.

"The Raven," I whispered. Not *a* raven or Raven Cursed. *The* Raven. There was importance to that title, although I had no idea what or why. Malific wasn't known as The Raven, just the god of destruction. The look on Mephisto's face continued to haunt me. Guarded and speculative, and in that moment something had changed between us. But what?

A knock at the door pulled me from my thoughts. I gulped down the water in the bottle and refilled it before taking a quick look in the mirror near the console by the door. My ponytail looked exactly as messy as it should considering the few seconds I spent on it. My brown eyes were brighter than might be expected of a person who'd spent most of the last day and a half drinking and drunkenly ruminating.

Taking a deep breath before answering the door, I vowed to address the situation with my parents. I hated liminal periods. Unfortunately, my life was becoming a series of them: The woman who didn't know how to control her magic, to the woman who killed for magic. The woman who was considered Raven Cursed, to the woman who was considered to be The Raven. The woman who had never heard of the Veil, to the woman who effortlessly moved through it. The woman who desired the *Mystic Souls* book that could give her access to magic, to the woman who—

compliments of the Alpha of the Northwest Pack—would have access to it. The woman who was once the daughter of Vera and Gene, to possibly being the daughter of Malific and a god—or demigod.

In a matter of days, my life had changed so dramatically it was unrecognizable.

Opening the door for Asher, my attention immediately went to the leather-bound book pressed to his chest.

He has the book. He has the Mystic Souls.

My heart pounded and my breathing quickened at the sight of it.

"No matter how often it happens, I'm always flattered when a woman is this excited to see me."

Ugh, this guy. I rolled my eyes. "Well, of course, especially if you're offering them priceless gifts. I'm sure the response is quite different when all you're offering them is you," I countered.

The insult rolled off him like he had on a repellent, the haughty half-smile continuing to lift the corners of his lips.

Ever aware of his assessing gaze, I moved aside to let him in. Clutching the worn brown leather-bound book even closer to him, he entered. Gilded words ran along the book's spine. A robust peppery scent wafted off it. Magic from it feathered over me.

He handed me the book and I spent several minutes examining it, my fingers running over its discolored edges. Some of the pages were beginning to fray. It looked neglected.

He got the book. I couldn't believe it. I couldn't pretend that I hadn't been skeptical and believed that the only thing he was more full of than his ego was his crap. It was good to be wrong.

His chestnut-brown hair was mussed ever so slightly from doing what he was doing at the moment, running his fingers through it. Something he did often. He went on to do something else he did often too: pose. Why was he always striking a goddamn pose? Could he not manage to be around anyone without giving them a full, unobstructed view of something he thought was worth looking at? It was, but the quirk of his lips ensured I'd never give him the satisfaction of knowing I thought it.

"Your fear and anxiety reeks," he announced with a grimace, finally abandoning his pose and plopping down on the sofa.

"Thanks. Because smelling people isn't gross and creepy enough, you insult them, too," I snarked back, putting a few more inches between us. It didn't matter. He could scent me from across the room.

"I can still smell you under it and as usual, it's delightful."

"Well, that's not weird at all and don't let anyone tell you otherwise."

The deep chuckle reverberated in his chest, a pleasant, sonorous sound that should have lifted my mood.

He grew serious—predatory enough that my eyes went to each place in my apartment where I had a weapon hidden, calculating which one I could get to first. "What are you afraid of, Erin?" His tone had dropped to a low measure, deep and commanding.

"It's been a rough couple of days," I admitted. He wouldn't get any more than that. I couldn't give him any more than that. Careful, intense dark eyes continued to study me. I returned to examining the book. Discreetly I inhaled its scent, taking in aged oak with low notes of pepper. A peculiar smell that I rather enjoyed, or maybe it's what it represented that I found so exhilarating.

Asher's smile widened. "I see that I've pleased you," he teased seductively. "I never thought that would happen."

"Yes, I am quite pleased," I responded in a tone that mirrored his, giving in to the smile he gave me.

I flipped through the pages, relieved when the first few

pages were in English intermingled with spells in Latin. I became increasingly anxious as I continued to turn the pages and found some spells in Greek, then toward the end, Arabic and three other languages I couldn't determine. Cursing under my breath, I flipped the pages back and forth. Of course things couldn't be simple. I would have to have the pages translated by someone I trusted.

"Erin." Asher's voice was raised, getting my attention, which apparently was something he'd been trying to do for the past few minutes. "The book must be returned in two weeks. It's just a loan."

Fine. Good luck getting it back. I still had library books I hadn't returned. I merely nodded and kept my comments to myself. Feeling the weight of his attention on me, the book secured against my chest as if he knew my plans and would take it from me.

"I need more time."

"I'd love to give you more time, but I can't."

Noting the wily glint in his eyes, I asked, "Does the person who had this book know that they are no longer in possession of it?"

"Do you want the book or not?"

Two weeks. There was so much in it. It was a time crunch.

"I don't really have any other choice, do I?"

He shrugged. The casual amusement drained from his face and his eyes grew fierce and hard—a reminder that he was a shapeshifter. "You *can* turn it down. If it were my property to give, you would have it. I owe you that much. But it's not, and there will be severe consequences if it's not returned. Bring the book back in two weeks."

If Asher was saying there would be severe consequences, then I would take heed. Not many people could make me do that.

Resting back on the sofa, his fingers clasped behind his

head, he regarded me with an unwavering stare. "I caused the increased heart rate and respiration—and I'm quite proud of that. The fear and the worry I didn't cause. Who or what did, Erin?"

Clutching the book to my chest like a security blanket, I shook my head. "Nothing."

He inhaled the air. "The lingering smell of wine and whiskey tells a different story. That's not 'nothing,' Erin. I'm a very resourceful man, maybe I can help."

He fixed me with a hard stare he probably reserved for his pack. It was the undeniable look of a man used to people responding to his requests.

"Nothing," I repeated.

"Erin, why must you be so stubborn? Have I not earned your trust?"

I choked on the laughter. "No, I don't trust you. Asher, no one trusts you but your pack. I'm sorry, Mr. Alpha CEO of Northwest Wolf Pack. The moment my situation or problems compromise them or put them at risk, I'll have track marks on my back from the bus that ran over me."

His knowing smirk made his way to his eyes that danced with sly amusement. Amusement I didn't share. "Erin." He purred my name. "Does it involve my pack?"

"No."

"Then let me help you."

I finally nodded and took a seat on the ottoman in front of the sofa. "Okay," I started in a grave whisper, "I have a pushy Alpha in my home who won't take no for an answer. We have a tumultuous past, so I don't really trust the bastard, but for some strange reason he wants me to. Can you get rid of him? I'd be ever so grateful."

Leaning in, he placed his face just inches from mine. A small smile quirked his lips, and warm breath brushed against my lips. Shifters didn't have active magic, which was a shame, because I would have loved to blame the little tingle that moved over my arms on that. "Of course. Whatever Erin wants, it is my pleasure to give."

Coming to his feet in a sweep of grace and stealth, he still seemed amused, like I'd inadvertently given him something. I'd seen his sleight of hand at work during the several jobs I'd worked with him. Despite knowing it was impossible for him to do it, I still slid my hands over the sides of my leggings and patted at my shirt to see if anything was missing.

My hand was on the door handle when he added, "I wouldn't be late returning it." The hint of threat in his voice had me whipping around to respond.

"Why does everyone claim to be a badass but tiptoe around threats? Just say what you mean."

He reached past me and opened the door. "Erin, two weeks isn't a suggestion, it's a firm date."

He looked at his watch, committing the time to memory, and so did I when I looked at the clock on the kitchen stove.

"You'll get it in two weeks," I confirmed.

CHAPTER 2

*G*oing through the book on the ottoman would fill my day and also give me an excuse to avoid the inevitable talk with my parents. Should I just blurt it out? "Hey, did you all know I'm not your kid and am possibly the offspring of a god who created an army and pretty much likes to destroy people and things for sport? How's your day?"

I plopped back on the sofa, resting my head and focusing on one thing: I didn't accumulate any debt with Asher to get the *Mystic Souls*, despite Cory's conviction that acquiring it would come with a heavy debt owed to the Northwest Pack. It's better to live life debt free, and even better when debt free from the pack. No, no debt, just a time restriction.

Cory knocked once and opened the door. His gaze immediately went to the book, a gasp escaping him as he looked down at it. Something he considered a fable, a work of fiction, a legend, was right in front of him. The weathered, sun-damaged pages were marked by Post-Its I had started inserting, noting the spells in English and Latin that I was aware of.

"So," he started off slowly, picking up the book, "it's not

an urban legend." He thumbed through the book, his brow furrowing at the same places I had—the languages I couldn't identify.

"What languages are these?" he asked, pointing to the last sections of the book.

I had no idea. Nor did Google.

"It could be anything."

I hadn't told Cory about my conversation with Mephisto the day before—or who Mephisto suspected my mother to be. I was still processing it. But the existence of the Veil opened up innumerable possibilities, including the fact that the people who lived there could have their own languages.

"Erin," Cory stated after an hour or so of us both looking through the book, "these spells seem really dangerous." He had studied it carefully, occasionally using his phone to translate some of the contents.

So it isn't just me. A quick perusal had shown many curses that addressed the death of a person or loss of a limb, restrictions of speech and function, and there were several cloaking spells I hadn't learned. I wrote them down for future use. Cory copied down one that allowed flight and a few elemental control spells and a lighting spell. We came to an abrupt stop at one spell that raised and controlled the recently deceased. That was definitely illegal. Necromancers weren't allowed to do that. There had been a political decision to ease the concerns of humans. Vampires were the only interaction with the dead that humans would tolerate.

I don't know why I thought archaic magic would be safe. Not just powerful.

"Well, this one seems simple and safe." I pointed at one. Cory stood behind the sofa, looking at the book from over my shoulder.

"Simple is good and safe is even better," Madison piped as she walked into the apartment. Her smile held the tightness of apprehension and disbelief. I'm sure it had been there since I called her this morning to let her know I had the *Mystic Souls*. Surprise shone in her eyes as she looked at the book. Her lips formed a small O.

"Not all the spells are simple and most of them aren't safe, and those are just the ones I can decipher," Cory admitted. Turning the book in her direction, he showed her the last quarter of the book.

Frowning, she leafed through the pages. "This language"—she pointed at the spells whose language we couldn't identify—"is an archaic language that witches and mages used for spells before adopting Latin." She paused, looking contemplative. "I'm sure these spells would work for finding a workaround, but they won't lift the curse. I don't know if lifting the curse is even possible. Which is fine. You just don't want people to lose their life so you can use their magic."

It was true. I needed magic to fill that never-ending void where magic should be. To have access to something that should be rightfully mine.

"I'd prefer to remove the curse," I admitted. "Spells can be undone, performed incorrectly, or even restricted. Removing the curse makes it permanent."

Madison was pacing the room, her hand absently moving to her hair to fidget with it and being reminded that her full coils of sienna hair were gone, replaced by darker, straighter hair, in an effort to give her a more mature look. In her jeans and button-down, it was another reminder that despite our parents' best efforts to raise us like sisters, we were polar opposites. Not only in personality but also looks. I'd never be accused of being cute, my features too sharp and defined for that. Sexy, maybe. It depended on who you were asking. But Madison's enviable balance between fit and curvy on a five-seven frame put her in the sexy *and* cute category.

"We're working on the assumption that a witch cursed a mage, right? That's the story we all know. A mage and witch were feuding, as they always do." She stopped to give Cory a reprimanding look, because he was willing to continue the feud, spurred by the need to be considered the superior of the two magic-wielders. I still didn't understand the rivalry between witches and mages, or their distancing themselves from each other as if there were a stark difference in their magic—there wasn't. Just different names for the same: a mage who could make spells and perform them with efficiency was called a spellcaster, a witch a spellweaver. The difference in what they did? Absolutely nothing. Daring to point that out only earned an unrequested history lesson about their origins, which were from the same god but different sisters. It was exhausting listening to it.

Madison continued. "The mage Caspian took the feud too far and killed a witch while she was transformed."

"She'd taken on the form of a raven," Cory offered. "Using a transformation spell. We know that. The witch cursed Caspian and his bloodline to never have magic without the penalty of death."

Raven Cursed. A line of mages who come from a cursed bloodline. Mages don't claim us, so we might as well be our own denizen group.

"This is where I feel there's a piece missing," Madison offered. "Everything we know about witches' magic doesn't support this. If the curse wasn't done by a witch but by a Caste?" She looked at both of us in turn. "There were so many Caste until fifty years ago when the Immortalis started to kill them off. If the Caste can only do their curses as a coven, then there aren't enough of them left to remove the curse."

Madison was back to pacing again. This had to be something she'd been working on since she found out about the Caste. How long had she wondered about this—about me? "Caste are the only ones who can remove their curses," she said. "And their magic is archaic. Magic, like anything, evolves."

I looked away, not because of her hypothesis but because I wasn't ready to tell her that my magic was different because I might not be Raven Cursed. I could be something different altogether.

"Then that means it can never be removed?" It came out sounding more hopeless than I intended. I was fine trying to treat the symptom and not the problem, but I had been hopeful that *Mystic Souls* would remove it. Break the curse and make me whole.

"I could be wrong. I'm sure I am. We just need to find something in the book that will do it." Madison's false optimism wasn't fooling anyone. "If we can't remove the curse, so what? If we can get you magic without you killing anyone, isn't that what we want?"

Giving her a smile, weighted by the knowledge that it might not work because of what and who I might really be, I said, "It's what we want."

After an hour and a half, we were only a little less than a quarter of the way through the book, scrutinizing each spell to make sure we didn't miss anything. Some wording was early modern English and some old English.

We'd culled only four spells from that hour and a half of work.

But just seeing the four spells lifted a heaviness that had burdened me. Whether the curse remained or not, at least we had found a way to circumvent it. There was a light at the end of the tunnel. Tomorrow, I could have my own magic without anyone ever having to die or be put in the state of in-between. Cory would no longer have to loan me his magic. Distracted by the prospect, I zoned out but was pulled back to the present when Madison coaxed the book from my hands.

"I still can't believe you have it," she said, leafing through the pages.

"Just for two weeks," I reminded her. She closed the book, keeping one finger in it as a placeholder for a spell she had been returning to throughout the session. It was an earth restoration spell. As an earth fae, she destroyed flora whenever she borrowed from them. Although she didn't seem to have a profound connection to the process, she had a look of discontent whenever she had to do it. I suspected that she, like me, was looking for a way to restore what she killed.

Her thumb ran along the worn leather. It was supposed to be inconspicuous, but I noticed her lean in and inhale, basking in the magic that emanated from the book.

"Asher got this for you?" she asked, her raised brow and tight lips showing her mistrust of him and the likelihood of him having used unscrupulous tactics to get hold of the book.

"I'm placing my bets on theft," Cory asserted.

"Why would he steal it for me?"

"I don't think he stole it *for you*. He stole it just to see if he could. He loaned it to you to get off your crap-list, and I suspect he's going to hire you for a job that is guaranteed to involve shady dealings."

"Now you're just showing your biases against him," I said, although there was doubtless some truth to his words.

"Well, I have to admit, Asher's reach is very long and quite impressive," Madison said.

"I'm sorry, Maddie." Cory grinned at the dagger-sharp look she shot him for calling her Maddie. "You said 'Asher is a thief' incorrectly."

"How do you know he didn't borrow it?" I challenged. I couldn't believe I was defending Asher, although I said it in hope as much as in his defense. I hoped the book was borrowed and that if we weren't able to get through all the spells, I'd have another opportunity with the book at a later time. Though I guess the same could be true if he had stolen it.

A small smile settled on Madison's lips as she listened to Cory and me debating the circumstances that led to Asher gaining possession of the book. Cory wasn't ready to rule out theft. I had settled on it being an attempt to make amends for betraying me.

"If he didn't steal it, why didn't he answer your question?" There was a rigid scowl on Cory's face.

"Let's say that he stole—"

"He did," Cory interrupted. "No need to give him the benefit of the doubt."

"He allegedly stole it. We have it now and there's nothing we can do about the alleged theft right now. Let's just do the spells and return it to him, and it will be his problem."

Madison deliberated over the last few pages of the book, her face twisted in concentration. "I think I might be able to interpret these pages. It looks like Akkadian or close to it."

Cory sputtered. "Close to it. We're dealing with a rare archaic book that most people believe is just a legend, and we're going to wing a spell because it 'seems like' or is 'close to'? Am I the only person who wants to be absolutely sure that we're lifting a curse and not conjuring something that might have cataclysmic results? Like this one." He took the book from Madison and flipped through a few pages to where he'd left pink Post-Its to mark spells we had no intention of trying.

"This one's worded nicely, but if you didn't know Latin really well, you wouldn't know that it's a demon summoning spell." He flipped a couple of pages. "This one here is a death spell." He flipped to another in French. "A cursory glance at this one and it appears to bind you to the person who evokes the spell. Binding isn't necessarily a bad thing, but the way this one reads, the person's life force is used for the magic. Do the magic enough, and it's certain death for the bound."

Cory spoke Spanish fluently and knew Italian and had picked up French from conversations between me and Madison in an effort to prevent us having our "secret" language. We all knew Latin well. If you were going to work with spells, it was a good language to know.

After three hours we had culled all the spells that we felt confident we had translated properly. My tomorrow could look very different. *Or it could be the same,* I reminded myself. I needed to be realistic, but I couldn't totally suppress the flush of optimism that kept rearing its head.

Our search only yielded nine spells. Two were to remove the curse, and the other seven were to prevent a donor being placed in a death state and sharing their magic.

"Borrow magic from me," Madison suggested once the spells had been divided into the two groups. We'd decided to start with the ones we deemed the simplest and safest. Madison then directed her attention to Cory. "You're a great spellweaver. If there are problems, you can intervene."

I'd never borrowed magic from Madison, and the thought of doing so felt heretical. Or maybe it was the ensuing guilt that would overcome me if the thought of keeping her magic crossed my mind even for a microsecond. It would, I knew. It did with Cory, despite my knowing I could never exchange his life for magic. My craving and need existed, and tamping it down was an ongoing struggle.

Please let this work. I didn't want this to ever be an issue again.

My lips were gripped between my teeth, unwilling to commit to the idea, so instead of speaking, I simply nodded.

We prepared all the ingredients for the spell, and

Madison handed me an opaque-looking stone to boost my magic.

"External sources of magic don't work," I said, reminded of a bounty, a vampire who had stolen an illegal magic object that gave him the ability to use magic. I hadn't been able to use the magic.

Madison tossed the stone aside, a weak smile lifting the corner of her lips. This was just another reminder of the complexity of my magic. If I were actually Malific's daughter, Madison didn't know half of the complexities. I pushed the idea aside. I wasn't Malific's daughter. I refused to believe it until I had more information. For now, it was just speculation.

Madison lay down on the floor a few feet from me, waiting for me. It took several moments before I advanced and hovered a few inches from her, preparing to say the words of power, to divest the magic from her. But I hesitated. I couldn't do it.

After years of coveting it but resisting, it seemed so wrong to take it now that she was offering. I didn't want to see her in any state of in-between. She'd taken too many risks for me.

"She'll be fine," Cory whispered next to me. He raised his voice. "Won't you, Sleeping Beauty?"

Madison opened one eye. "It's always fairytales with you," she teased.

"Sure, latch on to the fairytale part and not the compliment? *Beauty.* Nice." He chuckled.

"Thank you, Cory, for the wonderful compliment. Those are the words that will carry me for a lifetime and raise my spirit on down days. Brighten my days when the sun refuses to shine. Bring a smile to my lips each time I think of them. Oh, wonderful one, I appreciate the compliments you bestow on me." Madison winked at me.

"That's more like it. How hard was that?" he said, flashing

her a grin and placing a light kiss on her cheek. He was the only person who could get away with that.

Madison shut her eyes again and I hovered a couple of inches from her, inhaling the gentle breeze of magic that wafted from her, earth and lilac. As I started to say the words of power my body tensed. Magic curled around me like a blanket. It felt so different than Cory's, yet so familiar.

We had debated on which spell to try and eventually settled on the one that seemed the easiest, in which she would keep her magic and not stay in-between. If the spell worked, she'd wake and we'd both have her magic.

Not wanting her to be in-between for too long, I quickly went to *Mystic Souls* and did the invocation. The room became heavy with magic, a dull and gloomy pall filling the space. The temperature dropped so low, I could see my breath. Goosebumps formed along my arms. Dark and dolorous magic overtook me, and a sense of foreboding became an unbearable weight.

Cory and I waited patiently for Madison to get up. But she didn't. She no longer had the peaceful look she had just moments before. And her body became too rigid. Something was wrong.

A trickle of blood ran down her face like tears, then a trail of blood came from her nose.

"Bring her back!" Cory commanded. I said the words of power to return her magic. But nothing happened. Fear wrenched in me when I felt the tug in my chest that told me the person I borrowed magic from was slipping away to the other side. Madison would die and I would have her magic.

I was killing her. I said the spell again with no success. I kept saying it over and over until my voice was raw and reedy. I tossed the *Mystic Souls* aside and pressed my lips to hers and said the words of power again. And again. Nothing.

Out of reflex Cory started to administer CPR.

"That won't work," I yelled. Again, I repeated the words of

power, over and over like a prayer, my lips pressed so hard against hers the words were muffled. It was as if the proximity would give me more power. It didn't. Her body was losing heat.

"Say the spell again. Not your power words. Say the spell and add 'Rescindo,'" Cory urged. Leaping up to get the book I'd tossed aside, I flipped to the page, taking little care when turning the pages. This book was dangerous. It should be destroyed. Every page should be ripped from it and set aflame.

I said the words as quickly as I could. A sharp tide of air swept through the room. Madison lurched up, running her fingers over her face. There was horror in her eyes as she looked at her bloodied fingers.

"I'm so sorry," I said, my voice quivering, tears blurring my vision. "I'm sorry, I'm so sorry . . ." I repeated it so many times my voice became rough and dry.

"It's okay." I could tell she was trying to make her voice sprightlier than she felt. She kept blinking her eyes and wiping them until Cory gave her a damp cloth. When she was done Cory lifted her chin and examined her eyes.

"How's your vision?" he asked.

She blinked several times until finally her eyes were clear. Cory took the damp cloth from her and softly blotted her face, removing all traces of blood.

Finally he rested his forehead against hers. Madison was strangely calm, and I wasn't sure if it was for my benefit to keep me from panicking.

"That's not what I expected," she eventually said.

"That's not what anyone expected," I said, closing the book and putting it on the table.

"Are we done?"

"Of course we're done. I . . . I don't trust the spells in that book. That was the simplest one, and there's no way I'll put you or any of us through that again. I just won't."

"That was one spell. One attempt. We should try again. Just one more."

"What if that's the one that kills you? No. I can't ask you to take that risk. I . . . I just can't." The blood tears streaming from her eyes, the trail of blood from her nose, and her lying lifeless in front of me flashed through my mind. It wasn't worth it. I wasn't going to put her through that again, and it was heartbreaking that she wanted to do this to give me access to magic, change my life.

"No, we're done with it," I said flatly. My hope died with the words. A few days ago, *Mystic Souls* was just one of my two options. Now, as I recalled the emotional distance Mephisto had put between us, I wasn't sure if the other option remained.

I looked from Madison to *Mystic Souls*, feeling the weight of despair settling back on me. I was back where I started. Now I needed to look for an alternative. There were always other options. I hoped.

Cory and I were fearful of lingering side effects from the spell, but Madison didn't hold the same concern and had to be urged to stay. When she finally agreed to spend the night, we ordered pizza.

Cory and I munched on a meat lover's with extra cheese, but I couldn't help the eye roll I gave his salad. As if a bowl of lettuce could undo the damage our cheesy meat goodness had done to his diet. Cory split his attention between turning his nose up in derision at Madison's cheese and black olives pizza and studying the *Mystic Souls*. He placed another sticky note as a placeholder in the book and closed it.

"How is that even a food people eat?" he huffed out. Madison's typical pizza order seemed to become more offensive each time she ordered it in his presence. It was very weird for him to have such a strong opinion about it, but Cory seemed insulted to his core by her culinary blasphemy. Madison simply locked eyes with him and took another large bite, causing him to cringe.

"Are we really going to have this debate each time we order pizza?" Madison asked.

"If he hasn't stopped by now, he's not going to. I'm not sure how black olives wronged him, but I wish they would apologize. We all have our quirks, and this is his."

"It's not a quirk. Who wakes up one day and says, 'I think I'll mess up a cheese pizza by putting olives on it'?"

Madison's response was to take another bite, eating it slowly and obviously savoring it. With a sound of disgust Cory turned away and resumed studying *Mystic Souls*.

"He's so easy to rile," she whispered.

"I never thought olives would be such a controversial topic."

"It is when you're doing it wrong!" Cory said.

He mumbled a few more scathing remarks about the pizza before returning his attention to the book. I'd lost all interest in it, but Cory was curious to find a spell that would allow him to enter the Veil.

"I think this spell will open it," he announced. He read aloud. It seemed easy enough but so had the others.

With the book in hand, he moved away from us into a corner.

"Cory, don't," I pleaded.

The set of his jaw was enough for me to know he wasn't going to listen to reason. Curiosity and his desire to experience a world not available to many overrode logic. Or maybe he wanted to see the beautiful world I had described. I couldn't blame him for wanting to get a glimpse.

"Remember, Mephisto was guiding me when I did it."

"I'm not going to go in, I just want to see it. Just the opening, to know that it's real."

20

"I told you it's real. Isn't that enough?"

He huffed. "Fine. I want to see it, too."

He sorted through his bag of ingredients, pulling things out, while Madison and I gave each other sidelong looks.

A golden flare of light briefly obscured our vision. A powerful gust of wind tore through the room, then a pale golden shimmer rose and fell. The scent of red currant misted the air. But after the initial display, there was nothing. The Veil never revealed itself. No bright new beautiful worlds came into our scope. Just moments of nothingness. But I'd take that over what happened earlier.

The silence thinned as Cory flipped through the book and Madison joined me in discouraging him.

Darkness suddenly claimed the room, making it appear duskier than outside. A white pool of light flashed in the middle of the room followed swiftly by a loud boom that could only be my door being blasted open. Magic that I couldn't identify inundated the air.

I switched the lights on and, as I suspected, the door was off its hinges.

"You didn't open the Veil, but you did let something out," I said, assessing the damage. *But who, or what?*

The noise brought my neighbor Ms. Harp out of her apartment. She gave a sweeping look at the splintered wood littering the hall and my destroyed door, glowered, and shook her head before returning to her apartment. I deserved that. If only I could get her to come into my apartment to give Cory the same castigating look.

Cory and Madison were staring at the middle of the room where the bright white light had been. I couldn't bring myself to say "I told you so" because regret had put a worrisome crease on his face.

"What did I do?" he asked softly.

"Nothing we can't fix." My voice held more confidence than I felt. But I needed it. He didn't, and neither did

Madison who was still staring speculatively at the space where the light show and shimmer had taken place. I could see her need to fix things that were "Erin" or even "Erin adjacent." But nothing could be done.

Magic leaves a fingerprint. This was definitely magic, although I couldn't identify it. Fae, witch, mage; or even an "other". They all lived in the Veil. For all I knew it could have been a god. Malific? No, she couldn't be here. She was in the Veil, imprisoned by an Omni ward.

CHAPTER 3

*I*t had been three days since Cory had released the unknown from the Veil, and even the shifter Madison called couldn't track the scent. This was worrisome, especially when he said the trail had just disappeared. Trails didn't just disappear unless the person Wynded. I suspected the visitor couldn't Wynd, because that would have been the preferred mode of transportation rather than destroying my door.

Madison hadn't reported any suspicious activity over the past few days, but it was difficult to not think about it. My uneasiness intensified under Asher's overt suspicion when I returned the book yesterday. It lingered as I made my way to my car, and I could still feel the weight of it as I backed out of his driveway.

I simply told Asher I didn't need the book anymore, making an effort to keep the conversation as evasive and succinct as possible without giving him an opportunity to determine if I lied.

The unknown couldn't be dealt with, so I had to focus on what could—getting released from therapy.

Is there such a thing as spite therapy? I wondered. Because there wasn't anything remotely therapeutic about what was happening with Dr. Sumner. We sat in stilted silence while I sipped on my second cup of coffee from his Keurig.

The office had changed. Thick, room-darkening curtains were drawn. The fire extinguisher that I used to ward off the attack was closer to him—actually there were two now. The attaché case he kept on his desk was also closer to him, open and tilted against the chair. I'm sure that would make it easier to retrieve whatever weapon he had stored in it. An obsidian-colored stone was on the side table. Magic wafted off it—witch's magic, although I had no idea what it was for. I assumed it was like the electric pellets I used as a distraction. It didn't feel like a Crelic, which gave magical ability to non-magic wielders.

Seeing my interest in the stone, he picked it up, taking in the heft of it. "When it comes in contact with a hard surface, it creates a fire." Ah, just like my electric pellet, but a bigger distraction. His tone was stiff and guarded, completely unlike his usual relaxed tone with its hints of aversion and judgment.

"I'm sorry about what happened during the last session," I said.

"It's not your fault. Your life seems to lend to such things. Do you mind telling me why?" There was true curiosity in his face and his voice. He took off his Clark Kent glasses, giving me a full view of the ocean-blue eyes, softened by his intrigue. And perhaps even concern. Noticing my staring, he quickly slipped the glasses back on.

"Why what?"

"Wouldn't life be simpler if you totally emerged yourself in your humanity, ignored magic and the problems that come with that world?"

I'd cured him of his inane curiosity with the supernatural world. That had to count for something. Now he was back to being a Nike commercial. Just Do It.

"I don't think that's a possibility. Even more so now." Maybe this wasn't spite therapy but a disturbing game of chicken. I unloaded on him, dousing him with the frigid water of my reality to see if I could get him to bail on me, dismiss me from therapy because he didn't want to be bothered anymore.

I explained the Veil to him, the Immortalis being a creation of the god who might be my mother, how I got hold of the *Mystic Souls* and nearly killed Madison, and that going into the Veil to retrieve a mysterious box for Mephisto was now my only chance to get magic and, based on my last interaction with Mephisto, that might not even be an option anymore.

He listened intently to the deluge of information. As he mulled over it, scribbling on his notepad, I took another sip from my cup of coffee before lying back on the sofa. If he could wear a sports jacket with the accompanying elbow patches and his Clark Kent glasses, then I could lie on the sofa and complete the clichéd scene.

My arm was folded over my face to block the ceiling lights. He went to the wall and dimmed them, giving the room a warmer feel. His voice matched the melancholic atmosphere in the room.

"If the *Mystic Souls* didn't work and your other source might not be an option, what are your plans?" He kept his voice neutral, but I knew he was just setting the groundwork for the next discussion. A world without magic. Learn to fight the urges. Maybe another push for medication or something he believes will subdue it. Take the office job that Madison offered me. Submit to an insipid and banal life.

I sat up and looked him firmly in the eyes. "I'll figure out something. There has to be another way. If Mephisto exists, I can't believe that there aren't others." There were others, the very men in his inner circle. The similarities between them made me believe it. It wasn't a coincidence that the exact same marking showed up on all of them when we went through the fire at Elizabeth's, the Woman in Black.

Dr. Sumner was really leaning into his role as "therapist" with his introspective look while rubbing the bridge of his nose. He set the glasses on the table, and before I could give him a second appraising look, replaced them on his face. I really needed to work on not letting everything I think show on my face. I wasn't ogling him, just noticing that my therapist was not bad to look at.

"Really, Clark Kent?" I said, getting a glimpse of the smirk that was threatening to emerge.

"Clark Kent?"

"You don't need them. They bother your nose, so it's silly to wear them."

He gave me a light chuckle and deliberately pushed them farther up his nose. "Let's talk about"—he peered at his notes —"Malific."

With his face professionally neutral, I couldn't read whether learning that gods lived among us—or just a slip into the Veil away—had shocked him. Or that I might be one.

"What do you want to know?"

"What do you plan to do with this information?"

"Nothing. I don't even know if it's true."

"You do. That's why you're here. It's the reason I didn't have to urge the information out of you. Erin, let's talk about it. You—"

"'can't fight your demons if you don't admit they're there.'" I finished his favorite tautology.

His lips puckered into a moue. "Exactly. You might not like what I say, but it doesn't make it any less true."

"I need to hear it from my parents. Right now, it's all speculation and assumptions."

"You don't trust the source?"

I did, and that was what was most difficult. I didn't want to believe it. Part of me was clinging to me just being a death mage. Raven Cursed. Looking for a way to have magic without anyone dying. Weird as it might sound, I missed the simplicity of that.

"When do you plan on talking to your parents?"

I shrugged and became distracted by his bookshelf. Used to me getting distracted, he was silent when I stood and strolled to his shelf, scanning the titles. I was shocked to see two spell books. They weren't anything worth looking at, easily found in one of the occultic bookstores owned by the witch covens. That was one of the ways witches made money. They had spell books and harmony candles, which weren't anything more than vanilla and lavender, but humans considered them enchanted because they were made by witches. That belief was something the witches cultivated by whispering an invocation over each candle that was sold.

Many humans liked to believe they had untapped magical ability and were just one spell away from unlocking it. Mages made several attempts to capitalize on that, but it never worked as well as with witches. Humans considered witches more mythical, which I believed was another source of contention between witches and mages. Movies and TV shows supported the mysterious witch persona, the Charmed one, the one the vampires turned to for help when all had failed. That badass-magic-wielding savior who came up with the right spell in the nick of time to save everything and everyone. Witches were magic-chic and they used it to make money.

"You know these are just basic spells and only brush the surface of what witches can do with their magic, right?"

"I know. But I'm curious and these are what I could get my hands on. It's harder than I thought to get a real magic book. But it's interesting, nonetheless."

I wondered how bad he wanted a *real* magic book. Enough to release me from therapy? He was human, he wouldn't be able to do anything with it, and I was sure Mr.

Responsibility wouldn't let it fall into the wrong hands. And such a book wouldn't contain dark spells or spells that most witches and mages didn't have access to. Protection of such books from the mainstream was an implicit responsibility of supernaturals. Giving him one wouldn't be breaking a law, just a social contract.

Pushing the idea aside, I shelved the magic book and continued to pull books off the shelves, perused them and re-shelved them.

"Erin, let's discuss *the incident*." His tone was firm.

"We discussed it. I give you my word, I told you everything. I borrowed his magic, left the room to practice, and didn't feel the signal that it was time to return it. The feeling can't be ignored . . ." I let my sentence drift into silence.

"If you ignore it, then it's intentional?"

I nodded my head once in answer. "It's not something you can miss. It's a raging signal, and if I miss the physical signs, I start to feel like I'm draped in darkness. Ignoring it is my choice."

"And he was dead, and you're missing time from that day?"

Admitting it once was difficult; twice was something I refused to do. Standing with the book I had been perusing pressed to my chest, I took in several long breaths, hoping they would chase the memories away. They didn't.

"Could someone have set you up?" His voice was so low, I strained to hear him. I re-shelved the book and returned to the sofa. Dr. Sumner leaned forward. Concern marred his face. Intense inquiring eyes bored into mine, rendering me speechless. I had never thought about that.

"There aren't many death mages or Raven Cursed or whatever. You seem to be stronger than most, and that's probably because you're a god or half . . . demigod. If the man who tried to abduct you knew what you were, could he have been the only one?"

The words didn't come immediately as I processed what he said. "There would have been an attempt before," I eventually said. I had been in enough situations that if someone wanted me dead or set up there would have been enough opportunities to do it.

He nodded his head slowly as he leaned back in his chair, fingers clasped behind his head. Several minutes passed before he spoke. "What if it wasn't you they cared about, but him? You were a means to an end. The mage who killed her host? You have a history of not having great control."

"Our time is up," I blurted, jumping to my feet. Before he could say anything else or offer any more theories, I left the room. The air outside wasn't cool enough or fresh enough. Asphalt and pollution stained the air. Food, car fumes, and city staleness flooded my senses. I didn't care. I sucked in a deep breath.

Despite being in the open air, I felt like I was suffocating. No, it wasn't a possibility. I hadn't been set up. I didn't go through all of it, have my face plastered on TV, jail, arraignment, plea bargains, and a stay in the Stygian because of a setup. I had screwed up and was paying the consequences.

"Erin." I turned to find Dr. Sumner just a few feet from me. His frown deepened. "We're on the same team. I want what's best for you. If you need to stay away from magic, then that's what I will recommend and help you do. If you find a way to get it without anyone dying, then that is an alternative for you. But if you're here because it was ordered for a crime you didn't commit, then the truth needs to be discovered."

"I . . . I . . ." I stammered over the words. "I don't think that's what happened." I was firmly sailing full speed toward a place of denial. After *the incident* I was convinced nothing could break me. Now I felt like I was one small bump from shattering. I hated the feeling.

"If we can prove it, you won't need to see me anymore

because you didn't do what brought you here in the first place," Dr. Sumner said softly, approaching me like he was dealing with a timid animal. He shoved his fingers through his hair, disheveling it. He huffed out a long breath, and compassionate eyes met mine. His nearly inaudible curse was uncharacteristic. At any other time, it would have made me laugh.

"I should have kept that to myself. Sorry." Then he muttered more curses. "We should have another appointment this week. Unless you can stay longer."

I shook my head and backed away to my car. "I'll call and make an appointment," I lied.

Most of my drive home was spent recalling that night. *The incident.* Going through what I could remember with new eyes. The dissection was interrupted by my phone ringing. Victoria. My eyes rolled but I took the call, wondering if the bonus she gave me was worth dealing with her melodrama.

CHAPTER 4

*A*pparently, the hour-long discussion I had with Victoria as she ranted about her disappointment with my bodyguarding capability wasn't enough. She needed to reiterate it in person once I arrived at Kelsey's that evening.

"You aren't taking your protection duties seriously, are you?" Hints of egotism and entitlement twined through her words and flitted over her beautifully distinctive features. Her scrutinizing gaze raked over me. My off-the-shoulder eggplant-colored shift dress garnered a miniscule smile of approval.

"At least you're taking discretion seriously," she said. Her lips pressed into a thin line. Running her fingers over the soft curls of her dark-brown hair, she demonstrated a poise and casual elegance even in her faux-distressed state that most couldn't pull off. I was one of the few who knew she was a Caste, magical wielders who historically were talented at curse casting. Interbreeding with humans and the Immortalis's assault on their race had diluted their power. Based on the way Victoria was behaving about my alleged dereliction of duty, you would have thought she was magicless. Her weak magic wouldn't protect her against the likes of the Immortalis, but she was hardly as defenseless as she'd have people believe. She leaned into the role of elegant, helpless restaurateur.

With Madison's new information, I was seeing Victoria and the magic she possessed through new eyes. There were so few Caste now, it wouldn't change my situation—they couldn't undo the curse. I remembered Simeon describing them as "too self-absorbed to care about more than themselves." If Caste had intervened on a witch's behalf, I couldn't help but wonder why. Had the mages gone too far feuding with the witches? Crossed the tacit boundaries one too many times, drawing their attention to the supernaturals? Did the Caste intervene for money? Or to repay a debt?

The more I considered Madison's theory, the more plausible it seemed. Caste had been mistaken for witches in the past. Probably given credit for their work as well. Then it dawned on me that maybe it was a Caste that had been killed and not a witch.

"Can you do a transformation spell?" I asked Victoria.

"Is that your answer? I'm to protect myself by turning into . . . what? A mouse, and scuttle away? A crow, and fly away from my problems and leave my life behind? A flea, and live in an animal's fur for the rest of my life? Is that what you propose I do, Erin?"

I propose that you take it down a notch. Someone please give her an Emmy, Tony, or whatever so she'll stop the performance.

"No, I don't want you to do any of that. I'm just curious about you and what your kind can do."

She grimaced, then a look of nostalgia momentarily passed over her face. "Not what we used to. We were revered." A cruel beauty breached her elegant façade. "And feared. People would seek us out, plead for our help. One curse and we could ruin lives. Now, my magic isn't enough to really protect myself. I can't even do a hex. There aren't enough of us left to do our typical curses, and our bloodline has been weakened to the point that I doubt even if I gathered all who remain we could do anything that resembled our ancestors' powers."

If it hadn't been for that glimpse into her adoration of being feared and what looked like an adoration for cruelty, I'd feel sorry for her.

"Do you know if you all had anything to do with cursing a mage by the name of Caspian?"

"Caspian, Caspian . . ." She repeated the name several times without appearing to recognize it.

"He was the original Raven Cursed. Punished for killing a witch when she wasn't in human form. She'd transformed into a raven. The witches were said to have cursed Caspian, but they aren't strong enough to perform a curse that would affect his entire bloodline. Do you know if the Caste intervened on the witches' behalf?"

"We never intervened in the petty quarrels of mages and witches. They're still at it. No, Caspian didn't kill a witch, he killed one of us. There wasn't any way that could go unpunished."

Again, I got a peek into the malice Caste were capable of. They might have been self-absorbed, but they weren't above vengeance. I sucked in a sharp breath.

"My grandmother told me stories of how the mages petitioned for only Caspian to be punished. The Caste agreed. You would have thought it would have stopped the animosity between witches and mages. After all, that's what led to his curse." She shrugged, making it quite evident she was done with our trek down memory lane.

She gave my attire another long sweeping look and then an approving nod. It didn't matter if she liked the dress or not, it was functional. It allowed my little weapons to be hidden on my body, along with the weapons I had in my purse.

33

Taking the calming breath I needed to deal with her, I let a few moments tick by before I spoke. "Victoria, the full moon was almost a week ago. You're hardly at risk of being taken. The Roboro gem was destroyed. I've checked all my sources; there aren't any more. You're safe. You really don't need me here."

She was safe, for now. I wasn't sure for how long, but Immortalis had been searching for fifty years for a way to get back into the Veil. I suspected it would be another fifty before they could, because I had destroyed the object they were going to use. Victoria wouldn't ever be completely safe because she was a descendent of the people who cursed the Immortalis. They would always need her blood to remove the curse but for now, she didn't have to worry about it.

"Well you need to be here because I'm getting a feeling."

I wouldn't be able to get out of bodyguarding duties because her spidey senses were tingling. Victoria wanted me to protect her, so it appeared that I'd be spending my evening at Kelsey's "guarding her," despite the conspicuous guards already in the restaurant.

She abruptly stopped pacing around her expansive Parisian-inspired office. The cream-colored writing desk she lightly rested her fingertips on was just a few shades deeper than the walls. The luxurious rug in the middle of the floor had the same soft coral, beige, and blue hues as her silk shirt. With people like Victoria, it wasn't hard to assume that her attire was deliberately chosen to exude the same effortless luxury, refined confidence, and importance as her office.

"For the past few days, it's felt like someone here has been watching me. I want you here just in case," she said, returning to clacking her three-inch heels over the hardwood floor.

For someone afraid of being abducted, it seemed like shoes she could run in would be the practical choice. But who was I to judge? No, I was judging.

"I don't like feeling like this," she went on. "I've had to hire protection for Pearl, too. Just in case they try to use her to get to me. I would hate someone to use my kitten against me."

You can give her a pretty little collar and call her a kitten all you like, she's still an apex predator. But sure, worry about your poor little kitty.

"She has claws and weighs a hundred pounds. I think she'll be fine." I attempted to sound assured but instead it came out derisive and condescending. Victoria shot me a narrowed glare. If she had the ability to curse, I probably would have earned it for that snide remark.

"She's eighty-five pounds and a defenseless kitten," she retorted.

Was she screwing with me? She had to be screwing with me, but seeing her distress I quickly realized she'd slipped into the land of delusion when it came to her cat.

"Of course. I understand. I'll stay here tonight and look around and then I'll have someone set up a Klipsen ward," I offered. Klipsens were expensive wards that required a lot of magic and several days to set up. While most wards could be disabled with magic, using a number of techniques, Klipsens were very difficult to disable and kept people from Wynding in.

To satisfy Victoria, I did another surveillance of the restaurant exterior and the patrons. Standing outside Kelsey's was a reminder of its exclusivity. The alabaster stone building stood out among the brown and tan buildings on the block. There were floor-to-ceiling windows in the front. A mere glimpse was all they afforded from the outside because strategically placed art gave the patrons privacy. If the swanky exterior hadn't tipped me off that it was a posh establishment, the doorman that greeted me would have.

The outside was just a hint of the opulence customers were treated to inside. Cream-colored leather seats against dark wood, beautiful art on the walls, orbital lights adding to the contemporary look. The club's interior was more modern than one would expect from the exterior, but everything about it touted exclusivity. A place to be—a place you wanted to be. Which was why the club was able to enforce its no cellphone rule. Texting or taking a call in the place got you banned. Whoever was privileged to perform received the patrons' undivided attention.

Glass in hand, I walked through Kelsey's, sipping from what had to be the best Sprite I'd ever had. It wasn't. It was just a plain Sprite, like any of the others I'd had during my life. My drink served as a reminder of the effects of the D'Siren Victoria had in the restaurant, which amplified the experience. The man with the deep baritone voice, crooning at the piano, had ensnared the audience. They were hanging on to his every melodic tune, enraptured. I wondered if he was nearly as talented as his enthralled audience seemed to believe or whether it was another trick of the D'Siren.

Finally seated at the bar, I scanned the crowd; mostly supernaturals with a few humans intermingled. Magic inundated the spacious establishment. In the corner was a special section, with comfortable-looking club chairs giving the people seated a view of the crooner. It had a Great Gatsby vibe: the vivacity of the twenties and its aged charm, and Deco with a modern flair.

From my perch I had a good view of the large room. Taking a bite of the Key lime tart placed in front of me—an offering from Victoria, I assumed—I closed my eyes to savor the decadent mixture of sweet and tart, then shoved another large forkful in my mouth. It was sinfully delicious. When the bartender placed a glass of white wine in front of me, I took a small sip. Pinot Grigio. Crisp, with hints of lime and apple. While indulging in the heaven on my palate, I inhaled the flowers on the bar. They filled the air with sweet floral redolence.

Then I jerked my nose away and saw it for what it was—a plain, boring, run of the mill white tulip. The wine, nothing special, and the Key lime tart might have been from a box. In this house of mirrors, everything was an ambrosial experience full of decadence, delectable flavors, allure, and deception. I pushed that knowledge to the forefront and slid the tart and wine aside.

"You didn't like the wine?" asked Asher's smooth deep voice from behind me.

"I'm working, I really shouldn't be indulging," I said when he'd moved to position himself in front of me. The aged aromatic scent of the brandy in his hand was another deceptive thing about Kelsey's. I enjoyed the way brandy smelled but never the taste. Each time he brought it to his lips, the glassy-eyed euphoria it brought him made me rethink it. I wanted to try it again, and this time I wasn't going to discreetly spit it back into the glass.

"I figured you'd like the tart," he said, looking at the plate. "After all, it's your favorite."

"How do you know it's my favorite?" An edge of accusation swept over my words and I focused intently on him, looking for any signs that he was about to be deceitful.

"Our last job, I picked you up after you'd visited your mother. You smelled like Key lime pie, and if your visits with your parents are like most, I'm assuming one of them prepared your favorite dessert. Am I wrong?"

His hauteur made me want to tell him he was wrong.

"I prefer Key lime pie."

"We all prefer pie, and if I could have had them make it for you, I would have. But they only serve Key lime tarts here." His attention moved from the tart to the wine. "Did you enjoy the wine as much as the tart?" His smile widened.

That was from him, too. I should have known. Victoria was too busy working on her Oscar performance of the woman living on the fringe of terror who somehow managed to find the spirit to soldier on and make her grand appearance in her restaurant to greet her guests.

I shrugged. "I'm working."

His eyes slowly roved over the room. "What's the job?"

"Well, I wouldn't be worth my fee if I blabbed about my jobs to anyone who asked, now would I?"

"There should be no secrets among friends," he drawled, taking another sip from his glass before a lazy smile moved over his lips.

"That's not remotely true. Everyone has secrets. And we aren't friends. You were simply removed from my hate list."

"Then I need to work harder to get on your friends list. I will make that my personal goal. I'm sure it's a lofty goal but I'm up for the challenge."

"You can start by not being a backstabbing ass. That would help."

Now I was the one looking around the room, matching faces with the magic that wafted through the air. Witch, mage, fae, and shifter magic created a mélange of smells and energy that in a smaller space would have been overwhelming. I thought of Mephisto and the other three whose magic mirrored his. Would an expansive space like this prevent me from feeling like I was ensorcelled in magic? Drowning under the weight of it? It hadn't worked in Mephisto's castle-like home.

"Have we returned to this tired debate? I never backstabbed you. In fact, I warned you off."

"You got me the *Mystic Souls*, we're good," I said, immediately regretting opening the door for questions about its early return. But he didn't inquire about it.

"If you get a break, please feel free to join us." He nudged his chin toward the area across the room, the exclusive section where three men and two women were seated. I recognized one woman as the Alpha of the Northwest Lion's Pack, LLC. Like the Northwest Wolf's Pack, LLC, they had gone corporate to no longer be considered a pack. They weren't fooling anyone. The pack and a pride still existed.

As the woman's hazel eyes landed on me, the desire to ask her why they didn't call themselves Northwest Lion's Pride as opposed to pack diminished. It was just me being pedantic, but it was something I had always wanted to ask the Alpha, or rather CEO, who could give me some insight. Her predator's scope kept me in her line of sight. The angular features of her face framed by auburn hair gave her a feline appearance, sleek like a cheetah rather than the lion who shared her body. The sapphire-blue dress complemented her warm coral skin.

Asher took a seat next to her and whispered something. Her cool appraising gaze became more intense. When she laughed, her eyes sparked with amusement. My attention immediately went to Asher who raised his glass to me.

There's a level of immaturity we all maintain. We delight in the nostalgia of our youth and the silly things we could get away with. Sticking your tongue out as a child might not be appreciated but it was acceptable. Doing it as a fully grown adult was puerile as hell. I should have been ashamed of doing it. I wasn't. And I felt a special form of delight when Asher choked on his drink.

The warm glow of the lights in the restaurant gave the intimate feel of candlelight, adding to the allure of the place. There was just enough swank and exclusivity to appeal to the who's who of the supernatural world, and I knew that when I saw the vision in midnight ease into a small table off to the side, seating himself away from the crowd but able to observe the room and everyone in it. His lips curled into an inviting smile.

I would have known he was there even without the visual.

The subtle air of magic changed, becoming more intense, electric, and heavy. He blanketed the air with his distinctive magic. He knew how to subdue it but he wasn't even trying. He was leaving breadcrumbs for me. Mephisto.

Grabbing my glass of wine, I moved to the back of the restaurant, noting everyone and everything; nothing looked suspicious. Victoria reluctantly agreed to me leaving her with the other three guards when I assured her that I was just a phone call away. I also reminded her that she did have use of some magic; after all, she used it to evoke the D'Siren. It might not be as strong as some, but it could protect her.

Before I left, I took another look at the remainder of my tart, questioning whether its divine taste was the D'Siren at work or whether it was actually one of the best desserts I'd ever had and pairing it with the wine wasn't a bad choice. Unable to resist, I glanced at Asher and caught his gaze. I could see the invitation in his eyes. Still having some trust issues when it came to him, cozying up to him for a night of music, fun, and drinking was something I needed to avoid. Besides, I didn't need to get too comfortable in places like Kelsey's.

The cool night breeze was welcome, a palate cleanser after the magic-permeated room. The refreshing breeze that cooled my overwrought senses was interrupted by the magical signature of the fae, floral with hints of ground cacao. This distinctive magical energy wasn't just fae, it was Neri and Adalia, the fae king and queen. Their striking and stately appearance made them difficult to ignore.

They didn't have guards with them, and I wondered if the heightened security in Kelsey's wasn't just for Victoria but because of them.

Walking past me, they gave me a look as if they expected me to bow or show some sign of veneration. I ignored it. They would only receive the deference they expected from other fae. They were their leaders and therefore deserving of it. The Master of the vampires, the Alphas, Arch-mage, or the High witch were extended the same deference by those they led. If mutual regard was shown by one leader to another, it was out of courtesy, not obligation. I wasn't a fae; I owed them nothing. Since the mages didn't claim me, any regard I extended to them was a politeness not an expectation.

For some reason, Neri seemed to forget those unspoken rules. The bridge of his slender nose that he looked down with such condemnation was as razor-sharp as the lines of his jaw and enviable cheekbones. His wide mouth never moved into anything that resembled a smile, just a taut line. His appearance could be harsh, but there was always a glint of delight in his eyes and it brightened even more whenever he looked at Adalia. Her appearance was a contrast to his. Where he was all defined lines and unyielding angles, she was rounder, softer. Smooth edges and delicate curves. Heart-shaped face, supple lips that set in a resting smile, and soft brown eyes that held the royals' shared pretension.

Kelsey's catered to a clientele who believed in dressing in fine suits and beautiful dresses for the occasion, yet these royals were a little overdressed. His silver Cambridge suit paled his parchment coloring even more, whereas her vibrant yellow floor-length gown complemented her dusky skin. Adalia commanded the street the way a model would the runway, her legs slipping out from the slits in her dress that were wardrobe malfunctions waiting to happen.

But it wasn't their appearance or their command of the space that held my attention; it was their magic. And if they were any closer, I would have leaned in just to feel it again. At that moment, I wasn't sure if just a whiff of their magic or a need to bathe in their energy would be enough. I could see the headline now: "rogue death mage attacks king and queen of the fae."

I sped up to get away from them but came to an abrupt stop at the sound of the growls of three wolves with their teeth bared, pounding in our direction. Snatching off my shoes, I tossed them aside, preparing for whatever may happen.

One wolf lunged in my direction but I hopped onto the car closest to me and climbed to its roof. Neri sent a wave of magic, sending the other two sprawling onto their backs several feet away. They rolled and came to their feet and charged at the fae.

Glassy eyed and seemingly ravenous, they appeared to be driven by a force that had stripped away their volition. I looked around for the source. Magic could be used against shifters, but none of it could control them or their change, although there were rumored to be magical objects that could. Not that anyone had ever seen them. I suspected Asher was in possession of any that might exist.

More shifters appeared from the opposite direction. Neri and Adalia shot magic that stopped the coyote, hyena, and cheetah racing in their direction. In the short reprieve, the royals formed a protective shield around themselves.

The animals surrounded it, pounding, biting, and clawing. It wavered but held. If it gave, the couple would be surrounded by shifter animals, bigger, faster, and stronger than their human counterparts and with the human intelligence that allowed for better strategy and hunting skills. The animals were employing attrition, assaulting the barrier and forcing Adalia and Neri to fight to hold it up and keep repairing the slashes and rents.

"Stop," I commanded, hoping to reach the human part of them that could override the magical impulses driving them. I scanned the area again for the person controlling them.

It wasn't the scent of magic that caught my attention, though, it was the silver spark that flickered like lightning from the roof. It was like the magic in my home. My heart started pounding in my chest when I realized I might be looking at the very thing that had escaped. He was too far

42

away for me to make out his features, but the expansion of feathers behind the figure was undeniable. Wings. The person slipped farther into the darkness until he blended with the night.

One of the wolves broke from the pack and came after me. I moved to the middle of the car's roof. Its claws clacked as they dug into the metal for purchase. In my purse I had a Taser and a knife. Holstered at my leg was a Beretta Pico. There weren't silver bullets in it, so it would just hurt like hell, but even so, shooting a shifter when it wasn't under its own control seemed wrong.

My attention was split between the fae royal couple, the wolf attacking me, and the winged person responsible. Taser in hand, I changed position, prepared to defend myself if the wolf managed to get on the car.

"Down! Now!" Asher's nearly inhuman bellow of command even made me straighten a little. A slight thrum of magic was in the words. Shifter magic.

The shifters gave a strained whimper and rocked back and forth. I quickly realized they were struggling to answer the command of the Alpha to their right and the person behind me who was controlling them. The struggle was profoundly displayed on their faces.

"Brandon, Meredith, Ameri, Jax, Clarisse, down. Now!" The raw animalistic command flowed with another wave of power and magic I hadn't realized shifters possessed. I had never borrowed magic from a shifter and had been positive I couldn't. I wasn't so sure now.

My gaze moved to Asher, the glow of his eyes, the raw energy pulsing from him, the strain on his face as he forced his command over the animals, trying to override the person controlling them. Sherrie wasn't too far behind Asher and was also commanding her pack to obey. The wave of power commanding her animals to retreat and submit to her spoke to something so primal and intrinsic that I found myself shifting my weight, moving, readying to obey. Forcing myself to ignore them, I watched the Alphas wrangle for control.

Asher was upon one of the wolves surrounding the fae's barrier. He hoisted the animal back and it hit the ground with a thud, rolled to its feet, and charged him. Sherrie shoved the cheetah away, emitting a vicious growl that rang through the street. It surprised me that people weren't flooding out of the restaurants and businesses to look at the chaos. There were only two onlookers, who at the sight retreated to their car and backed down the street.

I was dividing my attention between the wolves in front of me and the figure that kept slipping in and out of view like a wraith. More bursts of silver and white sparked from his hands. Asher was on the ground, his hands clamped around the jaw of the wolf to prevent it taking a chunk out of him. Risking a snap, he rolled from under the wolf and secured his hand around the animal's neck. For several minutes, Asher's face was strained, the muscles of his arms tensed, his eyes not even remotely human. The wolf eventually stopped struggling as he lost consciousness. Asher was gentle when he lowered the animal to the ground.

Hello, Mr. Alpha. I made a note to never go after Asher hand to hand.

The other wolves were still trying to get to Neri and Adalia. The wolf who had me as its target had backed away. I assumed it lost interest in me in favor of its main objective—the fae royalty.

I was wrong. Instead, it was gaining enough space to get a running start in order to lunge onto the car. I clambered onto the back of the vehicle. The wolf was sliding, unable to get a grip, clumsily chomping at me. I shoved the Taser into its side and kicked it off the car.

Sherrie was trying to wrangle her shifters away from the noticeably weakened barrier. Its luminous bubble was dim and translucent. I drew out my holstered weapon and aimed it at the wolves assaulting the magical barrier protecting the fae.

I couldn't pull the trigger on the animals. They were innocent. The puppeteer of this madness was using them as weapons. I swiveled and aimed at the winged person on the roof, but a bullet from a handgun wouldn't reach him. I needed a rifle.

The figure moved out from the shadows and was slowly winnowing down. The unexpected thump that accompanied his landing had its intended affect—dramatically announcing his presence.

Deep pools of coffee-colored eyes with hints of ocher should have been soft, warm, and inviting, but they were hardened to the point they looked hateful. He leveled a look at the king and queen and recognition flared in their eyes. His sheaf of sandy-brown hair blew lightly with the wind. His black and midnight-blue wings commanded the night. Concentrating on the magical protective barrier, his cool driftwood-colored skin flushed. The streets became bathed with his magic, mixing with that of the royals. Long fingers tapped at the air as though striking the keys of a piano.

"Ian." Asher growled the name through gritted teeth, in a curse.

Ian skewered Asher with a hard stare before redirecting his attention to the royals, his fingers resuming its peculiar beats and only stopping once the barrier floated away like paper on the wind. Asher was a blur of movement as he hurled the royal couple back and out of the way of the lunging shifters who were warring to attack.

I squeezed off two shots a few feet away from Ian. A warning. The next shot intentionally whizzed past his face. His eyes widened and locked on me. I made a show of repositioning, hoping he realized that the next one would hit him.

He put his hands up, not in surrender but to expose a network of markings on his arms. Coils, shapes, and intricate

45

designs that denoted a magical restriction. His gaze moved from me to Asher. Neri and Adalia were just coming to their feet, straightening their clothes as though they weren't surrounded by raging animals.

"There will be retribution for what you did to me, Asher!" Ian vowed, then he soared into the sky and was swallowed by the darkness. For a moment, I thought he had Wynded, but his flight was just that fast. From where I stood, the strong magic that remained in his wake told me he possessed a great deal of it.

People had finally spilled out of Kelsey's and other buildings to stare at the aftermath. I could see the measured rise and fall of the shifters' chests. They were lying on the ground, alive but depleted.

Mephisto's attention landed on me as I moved from my position on the car. Hearing the approaching sirens of the police department and Supernatural Task Force, I concealed my weapons. Mephisto was gone when I looked for him.

There was a commotion among the officers getting out of their cars and the STF trying to head them off. There was going to be a debate over who would handle this situation. Because it involved shapeshifters, it should be handled by the STF, but I figured the police would argue that because the attack was against me and that some people in the crowd were human, it should be in their jurisdiction. It was always a battle in situations like this.

While they discussed it, a dark-blue sedan drove up and parked next to the police cruiser. River got out of the car and looked directly at me, a shadow of accusation creeping along his square features. His eyes were stone cold, convicting me of wrongdoing without even knowing the situation. His thin lips drew into a tight narrow line. Dressed in a simple button-down and khakis, he was clearly not appropriately attired for Kelsey's, but he struck me as a person who typically violated dress codes. His badge wasn't on display, so this wasn't a professional stop, or maybe it was. He could have been on his way home and saw an opportunity to arrest me and get it to stick this time. As the second person on the scene after *the incident,* he got an up-close and personal observation of the spin, red tape, and manipulation of the system used to make sure I didn't spend any time in prison. Putting me behind bars became his new goal.

His stern gaze stayed on me while he reached into his car, I assumed getting something from the glove compartment, before returning to his position next to his car. Yanking his gaze from me, he split his attention between the STF and the police officers discussing the situation and the scene.

Asher eased up next to me.

"What did you do?" I hissed.

"What makes you think I had anything to do with this?"

He couldn't possibly have thought I missed Ian's dramatic pronouncement.

"The whole 'There will be retribution for what you did to me, Asher' part was a tipoff," I shot back, rustling through my purse for a pen. "Give me one of your cards," I demanded. If I hadn't been attacked by a wolf—Asher's wolf—and forced to shoot at someone, which was going to lead to me being taken in for questioning, and the magical troublemaker implicating Asher, I would have found it in me to ask instead of demand.

His brow lifted in inquiry. I waved my hand at the scratched paint and dents in the car.

"Your wolf, your bill."

He chuckled, reached into his suit jacket, took the pen from my hand, wrote something on the card, and tucked it under the windshield wiper. Standing next to Asher was the STF, who I suspected had won the debate over who should handle the situation. The unenthusiastic looks on the officers' faces clearly showed that the win wasn't a real victory.

"Do I need an attorney?" Asher asked the officers while

47

they studied the naked people sprawled in the middle of the street.

Instead of animals on the pavement, there were now exhausted humans. Someone from Kelsey's hurried out and covered them with a white tablecloth. It was a sweet but unnecessary gesture; you were unlikely to find a vampire unworthy of a double-take or a shifter without a pleasingly fit body. In human form, they were extremely strong. I don't think the immodesty was an animal thing but more an awareness of their attractive physique.

"If she presses charges, then yes, your shifters will need an attorney and probably bail. Neri and Adalia said there's nothing to press charges for. But that's not the story I'm getting. It looks like the shifters went rabid without any explanation." Giving Asher a sharp look, the officer said, "Do you happen to know why?"

Face placid, Asher remained silent, answering with just a shrug.

"I'm not pressing charges," I said, interrupting the tense silence. "It was just a misunderstanding. A game that got a little out of control."

"A game that got 'out of control,'" River chimed in, violating the implied jurisdiction compromise established by the police. "Things have a habit of getting out of control when you're around. Do I need to call your sister? Maybe she can help with this incident, too." Cool assessing eyes moved from me to the scene. He drew his lips down and raked his hands through his graying hair.

"No, I'm good." My dismissal and the lack of attention I gave him was a win. I could feel the heat of his anger. He had DA ambitions, and I really hoped by the time he made his way to that position, his animosity and vendetta against me would be resolved.

Disbelief ringing in his voice, one of the Supernatural

Task Force officers said, "Tell me about this game that got out of control?"

"You know, the Little Red Riding Hood and wolf game. It's really popular."

Asher turned his head and tried to hide his snort of laughter.

The officer's eyes narrowed in irritation. My brand of humor was just making things worse.

"So," he said, "you want us to believe there's a game that incites wolves to chase you." Although he kept hard, inquiring eyes on me, he directed his question to Sherrie and Asher. Their shifters, their problem. "It seems like a very dangerous game. Someone could have been killed."

You know there's no game. But you're going to go with it, aren't you? Fine. Let's do this.

Schooling a neutral look onto my face, I returned his scrutinizing look. "It's more complicated than that. Like I said, it got a little out of control."

"Ah, it's all fun and game until someone dies," River countered in a voice filled with barely suppressed loathing.

I broke the intense stare with River when one of the STF agents shuffled his feet. Both of the STF agents gave River a quelling look that he missed because his focus was still on me.

I had no idea why Asher wasn't telling him that a winged man with animancer powers controlled Asher's animals and made them attack Neri and Adalia, but I planned to find out.

There was some relief in Asher not telling what really happened, because I was sure Ian wasn't supposed to be here. Cory was responsible for Ian's presence, and Madison was there when Ian appeared. I didn't know how it would affect them and I didn't want to find out. Human knowledge of supernatural existence created a delicate situation. Magic rules were inconsistent, and while an anomaly in science was met with reservation, with magic, it caused fear.

"May I see your ID?" one of the STF officers asked.

That was the last thing I needed. If this person didn't already know who I was, my name would definitely ring a bell. Having been accused of murder and subsequently getting away with what most people considered a slap on the wrist hadn't sat well with the human police department or the STF. It was a political nightmare that hate groups used to assert that supernaturals were out of control, and human police to debate the need for humans in the STF or the merging of the two agencies.

Police didn't like that they didn't have any jurisdiction when it came to supernatural crimes. I once heard Madison say the police should be happy because they didn't have to deal with the shifters and their team of aggressive attorneys who were far more vicious and predatory than the half-animals they represented, and the vampires' representatives were considered even worse.

The officer looked at the name, then me, and then the name on the ID again. Face stolid, he handed it back to me.

"Why don't you come down and give us a statement?"

"There's not much to say. You know the wolves tend to run in the streets sometimes. They shouldn't, and I know there's a fine for doing it. I saw them, started playing that silly game with them. I got startled by something and ran. Their instinct kicked in. They weren't trying to hurt me, just enjoying the chase. Then Asher came out and commanded them down."

The STF consisted of supernaturals, and I was so glad neither of them were shifters because not only would they sense the lie, they would have definitely called me on the BS story.

A game? Really?

But I got it out and Asher would repeat the story if they were taken in. And the shifters now in their human form, barely staying under their coverings, heard it, too. I

50

wouldn't have to make up something to go with my "game" story.

I moved over to Meredith to cover her better and hide "the girls," something that didn't seem to be a priority for her. I wanted that level of confidence and immodesty. On second thought, maybe I didn't. I did the same with Amerti, even though she was equally indifferent about her nudity. I gave Brandon a look and pulled at the cloth to cover his man berries, too. The others weren't any better. Eventually I gave up trying to help them with their modesty. They weren't worried about it, so why should I be?

The officer's lips were pulled into a tight stiff line, and he kept an accusatory eye on Sherrie and Asher. "Everyone come down so we can sort this out."

"Are they being arrested?" Asher asked, taking out his phone.

"No, if no one is pressing charges then no. But I'm curious why they were out in the streets. It's illegal. There are torn clothes over there." He pointed at the clothes strewn about the street. "That's not typical. Don't you all usually take off your clothes instead of tearing through them?"

The officer looked at the three wolves and they looked at Asher. "I had too much to drink," said one, "and I shifted to burn off the alcohol. I wasn't thinking. I just wanted to burn off the alcohol. Sorry, Asher."

Asher shrugged. The woman continued. "I'm dominant and it triggered the others to change." She looked at the officer. "You realize that happens, right?"

We all looked at the man and he nodded, but only because he didn't want to seem ignorant about shapeshifter physiology. I appreciated the lack of knowledge—it worked to our advantage—but I would have to tell Madison that her department needed to brush up on shapeshifter norms. A dominant can force others to change but not without touching them. Only an Alpha can do it without touch and that's on the rare occasion that he lacks control during his change. I call it a Hulk Out. But an unbalanced Alpha with the inability to control his emotions doesn't stay in his position long.

Sherrie's shifters gave similar stories and offered their apologies. Either the STF believed us or were rewarding us for our absurd storytelling. The officers cast another look in Sherrie's direction and then at Asher. The self-assured lift of Asher's lips seemed to discourage them from wanting to deal with his team of attorneys. It's a good thing I wasn't in their place; that smirk would have had me cuffing him and putting him in the back of the patrol car just for the hell of it.

After several moments of deliberation, fines were issued to the shifters. I looked at the paperwork. If I were a shifter, I'd make sure I was so far away from the city they'd never be able to accuse me of changing in a highly populated area. Thinking of how many times shifters took their animal form home from clubs as opposed to using a share ride made me question their money sense. An Uber would cost them seven times less than a fine. Most people were used to seeing animals in the streets, so it was unlikely they'd call the authorities. And if people had grown accustomed to seeing humans running around after they changed back, with their woman and man parts just breezing in the wind, then seeing an occasional wolf, jackal, fox, lion, cheetah, or whatever wasn't a big deal.

"You two need better control of your packs. A frightened woman and they go after her like rabid animals." The officer was getting too much pleasure out of chastising the Alphas.

"They didn't go after me like a rabid animal—"

"Sorry," said the one who had taken responsibility for the change.

Frustrated, the officer seemed to be looking for additional things to fine them for. But instead I was requested to make a statement. I did, repeating what I had said verbatim.

Once the officers were gone, I turned to Asher. "You meet

me at my place in an hour. I need to get to the bottom of this," I pushed out through clenched teeth.

"No need. I'll handle it."

"Like you handled it before—leading to a wrathful . . . whatever he is."

"He's a fae. Which is why he attacked Neri and Adalia."

This just got worse, and I needed to know exactly what type of fae Cory had unleashed and how to put him back in the bottle.

"An all-powered being who can fly and control animals is someone I want to know about. I also want to figure out why he's doing it."

Asher wiped a hand over his face. "He shouldn't be here," he whispered so softly it was nearly inaudible. "I need to fix it," he said, walking away from me. I took hold of his arm.

"Asher, I need to know"—I considered telling him that if he didn't tell me, I was going to recant my story, but I had dealt with Asher long enough to know that wouldn't work —"I want to help you." My words rang sincere because I was sincere. I needed to fix whatever Cory had done, especially if it could be linked to us and Asher realized that we had used the *Mystic Souls* book. I didn't know if he had put the pieces together yet or even if he would, but I needed to do something about Ian.

CHAPTER 5

"We really have to amend the 'When you call, I come,' rule," Cory complained, folding his arms over his chest before dropping onto the sofa.

"It was your rule, remember?" The pact we had was that before I borrowed anyone's magic, I would call Cory. Then that warped into each other being the first call for anything and everything. And he was my first call, with the exception of *the incident*. I had to call Madison for that because she was the only person who could help.

Cutting his eyes in my direction in frustration, Cory gave me a reluctant smile. "I know. I just didn't know the calls were going to come so frequently and so late at night."

"It's eleven, grandpa."

Waving his hand from his head to his toes, he said, "*This* requires sleep, exercise, good food, and occasionally a glass of fine wine. I'm not sure what deal you made with a dark lord that lets you function on whiskey, the garbage you eat, and naps, but let me know if it was worth it."

"I was right. You're an old soul," I teased, my chest wrenching at the thought of my mother—or rather, the woman who raised me. No. She wasn't just the woman who raised me. She was my mother. And my father was my father. They were my family.

"Erin, what's wrong?"

I gave Cory a forced smile. "I think I know who you released from the Veil. He wanted out and it involves Asher, who will be here in a few. Hopefully he can sort things out," I said warily, allowing my mind to drift to the worst-case scenario. An Alpha shifter, the king and queen of the fae, and a powerful winged animancer fae—what kind of trouble could that involve?

"We're going to need magic on this. Probably a lot."

"For the record, I don't have an egomaniac or jackass removal spell to help Asher. He might just need a hug from his mommy or something, but hopefully I can help with the other problems."

The resounding hard knocks interrupted my laughter.

"I don't think my ego is at a mania level and frankly, being a jackass is underrated. It's quite fun. There's freedom in it. I get to brass tacks and no one expects anything more of me. Allows me to be quite efficient and productive with my time. And"—Asher strolled into the room, his ever-present smirk intact—"regarding hugs. I think my mommy doted too much on me. Or that's what I've been told. I distinctly remember little things like 'you're perfect,' 'the best son any mother could have asked for,' 'little angel,' and 'a perfect little god' being said." The arch in his brow mirrored his smirk.

I hated to blame the mother, but . . .

"Then he was made into an Alpha," Cory breathed to himself, but Asher's enhanced hearing made it as audible as if Cory had yelled it. Asher bared his teeth in a smile that contained a hint of warning. The menace directed at Cory bothered me.

Asher slowly turned his attention away from Cory, who was glaring at his back, elevating the testosterone level in the room. "But I do enjoy hugs," Asher purred, a playful grin replacing the menacing one. He opened welcoming arms.

"You really don't want me anywhere near you right now. Who the hell is Ian, and how did someone without the ability to use magic magically restrict him?" I asked. Whatever Asher had done to Ian had made him very determined to return. Cory wouldn't shoulder the full brunt of that blame.

"Like you said, I couldn't do it."

"Based on the hate glares he shot at Neri and Adalia during the attack, I'm going to assume they're your partners in whatever happened."

Asher swallowed what he was going to say and turned his attention back to Cory, making it apparent that I'd earned his trust, but Cory hadn't.

"Asher." My voice dropped to a whisper. "This is a problem. You can't possibly want a person like that out there. Someone with the ability to control shifters and who has a vendetta against you. Let me help."

I moved closer to him and he studied me for a long time, his eyes narrowed to a sliver of silver. His ears twitched slightly. That was what I hated most about shifters. Everything was under the scrutiny of their internal polygraph. If he were a vampire, I'd be concerned by the way he was looking at my neck, his gaze dropping to my chest—not my breasts, but the rise and fall of my chest. His gaze finally dropped to the floor.

"Repeat your last statement," he said. It was a weird demand, but I did as asked.

He devoured the few inches between us, his voice a whisper for my ears only.

"Something's off," he admitted.

"With me?"

Fates, his skill wasn't just peculiar, it bordered on creepy. Did he know that we were somehow involved with Ian being released? Did something about me give it away? Asher's eyes slid to Cory and then back to me.

"I have no idea how he got out. He shouldn't have been able to return. I was there when he was extradited back to the Veil. I couldn't see it," he said in a hollow voice. I became hyperaware of his intense observation of me and Cory. "When the spell was performed, he was there one minute and the next, he was gone."

Several awkward moments of silence passed.

"My pack will be affected," he said, mussing his hair as he ran his fingers through it. Stopping, he directed his full attention to me. "I know we still have problems, but I trust it won't influence how you handle this. I need to know you will do whatever you can to help me."

When it came to his pack, he lost all pretensions, leaving a person raw and desperate to do whatever was necessary to protect them.

"Of course. I don't want this guy on the street either. If what he displayed today is an indicator of what he's capable of, it definitely needs to be handled."

Asher regarded me for another long moment before he moved his head slightly into a nod. Then he took a step back and looked at Cory; it was apparent Asher didn't want him there. He'd have wanted him gone even more if he knew Cory was responsible for Ian's release.

"If magic is needed, Cory will be involved. He can be trusted," I said.

Asher paced the floor, perhaps to give him time to edit the story he was about to reveal.

"I was assured he couldn't cross the barrier."

"Barrier?" Cory asked. I shot him a look. Cory realized his mistake and snapped his mouth close.

"The marks on him work like an electronic monitor. Once we put the markings on him, he couldn't cross." Asher wasn't telling us anything we didn't know. "He's been here before and pulled the same stunt. He'd created an army of shifters and was attempting a coup to take Neri and Adalia's position." Asher shrugged. "I don't care about fae politics. As far as I'm concerned, he probably couldn't be any more of a pain in the ass than they are. Neri and Adalia are arrogant, pretentious, and morally questionable when it comes to the fae and the protection of their position as royalty."

I shot Cory a quelling look before he could point out the pot/kettle situation.

"He returned four years ago," Asher went on. "I attempted diplomacy and requested he make a binding blood agreement that he wouldn't use his animancy abilities, but my proposal was rejected."

I was going to go out on a limb and assume the "diplomacy" was a thinly veiled threat that if he used those animancy abilities, he would live to regret it. Based on the gleam and predatory sharpness in Asher's eyes and the dark minacious look that flashed over his face at the recollection of the conversation, I was sure I was correct.

"And when that meeting didn't go as planned?" I inquired.

"We took other measures. I was prepared to pump his ass full of iron and drag him back to wherever he came from." His lips lifted into a snarl. "But the bastard's immune to iron. A fae who isn't weakened by iron. What the hell exists in the Veil? A person without any discernable weaknesses is too dangerous to exist."

Then why does he? I wasn't under the illusion that a threat like Ian would have been allowed to survive. If the pack hadn't sought to eliminate him, the fae definitely would have. It didn't make sense.

"Neri was concerned about his immunity. Then he remembered warnings he'd heard about a protective spell being placed on the people in the Veil. Neither he nor Adalia can see the Veil." He let out a dark, mirthless chuckle. "They probably didn't believe it existed until Ian showed up. Neri said he heard rumors about a penalty for taking their life—loss of magic. We sought out the Woman in Black. She didn't confirm it but wasn't able to disprove it. No one wanted to take the chance. She was able to send Ian back and put a spell on him restricting his return." His gaze slipped in my direction, knowing the stories that accompanied visits to her.

"What did she want in return?" I asked.

"A sample. One from each species. Hair and blood." He must have been more desperate than he was willing to admit.

"Then we send him back again, using the same spell."

"It's not that simple. The Xios was destroyed in the process. That's the price for using it. And I don't know if there is another."

"What did it look like?" I asked. I never took any names at face value when it came to magical objects because they often went by different names, and if you were dealing with a witch and mage, they would definitely call it something different. Dealing with them and their petty squabbles was exhausting. It was like the difference between Coke and Pepsi. *You're the same thing!*

Asher scrolled through his phone and showed a picture; the plum-colored object with its irregular curves and shapes reminded me of a porcelain lotus flower. He scrolled to the next picture, which showed a pile of dust.

"It was destroyed."

"Did you all keep the remains?"

"I considered that, but part of it was swept away with Ian so it wouldn't have been able to be used. Ian didn't have those marks when he was sent back to the Veil. I assume the remains of the Xios are what made them."

It was always a good practice when destroying a magical object to shatter it and remove a piece so it could never be made whole again. Even if ground into dust, the remnants should never remain together.

"I need to do some research, but I plan to send him back and ensure he doesn't return," I said.

The hardness in Asher's eyes expressed eloquently that he'd prefer an irreversible option, and it was only the spell on the Veil that was keeping him from it.

I made sure Asher was out of the building to prevent him hearing anything I said. When I closed the door, Cory jumped to his feet, his long legs devouring the small space as he paced the room.

"I did that. I'm responsible for unleashing that man on the city and doing that to Asher's pack. Neri and Adalia . . . the fae." He cursed under his breath, scrubbing his hands over his face.

I took his hands and held them and looked him in the eyes. "And no one will ever know," I assured him. The pseudo confidence in my voice made it seem like I had a plan. I didn't. Cory's brow remained furrowed. He was a powerful witch and he shouldn't have feared the shifters. But covens were small and not set up like packs. You mess with one coven, that's it. You have one coven angry with you. You screw with one pack and you suddenly have hundreds of enemies.

I liked to poke the bear, wolf, cheetah, lion, or whoever, but I wouldn't knowingly pick a fight with one, and showing my disappointment with Asher after his betrayal could have ended badly for me. But he kept it to himself. Even if I'd nicked him . . . or stabbed him, depending on who told the story or which officer was filling out the police report, Asher would never mark me as an enemy of his pack. He was too arrogant for that. Most of them were.

"We're going to fix this," I said, "and no one will ever find out. Chances of it being discovered are slim." Not as slim as

I'd like, especially since my returning the *Mystic Souls* to Asher coincided with Ian's appearance. Would he piece it together?

"How?" Cory sounded as anxious as he looked.

"We need to send Ian back to the Veil. If it was done once, it can be done again. I just need to find a way." There was always more than one object that could be used to accomplish a goal. It might require more magic, adjunct objects, and be a Herculean task, but it could be done. I hoped.

"What about the dragons, Mephisto, even Asher? They all collect magical objects, so they should have something," Cory suggested.

"And the STF. We have options."

The options weren't nearly as abundant as they seemed, though. The STF had to justify the use of a confiscated magical object, and that started the whole bureaucratic process, which often took longer than finding the object, even if I could use Madison's connections. I really didn't want this to be traced back to Madison. River would be skulking around, trying to find a way to pin it on me. My stay at the Stygian wasn't satisfactory sentencing for him. And I got it. It wasn't for a lot of people.

I had to find a way to get Ian back into the Veil and reactivate the restrictive marks on him. It was doubtful that Asher had any useful objects, although he'd freely give them up if I could rid him of Ian. The dragons might have something. If they did, it would prove I was right to strike up a business association with them after discovering they were responsible for the theft of several expensive objects from some very high-profile people. People they didn't want as enemies. I could purchase the object from them. Mephisto would be harder because he was a collector and unwilling to share. He'd have to be my last option.

But before I could find who had the objects, I needed to figure out which ones I needed.

CHAPTER 6

"*W*hat's wrong, Erin?"

Madison's voice was tight, the weariness in it leading me to believe she already knew what I was about to tell her.

"I know what came through the Veil, when Cory did that spell."

"Let me guess, does it involve the shifters?" Her sharp exasperated breath made me wish I had stopped Cory from doing the spell. "Someone's driving the shifters mad?"

"Mad? No. Someone's able to force them into shifting and then controls what they do. He's a fae." I shared everything Asher had told me. It was met with a string of curses, some in French, many in English, and a few that were a mélange. After the first ten *fucks*, I lost count.

It wasn't dealing with the shifters that bothered her. Neither they nor their lawyers bothered my sister. It was the fae. She was a fae, so technically Neri and Adalia's subject. It was a peculiar dichotomy, but all the species dealt with it. The vampires' lives were easier because they were their own subculture. They rarely worked for agencies or in the community. If they worked at all, it was usually for their own pleasure.

Shifters tended to work for companies owned by their corporation. Most of their business was in security contracts and real estate. It seemed like they had a contingency plan to separate from the community if needed. When they came out, they weren't easily accepted, so perhaps they were waiting on humans to turn on them again.

"I hoped it wasn't anything like that. I heard about what happened at Kelsey's, and of course, River definitely thinks you're involved. I'm dealing with a situation right now."

"What situation?"

"One at Hagard's Park."

Turning the car around, I headed toward the park while giving Madison the details about Ian, including Neri, Adalia, and Asher's part in Ian feeling aggrieved.

"If he was trying to get back at Asher, why did he have them attack you?" Madison asked.

"I don't think it had anything to do with me. It seems like he's trying to force their hand. Imagine rogue shifters attacking people and the Alphas unable to control it. A fae being responsible. Humans won't see the nuances. They'll blame us all."

Madison released another string of curses in blended French and English. Some made absolutely no sense. *Fuck-buster isn't a thing, Maddie.*

"Neri and Adalia are okay?" she asked. Genuine concern overlay her words as she spoke about them with a level of reverence I wasn't able to understand. It was the same way I'd heard vampires speak to Landon, the acting Master of the city, since the actual Master had lost interest in living among

63

humans and supernaturals. We were nothing more than the "unremarkable," a denotation given to humans and supernaturals alike. As the years passed, he found us less deserving of his time and no longer entertaining to watch. If I didn't know any better, I would have thought he believed we existed to entertain him and had failed to do our job. That's the problem with living hundreds of years, life becomes mundane.

But Madison's situation was different. It wasn't just reverence; she was Seelie fae, technically under their rule, and tasked with serving both the royals and the STF.

"It gets worse. Ian has an immunity to iron. Asher believes there's a spell that protects people from the Veil. There seems to be a penalty that goes with that. No one knows the specifics. What if it's something as draconian as if you kill him you forfeit your life?"

"I wasn't considering killing him, Erin."

"I didn't say you were. But sometimes things happen. And he's strong so he won't go down easily."

"I wish they'd handled this differently. Why didn't they get the STF involved? We could have done something about Ian. Put restrictions on his magic, fine him for violations."

Sadly, Madison believed that would have worked. The worlds that we operated in were antithetical. Rules and regulations dictated her behavior, controlled her world, ensured that chaos wouldn't prevail. In her mind, if something was the law, you followed it.

As a good citizen, you weren't supposed to have magical objects, and if one came into your possession, you turned it in. Sometimes my work had me dealing with people who considered the laws an unpleasant suggestion that if ignored came with a fine or a vacation, compliments of the STF penal system. And there were a select few who thought they were above it all.

"Asher would never come to you, nor would Sherrie if it

involved the Lion pack. If she found out first, she would have taken matters into her own hands, too."

Madison was in the Rune and Recovery department and wouldn't handle the park situation. It still fell under the Supernatural Task Force jurisdiction, but with humans involved, like yesterday, there would be a debate over who should handle it.

"I hope they can stop the shifters without hurting them. They aren't acting on their own volition."

"It's not our department, but I sent Claire to assist. She has a good relationship with their Chief. I'll put in some calls." Claire was one of the strongest witches in the department, and it gave me some comfort that she'd be there, if for no other reason than to mitigate the damage Ian was causing.

"She lives with Jessie. I hope she has a good relationship with her."

"Captain Flores," Madison corrected me. Although they were the same rank in the department, Madison would never call Jessie anything other than Captain Jessica Flores. And if she thought she could insist, she'd demand I call her Captain Calloway. She should count herself lucky I didn't just call her Maddie.

"Exactly, and they work for different departments that are often in a state of contention, and neither one has kicked the other out. I'd say that's a good relationship." Despite the tension, Madison was able to let a little humor into her voice. I let her know that I was just fifteen minutes away before disconnecting the call.

The park wasn't in the chaotic state I expected, but I had to make my way around the news trucks and the slowed traffic of people observing the aftermath. Five wolves lay on the grass, chests heaving in slow rhythm. A coyote and a fox lay a few feet from the picnic bench in a state of stillness. On the far end, I saw three members of the Lion pack in their animal form sprawled on the ground, subdued by tranquilizers or magic.

I didn't get out of the car once I saw Claire. She was hard to miss. Streaks of midnight blue twined through her dark-brown hair. A black distressed denim jacket was over her Harley Quinn t-shirt and slacks, to show some semblance of compliance to the STF dress code. Recognizing me as I passed her in my car, she gave me one of her overenthusi-astic smiles and waves. The contrasts in her appearance always baffled me. She was a walking contradiction—an indictment of judging a book by its cover.

I'd seen what I needed to see. The shifters seemed to be safe, although I wasn't sure they were going to be free to go. Sherrie and Asher were talking to Captain Flores, and nothing about her severe expression and tight-lipped frown gave me the impression it was going to work out in their favor. Flores stood several inches shorter than Sherrie, the Lion's pack Alpha, but she had a commanding presence despite the softness of her appearance. Hazel eyes with flecks of green held an intensity that at times made her gaze hard to hold. Light-brown waves of hair surrounded her olive skin. Her stance was a reminder that she wasn't just a mage but could also handle situations without the use of magic, if necessary.

Captain Flores seemed hyperaware of the cameras and that she was being recorded and photographed, and it was apparent she wasn't happy. Her decision would have to be based on making sure that humans felt safe. The STF's handling of shifters who weren't able to control their shift or their behavior in a public park, where families were present, would play out on the cameras and be scrutinized.

It was another reminder why I couldn't take a job at the STF, no matter how much Madison wanted it. I might get away from magic, but I'd be thrown into the labyrinth of bureaucracy and public opinion.

Parking on the outskirts of the park, I walked the few feet to the shops, cafes, and restaurants that made the park a city favorite. I was looking for the winged fae, positive he'd be somewhere close watching the aftermath of his work.

Wings hidden, he looked relaxed sitting on a small bench outside a creamery and lazily licking a strawberry cone. I guess that's what you do after you cause this level of chaos— you go for ice cream. His dark hair was swept behind his ear, his mood too blithe for a person who had caused so much mayhem.

At my approach his gaze languidly roved over me from head to toe.

"Is it safe to assume you are their emissary?" He leveled his eyes on me and ground out the title as if it were an insult.

I didn't correct him.

"Tell me, what makes you follow them so blindly? Do their will. Come here on their behalf when it should be them begging me to stop. Do the king and queen know that with just a little wiggle of these"—he waggled his fingers—"I could send an onslaught of attacks that they wouldn't be likely to survive? There are hundreds of shifters. I can attack from all angles. They wouldn't stand a chance. Now who should be the king?"

His power was undeniable. My need was blazing in me like an inferno. Tamping it down seemed impossible. In just a few steps, I could have it. Mephisto was from the Veil, and I could take his magic indefinitely without him dying. I wondered if it would be the same with Ian. Or would the results be the same as if I'd borrowed it from any other fae? How long would I be able to keep his magic?

Shrugging off the thoughts were hard, both because of my need and because the desire to punish him was intense.

His gaze leered too long on a mother and her child passing by.

"No more shifter attacks," I commanded, moving a little closer. A silver thread of magic sprang from his finger and he zapped me with it, causing me to back up several feet.

"I know what you are, emissary. Don't come any closer, you little raven." He was from the Veil; which raven did he know me as?

"I'm Erin."

"I don't care who you are, emissary. Will you be removing my restriction or not? Wait, you can't unless you borrow magic." Leaning forward, he jutted out his narrow chin as if trying to feel a breeze or something against it. "No magic there. There is something, though . . ." He shifted his weight, considering me carefully. "No active magic."

I knew. Mephisto was the only person who said he could feel magical energy from me. I bet the Others did as well. Attuned to the magic and its energy in a way like no one else, Mephisto instantly knowing what I was didn't surprise me. The winged fae recognizing it did.

"I don't think you are in a position to do it, are you?" he challenged.

"I will have your restrictions removed, just give me some time," I said.

His smirk was cruel and rife with malicious intent. "I'll give you as much time as you want, but know that I need to entertain myself." Cone in one hand, he took another lick and stretched out his other arm along the back of the bench, aloof. "How will I do that?" he mused. "What will amuse me? More attacks in parks? If it keeps up, people are going to start seeing the shifters as a danger. Or maybe the shifters will attack the fae. Hmm, that would be interesting. Maybe I won't have to overthrow them. Their own people will turn against them when they see they can't stop the attacks, and whatever will become of the shifters? I do remember so much distrust for them." His voice became a falsetto: "'They turn into animals, think about the children.'" He laughed, a deep mellifluous sound. Coming from him, I expected something harsher, something maniacal.

His dark smile spread even wider. "Or maybe I'll have the shifters turn on each other. They used to have fights to the death. Maybe we should return to that. Give them a little probe with my magic, turn them loose on the streets, and see who the real dominant animals are. How will people deal with witnessing such savagery?" Overly dramatic in his delivery, I could see the miscreant thoughts that lingered behind the ginger-colored eyes that reveled in the causing of what he considered justifiable havoc.

"I don't respond to threats." The edge that sharpened my voice didn't work in my favor. His smile broadened.

"Erin." My name was airily spoken between his lazy indulgence of his dessert. I couldn't decide if this was comical or scary. Probably the latter. The fact that over ten shifters were lying in the most popular park, sedated and magically constrained, while he enjoyed his strawberry dessert made him a special type of ass. "If only it was a threat. It's a decision. Choose: your city or the removal of my marks. I want my ability to move between here and the Veil returned."

"I'll try to get you what you want, but if you continue at this rate, the only option will be for people to do whatever is necessary to stop you. Do you want that?" I asked.

He showed me his markings as though they were a justification for his behavior.

Then he evaluated me for a long time, his brows furrowed. "Why are you working as Asher's emissary? What draws you to a man like him? His libertine ways? Confidence? Being an Alpha? Power seems to appeal to people in a way I'll never understand."

"I think you understand it just fine. This stunt is nothing

more than a power play. Well, you've got my attention and I don't think you really want that." Whatever look was on my face made him straighten up a little. Realizing I saw the change too, his air of conceit bloomed more and he took another idle lick from his dripping cone. Thoughts of smooshing it in his face brought a smile to my face.

His light, hearty laughter was carried by the small breeze. "I do see why Asher chose you to represent him. I find the Raven Cursed quite alluring." He said "Raven Cursed" with undisguised reverence. Being called Raven Cursed as opposed to The Raven brought me a small amount of comfort; at least I knew what Raven Cursed was. The Raven Cursed had parents, limited magical skills, and didn't know about Veils, Immortalis, Caste, or Malific.

"Yes, I find you alluring," he repeated, a small smile lifting the corners of his lips.

"Ick," was all I could manage. In different circumstances, he might have gotten my attention. Right now, I wanted to draw his magic from him and send him into the in-between without guilt. Not an iota of it would be wasted on him.

His gaze slipped to the right. "And the Alpha arrives. No, stay where you are," he chided Asher. Anyone would have requested the same thing if they'd seen the carnage in Asher's eyes. I had never seen a graphite ring pulsing in his gray eyes. Was that the last thing anyone saw before they felt Asher's wrath? No one could deny the heart of a wolf behind the expensive, tailored steel-blue suit—he was a predator, and if it ever slipped from the mind, this was a reminder. One that I needed myself. To me, he was just the flirty Alpha with a questionable moral compass. But right now he was the Alpha never to be underestimated.

"You don't have anyone else with you, so it's safe to say that you're not here to remove my markings. And your emissary is a magical dud. Ineffectual. Why are you here?"

"Leave my pack alone. No more of this or—"

"Or what, you'll shove me into the Veil without any means to return?" Ian snapped, his lips drawn back to bare his teeth.

Distraction and emotions that I used to my advantage. The electric pellet I tossed to the left of him drew his attention away from the shurikens I threw. The first one hit his shoulder, and his initial shock was replaced by outraged incredulity. The second one in his chest caused him to roil with anger. Magic thrust hard into me, knocking me back several feet and dislodging the shurikens. I was too far to get to him and take his magic. Panting through clenched teeth, he dropped his cone and erected a diaphanous field around him.

He seethed as he pulled out the shurikens. Hate flared in his eyes. "Asher," he hissed, "you're going to feel terrible about ripping your emissary's throat out." His throat bobbed as he swallowed down the rage that seemed to be distracting him from being able to perform magic.

Robust energy formed in the air. Asher folded over then dropped to the ground. His hands balled into tight fists. He was panting hard. Streams of perspiration formed along his hairline and eventually dropped from his nose. His eyes glowed, and the thin ring around them became more pronounced. I realized I'd never seen that look because it was a warning that Asher wasn't fully himself. Paws replaced his hands, and I pulled out my concealed gun, prepared to stop Asher the wolf.

The self-satisfied look on Ian's face wavered and eventually vanished after several minutes when there wasn't a massive wolf in front of him but an exhausted man whose paws had receded.

"Keep fighting, I have all day."

"But you don't," said a voice to my left, a sphere of magic shooting from her finger into the field. It was strong enough to buckle the field. While Madison battered at the protective barrier protecting Ian, Claire walked around it, examining it. *Smile more menacingly, woman. You look like you're about to invite him to game night. Bare your teeth, narrow your eyes. Growl for all I care, but stop smiling at him.*

He dismissed her at first, and with the goofy smile on her face, I didn't blame him. Then her smile disappeared and her lips started to move. Her eyes were pits of darkness as she reached into a pouch at her waist and sprinkled dust around the field, keeping her eyes on him the entire time. Her attempt at a menacing snarl was a miserable failure. It reminded me of a child trying to figure out how to pout. I definitely planned to give her a lesson in the art of menace. Ian sucked in a breath when her words came more fervently and the barrier undulated, buckling further and thinning with each moment.

He struggled to keep it intact around him while still trying to force Asher to change, who was resisting the magic. Ian's face relaxed, wings sprouted, and he shot into the air.

"You cheating jackass," Claire yelled after him. But he was too far away to hear.

"Thank you," I said, moving to Asher, who was lying on his back, arm over his face to block out the sun. His breath was labored, but not as much as I would have expected. He was flushed. It was like touching a stove when I pressed my hand to his cheek. Shifters ran hot, but I was concerned he'd have irreparable damage if he stayed this hot for too long.

"You're hot," I informed him.

"I know," he whispered. "But should you be groping me in front of an audience? I'm cool with it but we're probably violating a social expectation of decency." He moved his arm from his eyes.

"Are you okay, Asher?" Madison asked.

He nodded and sat up, shrugging off his jacket. "Just give me a few minutes."

I stood next to Madison, equally intrigued by his transition from physical distress to normal. The sheer control of it. Once again, I found myself coveting shifter magic. Alpha magic was something I hadn't tried. It might be possible. What would happen? I let my gaze drop to the ground because I was sure he could see my interest. It was confirmed when I lifted my eyes to meet his. A faint smile feathered along his lips.

Giving me a rueful look, Madison took a bag and picked up the shurikens that came off Ian. She handed the bag to me along with an accompanying warning look. They were illegal and should have been confiscated. But they had his blood on them, which meant I would be able to track him. This was one of the moments when she would tell me she was taking off her badge and we were working as sisters.

Claire looked away, assessing the area.

"So that's . . ." Madison waved at the empty space where Ian had been.

"Ian. He escaped from the Veil." I didn't elaborate on how he did it, not with Claire there. Madison trusted her and so did I, but plausible deniability was always a good thing.

"Veil?" Claire asked.

I gave her the Cliff Notes version of the Veil and how few people can see it and even fewer can navigate within it. I explained that Ian came through a couple of years ago and decided he would be a better fae king and to prove it, demonstrated his unusual power of controlling shifters. And how his threat led to Asher forming an alliance with the royals to send him back, and now that he'd returned, he was looking for a way to remove the markings that seemed to restrict his ability to move between the Veil and here.

Claire struck me as an open-minded type of person, but even though she nodded while I spoke, her face held a scowl of skepticism. She remained unconvinced even after Madison confirmed that the Veil existed although Claire wasn't able to see it. Ian and his antics didn't appear to convince her either.

I understood her skepticism, but I had to leave it to Madison to convince her. Ian had to be stopped, and I needed to find another Xios or its equivalent.

CHAPTER 7

The royals looked out of place on the sofa in Asher's home. I'd only visited their home once and was quite content to never do it again. Walking through it felt like walking through a museum, sterile and uninviting, projecting the same feeling that touching anything in it or taking photographs was prohibited.

In contrast, Asher's home radiated an easy comfort and casual stylishness. If you've been to one shifter home, you've been to them all. There were subtle differences that matched their personality, but all shifters seemed to have an affinity for earth tones; various warm shades of greens, tans, beige, moss, dark browns, and clay. Asher's home wasn't any different. Sleek dark leather furniture against a backdrop of warm light browns. The large area rug reminded me of the forest, though it had richer hues, and instead of a regular coffee table he had an eclectic-looking tree trunk.

His home was him: clean lines and modern. A direct reflection of him even now, seemingly at home relaxing but still wearing a business shirt and slacks, his jacket lying over the arm of a club chair.

Asher offered me a seat across from the fae who tracked my every move with interest.

"Erin." Adalia's voice was as wispy and light as a feather's touch. The tiny bevel of her lip was faintly similar to a smirk of hubris, daring anyone to do anything other than direct all their attention to her when she deigned to speak. Having her repeat anything earned a tone even fainter, with just enough derision to ensure you felt properly chastised for not hearing her the first time. "I have no idea why you've dedicated yourself to helping us when you have no cause. This won't go without notice or appreciation. If you can find a way to return Ian to the Veil, we—"

Neri placed his hand on his wife's thigh and murmured, "Adalia, are you sure you want to continue?"

"Yes, I do. I was nearly mauled by a pack of animals just two days ago."

Neri's lips pressed together, biting back words, and I assumed his wife had a flair for dramatics. She was likely more insulted by the gall of the attack rather than the actual attack.

"He's stronger than we are." The strain in her voice at that admission hinted at fear that extended further than just the potential loss of power. It was something I'd seen often; powerful people feared the loss of power. The privilege that accompanied it. Although I hadn't seen this couple exploit it, there had to be a certain level of comfort in knowing that very few had magic that rivaled theirs.

Placing a hand over Neri's that was still on her thigh, she said, "If you can send him back, preventing us suffering consequences from alternative actions, we will owe you a debt. Spare no expense; we will pay your fee."

Neri wasn't about to accept what appeared to be unsolicited help so easily. "Why are you helping us? You have no fealty to the shifters. In fact, I have on good authority that you and Asher have had some discord for several months."

Neri's gaze snapped to Asher and then back to me. "You're a mage, but one wouldn't know such a thing because of how little you associate with them. They have no claim to you, either."

That was the problem; I was a magic wielder without a home—a denizen group to call my own. The purveyor of magic that came with a penalty. Magic that peddled in death didn't allow me to have a home among the others. They considered me dangerous and a blight on the magical world and the perception of it. Association with me meant association with my magic. And my crime.

"So, why are you helping us? You can't truly be this altruistic?"

"No," I admitted, "I'm not. You're right, I have no fealty to anyone other than my friends and family. Madison is a fae, and what Ian is doing doesn't just affect her as fae, but her job. She pledged to protect this city and she will. But she's limited by the Supernatural Task Force's organization. I'm not. An unchecked powerful fae wreaking havoc on the city will lead to humans noticing, inciting the same fear that led to us being secretive about our existence. If we don't do something about Ian, the humans will, and I doubt they'll just stop with him. They never do."

Although I'd taken some creative license, most of the statement was true. I was trying to save my best friend's ass. I felt a personal responsibility for having possession of and using spells from a book that had already caused so much devastation. My dedication to my sister and the supernatural community, despite me not having a true home, obligated me to keep the royals safe.

Neri's face relaxed, his arctic eyes melted, and he extended an appreciative nod in my direction.

"Madison is one that we value a great deal." It would probably mean something to her, and I attempted to show some hints of caring.

"What have you discovered so far?" Asher asked me.

"Not much. We need to immobilize Ian's magic, and since iron doesn't affect him, it will have to be a spell. I haven't found one yet that will stop him." I had spent most of the previous night looking for a spell, and the fae looked as though they were experiencing the same level of frustration I was. With the ability to take flight and an army of shifters at his command, apprehending Ian was going to be a problem.

I wanted to clip his wings and render him earthbound. If I could get close enough, I didn't have to clip his wings; I could render him defenseless for at least a short period. But I didn't have the element of anonymity on my side. He knew what I was and what I could do. Was that an option? I wasn't totally convinced it was. And Mephisto and the Immortalis were proof that it might not be, because borrowing their magic didn't render them helpless by putting them in a state of in-between. Was Ian being overly cautious in keeping his distance from me and preventing me from trying?

"Do you have any leads on another Xios?" Asher asked.

I shook my head and directed my attention to Neri and Adalia. "I don't." I opened my bag and retrieved my phone, showing them a picture of a Cyax. "This might be an option; it will bind someone to a location. It requires a blood spell, but it's just as effective as a Xios." Blood spells were really effective, but they linked the caster to the spell, which usually depleted the caster's energy for days. The caster's lifeline was also linked to the object throughout the spell, and if the object was broken during the spell, there were deadly consequences. Blood spells using magic objects were a last resort. I planned for this to be one as well. I could borrow Mephisto's magic, and I could get Ian in the Veil and bind him there. It was an alternative to using the Xios.

"I'd like to look at your collection of magical objects," I said. "Even if you don't have this, you might have something useful."

"We don't collect magical objects. It's a waste of resources and effort," Adalia said with a shrug. "It's only a matter of time until an object that was once deemed legal no longer is. Such an unnecessary hassle."

We all looked at Asher, who didn't let such trifles as legal and illegal classification keep him from collecting magical objects like a child on an Easter egg hunt. Unfazed, he returned an insolent smirk. Ridicule, looks of censure, or derision would never be a deterrent for Asher. Seeing that Asher's acquisition of a Xios led to vanquishing Ian the first time, we weren't in a position to condemn him for his collecting.

"Aren't you able to disable him? It would only be necessary for a few minutes. Time to send him back," Neri asked. He was making a substantial effort to hide his antipathy for my magic.

"I don't know if that's an option," I admitted. They didn't need me to elaborate; our rules outside the Veil didn't seem to apply when in it.

The royals stood but I didn't. Based on their frowns, I'd committed another social faux pas. How hard was it for them to understand that I wasn't fae? They were just two haughty people that were higher maintenance than I was willing to provide. I managed a genial smile.

"Erin, we will owe you a great debt once you right this situation," Adalia assured me. "I still have no idea how he escaped. He shouldn't have been able to." She exhaled a weary breath.

Face schooled to neutral, I simply offered a shrug as an answer.

"Which one of you let him out? You, Cory, or Madison?" Asher asked moments after Neri and Adalia had left.

"I'm not sure what you're asking," I offered, stalling for time to figure out how to answer without answering.

"Really." His brow arched. "Let's not do that, Erin. Who

do I hold accountable for releasing the person who now has many members of my pack living in fear? Afraid that they will be used to harm others. Horrified that they no longer have the ability to stop their change or control their actions. Reduced to nothing more than attack animals. Even injecting themselves with silver isn't enough. Ian has magic so strong it even overrides that." Asher closed his eyes, inhaling slow breaths, his frustration palpable. I could imagine how difficult this must be for shifters because they couldn't use magic. Their shift was their magic, and someone was now able to hijack the only magic they possessed.

I remained silent.

"Is it a coincidence that Mystic Souls was in your possession and that you returned it the day before Ian made his appearance?"

"Coincidences happen."

"They do, but I don't believe this is one. So, who do I hold responsible for releasing Ian? You? Cory? Or Madison?" He was stalking the room like a caged animal. He scrubbed his hands over the shadow of beard starting to form.

Stopping abruptly, he looked at me. "I guess one could say that I'm ultimately responsible because I got Mystic Souls for you."

I didn't want to lie to him and fought the urge to reveal everything, but I could see the frustration and helplessness that shaded his face. Feelings like those made bad bedfellows. An unreasonable shifter was dangerous. My silence probably made me the likely suspect. He'd extend me some leniency. I wouldn't be an enemy of the pack. I wasn't positive that he'd give the same courtesy to Cory.

The long uncomfortable silence ended once he realized I wouldn't answer him. Standing in contemplation, I was reminded of his magical display and the curiosity it piqued in me. Something I wanted to explore. Near him, I couldn't remember the argument I made earlier against exploring my curiosity.

"I'll need to see your stash," I told him.

Reluctantly he accepted that the questioning was over. Running his fingers through his hair, disheveling it, he exhaled a noisy breath. "I don't like dishonesty."

I choked back my laughter. "Are you sure about that? You aren't winning any Boy Scout merit awards for your honesty."

The small smirk twitched at his lips. "I never lie. If I don't want to answer the question, I don't."

"I answered your question."

"I feel like you aren't being totally upfront with me. I don't like that."

"But you don't mind doing it to others?"

He shrugged. "I don't like it when it's done to me."

He said that with a straight face. I guess the royals hadn't left. Several moments I stood in abject awe waiting for him to laugh, say he was joking, poke fun at his arrogance and entitlement, or at the very least admit how absurd his statement was. Nothing.

"I'm going to step out for a moment and leave you alone with your ego and let you think about what you just said. You're getting a big boy time out. When you're finished, you need to show me where you have your collection of objects."

I'd taken a few steps from the door when I returned and poked my head back in. "I'm sure your mother said a lot of things to you other than telling you you're a special little boy, a god, and prince of all princes. There had to be a few things thrown in, like humility, don't be an ass, the world doesn't revolve around you, be nice to strangers, pick up your garbage. You get the picture. Yet the former are the only things that stuck?"

Asher didn't take me up on his well-needed time-out and was out the door seconds after I left. I followed him to the pack's home where they kept everything. Saying you have a vault sounds impressive until you discover it's nothing more than an oversized stainless steel safe. Usually there are cameras, and sometimes it might even be located behind a door with a fingerprint lock, facial recognition, or both.

But Asher's vault in the Northwest Pack's compound couldn't be considered anything less than a vault in every sense of the word. After we'd descended a flight of stairs, I followed him through a narrowed corridor, through a false wall, and to a door that required a code and had a fingerprint reader. Finally, I was led into his eight-by-ten vault. Surrounded by steel-reinforced concrete, I was given access to his collection of magical objects.

I frowned at his acquisitions as I moved from shelf to shelf. Several were class five objects, and a cursory count revealed that twenty-five percent of the things he owned were classified as illegal by the Supernatural Task Force's Runes and Recovery Department. Based on his sly look, he was quite aware of it.

"You shouldn't have some of these," I pointed out, picking up several of the items. They seem to have stocked up on Glanin's claws, which prevent shifters from intentional shifts. There were several moon rings, which prevent shifters from changing during a full moon. I was under the impression that they were in limited supply, but apparently not to Asher and the Northwest Pack. Aside from objects related to shifters, he had an assortment of protective objects, stones, magical ingredients, daggers, and magical books that would have made any magic wielder's day if given a chance to spend time in this vault.

I studied him with new eyes. Perhaps I had passed judgment too harshly and too soon. The way he had offered comfort to the wolves was in stark contrast to what I knew of him. And recalling how hard he fought not to change when Ian was trying to force him to, I wondered whether he struggled in order to challenge Ian or to make sure he wouldn't hurt me.

When Asher closed the distance between us, I no longer cared about my opinions of him or if they were without merit. I became aware of shifter magic and how different it was to others. His close proximity and the cavernous eyes that studied me were a reminder of the esoteric magic he possessed. That all shifters did. But as the Alpha, Asher had something different. I saw and felt it when he attempted to pull control from Ian and get the shifters to revert and again when he prevented his change at Ian's hands. He had command of the raw, primal, and archaic magic that embodied shifters.

"I'd be very well compensated if I were to call Madison," I said, a hint of teasing in my tone. It was a toothless threat; before I could even make the call, Asher would have his pack lawyers making every attempt to block STF's entry. While they had them busy with red tape, the vault would be cleared out and I'd look like the liar.

Glints of mischief played in Asher's eyes. "You wouldn't do a thing like that to me, now would you?" he purred, knowing as well as I did that it wouldn't work in my favor.

I put some distance between us, hoping to subdue my mounting curiosity about his magic. I had never borrowed magic from a shifter, had always assumed it was impossible. Now I was wondering if I could.

"You keep staring at me with an odd curiosity, and your breathing and heart rate have increased more than usual. What's different?"

My curiosity about shifter magic hadn't been squelched since I experienced the extent of it at Kelsey's. Each moment with him in the vault made it more apparent I really wanted to soothe it.

I shook my head and took out my phone, but his hands closed around mine before I could snap a shot.

"What are you doing?"

"I need to take pictures so I'll know. Most of these items I'm familiar with, but there are a few that I'm not. I have to research if they can be used."

Asher was slow to release my hands, but I didn't think it was because he didn't trust me. Possessing these objects provided a sense of security. Before, I had considered his behavior extreme, even criminal, but having seen shifters lose control and have their volition stripped from them, I understood his need for caution.

Asher watched me carefully as I inventoried everything. Once my phone was back in my bag, he asked, "Are you going to tell me what's changed? Why are you like this around me now?"

It took a long time for me to answer and Asher shifted from foot to foot. "I can control my wolf," he said. "You never have to fear me hurting you, Erin."

"It's not that!" I blurted, realizing he thought I was afraid of him. That I saw that side of him, a vulnerability, a weakness in his armor, and I was uncomfortable or even feared him. "You know I'm not human, right?"

He smiled. "You don't have active magic, so you are human-ish."

My words wouldn't come out as easily as I wanted them to. I wanted to test a shifter, see if the results would be the same as with Mephisto. Would Asher stay alive but only lose the ability to shift?

He'd closed the distance between us. Patiently he waited for me to continue, but the words wouldn't come out. It wasn't easy asking a person to allow you to put them in a death state. If they showed anything other than aversion, it was hard not to consider them a freak. What type of person agrees to that?

His breath was warm against my lips as he whispered, "Ask the question."

I took several steps back to give us space. "I'm curious whether I can borrow magic from a shifter," I admitted. "I've never tried before."

His eyebrows arched. "Why haven't you tried a shifter before?"

I shrugged. "Don't know. Shifter magic is weird."

"You kill people with a kiss and shifter magic is weird?"

"Shifters grow tails. It's weird magic, just admit it," I teased. "And you can partially change. You do a shifter shimmy, and a tail may very well appear."

The corners of his lips lifted. "Shifter shimmy?"

I gave him several moments to think about it. Seeing my hesitation, he inched in closer.

"Okay. Go ahead." Leaning in, he attempted to kiss me.

Stumbling back, I blurted out, "What are you doing?"

"I'm kissing you?"

"Why?"

His brows knit together. Tension quickly overtook his face at the idea of having incorrect information. Asher never wanted to have wrong information. "It's a death's kiss."

"It doesn't *have* to be a kiss. I just have to be close and speak the words of power."

"Then do it," he whispered, his voice warm and encouraging, taking the chill and emptiness out of the room.

This time, I was the one who removed the distance between us, intrigued by his lack of fear that didn't seem to come from a strange place of pleasure, need, or dark curiosity. It was just absolute and unambiguous. His eyes told me to borrow his magic and sate my curiosity.

"Say the words and let's see."

"You don't fear being so close to death?"

"I've been the emissary of death far too often. It's not healthy to fear what at times you are forced to deliver."

Is it just me or is that simply a fancy way of admitting to homicide?

"We don't have dominance fights, *technically*, although there are some who will only abide by our old ways. It's difficult to accept, but to maintain my position, it is unavoidable." He leaned in even closer, his lips curled into a lazy smile. "It's not death I fear, it's loss of control."

Which explained his position on Ian. I wanted to send him back to the Veil, but Asher wanted a more permanent solution.

"Okay. You probably should lie down," I suggested.

"I'm fine." Shifters are a strange group, I decided. Or maybe it was just Asher. *No, I won't lie down, I prefer to collapse on the concrete.*

I whispered the words, my lips brushing his as I spoke them. Then I pressed my lips lightly against his. Nothing. The words flowed from me again, just to make sure. Nothing. Maybe I shouldn't have been surprised. The distinctness of their magic baffled so many. Neither one of us moved. The heat of his body wrapped around me. His warm breath breezed against my lips.

He leaned in closer, pressing his lips harder against mine. It was time to move. *Move, Erin.*

I stepped away and smiled weakly. "I guess that answered the question."

"Which one? Are my lips as soft and sensual as they look, or if you can borrow magic from a shifter?" He flashed me a smile.

"Just wondering if you could be any more arrogant. I was *so* right," I countered, sneering at the smirk on his face. *This guy.*

His smirk didn't waver.

Breaking the uncomfortable silence, I studied the items in the room again. "I have two other sources," I informed him. "I'll let you know what I find."

CHAPTER 8

*S*imeon looked away from the deer he appeared to be engaged in an intense conversation with when my car moved up his driveway. I guessed that when you are a person with the ability to communicate with animals, you stand in front of your porch and just do that. I waved from my car, but a weak smile was all that he offered.

Although Simeon had offered me the use of his library, he probably hadn't expected me to follow through with it. He preferred the company of four-legged animals, so I didn't take it personally.

The large cabin in the middle of the dense wood was exactly what I expected. Tree stumps remained as a vanguard surrounding the home, edged by verdant woods. To the right, a slow-moving river flanked the walkway and curled around to the back of the home to form a bay where a person could fish. I doubted Simeon fished; he likely opted to use that time to talk with the animals. Oak, dirt, and muddy water inundated the air.

Kai was off at a distance, cutting down a tree, his shirt clinging to his sweat-drenched body and his face flushed from effort. Frenetic bursts of energy accompanied each swing. If I stepped closer, I knew I would feel the hum of magical energy coming off him like a live wire.

An ocelot startled me as she ran past me to Simeon, chirping at him. Smiling, he moved into the house and returned. He stroked her back before he dropped something I couldn't identify in front of her. She devoured it and made a contented mewl before darting back into the woods.

"Friend of yours?" I asked.

My comment didn't even earn me a twinkle of amusement. Regarding me with cool indifference, he stepped aside to let me in.

"You want to use the library, right?" he asked, keeping me on task. Clearly we weren't going to have coffee and pass the time in mundane conversation.

Hiding my surprise was impossible when I entered his home and saw the stark contrast to the naturalistic architecture of the exterior. Except for the hardwood floors, the home was modern. Black stainless-steel appliances in his farmhouse gourmet kitchen. A double-sided stone fireplace divided the kitchen from the great room, wood piled neatly next to it. The great room was simple in design, with just two large sofas and what looked like Amish wooden chairs. In the corner squatted a large wood writing desk. The legs were the trunk of a tree. If it was a replica, it was exquisite.

There wasn't a TV in sight, but I wasn't convinced he didn't have a high-tech contraption where he pressed a button and one rose from the hardwood floor. I schooled my face to neutral so it didn't show what I wanted to say: hypocrite. After the derisive remarks he'd made to Mephisto about his home, I'd expected something more simplistic.

"Did Kai lose a bet or something?" I asked. From my spot in the house, I could see him cutting away at the tree with determination.

"No, he asked." Simeon looked out the window, a small

smile curling his lips as he watched Kai finding pleasure in something most people wouldn't.

"Why is he using an axe instead of a chainsaw?"

He shrugged. "Because it's Kai," he said. He didn't elaborate. I assumed in their circle, that answer sufficed.

"The library is this way."

There weren't many rooms, but each one was large. His bedroom door was slightly ajar as we moved past it and I only got a glimpse of a king-size bed in the middle of the room that would take up half the space in my two-bedroom apartment. A natural stone fireplace had a large rug on the hearth in front of it. Sage-colored walls gave the room an inviting, earthy feel. The oversized window provided a serene view of the lazy river. In front of the window was a meditation cushion. Oversized potted plants were placed in each corner.

What was meant to be a quick glance turned into a full stop as I took in the room. Beautiful and calming. It was a serene space that made the room I used for meditation pale in comparison.

"That's my bedroom, not the library," he offered softly.

Really? I guess the bed in the room should have tipped me off.

He nudged me, his steps quickening and moving with the same ethereal grace and fluidity that Mephisto no longer hid.

Simeon's home was beautiful, but the most impressive thing about it was the library. Ceiling-to-floor built-in bookshelves lined each wall in the massive room. There was an oversized chair in the corner, with a small table, and in the middle of the room, a table made of reclaimed wood. It was an odd choice to complement the white shelving, but it fit.

"Kai?" I asked, pointing at the table.

Simeon nodded. "How did you know?"

After seeing him wield an axe to cut down a tree, it wasn't an illogical leap to assume he was a craftsman.

"This is the section you will be most interested in."

Simeon pointed to a section of weathered-looking books and tattered binders with papers and journals.

Three hours and I didn't have any more information than I had before. There were many accounts of the Veil. I was referred to as a *Naut*—one who could move between the Veil with ease—unless I was a *Pars,* who had some restrictions in parts of the Veil. I hadn't navigated the Veil enough to determine which. Was seeing the entire Veil possible, or was it equivalent to trying to see the entire world? *Sers* could see the Veil but couldn't go through it. I wondered what Elizabeth was; she had extensive knowledge of the Veil. Had she resided there? The more I learned about the Veil, the more I wanted to explore it . . . until I remembered people like Malific were there. And Ian. He was desperate to return although I didn't know why.

Despite a thorough search, I couldn't find a single spell to lift a person's inability to return to the Veil.

I raised my forehead from its position on the table when the scent of cedar and mint wafted into the room. Staring at me from the doorway was a silent Kai, freshly showered and dressed. His dark hair was damp and disheveled. Cognac-colored eyes ran along the length of the table, taking in the crumpled bags of chips, candy, and nuts that I'd been munching on. His eyes jumped to the trash can in the corner, then to my pile of garbage on the table.

"You're messy."

Note to self: Kai is a neat freak and a little rude about it.

"Hi, Kai," I sang in a cloying voice.

Kai's eyes didn't move from the pile of mess until I gathered it up and moved past him toward the trash can. I could feel the live wire of magic pulsing off him, beckoning me in a manner that was hard to ignore. Quickly dumping the trash,

I made it back to the chair and locked my feet behind the legs to root me in place. Kai took several steps back, perhaps because he saw something in my face that made him want to remove my urge. It didn't, because I suspected that, as with Mephisto, I could borrow Kai's magic without dire consequences. And I wanted it so badly that it was becoming distracting. I jerked my attention from him to the books.

"What are you looking for?" Kai asked, his gaze going to the books open in front of me.

"I'm not sure. A way to get into the Veil, maybe?"

"But I thought you can."

"With Mephisto's magic, I can. But I need to get someone else in there and make sure he can't get out."

Hopeful interest sparked on Kai's face, but he tamped it down quickly. It confirmed what I suspected: They also wanted to return to the Veil but couldn't. I hadn't figured out if they were kicked out and cursed never to return. They didn't have the same markings as Ian, so I had no idea what was keeping them from doing it. Mephisto had told me he was restricted, but he hadn't offered anything more.

"How was he restricted?" Kai asked.

"Elizabeth did a spell using the Xios. It's a single use object and was destroyed in the process."

His brows pinched together. "The destruction of the Xios sealed the spell, so how did the person get out?"

"I don't know," I lied, watching his face carefully to determine if he could detect the lie. If he did, he didn't show it. "He's upset and wants it removed so he can travel between here and the Veil as he did before."

"What is he? Fae? Witch? Mage?"

"Fae. And it's becoming a huge fae problem. He has his sights on Neri and Adalia's position." I could hear the annoyance edge its way into my voice. This wasn't just a fae problem; it was a shifter, STF, and my problem. I suspected Ian's thirst for power and domination wouldn't stop at just having the fae under his control. If I didn't get rid of him, more people would become curious about his escape and the Veil. Obviously, the Veil's existence wasn't a secret, but I was comfortable with it not being widely known. Curiosity often creates a relentless desire to satisfy it. I didn't want another Ian escaping.

"Not just any 'fae' problem, you have an Ian problem," Mephisto corrected, entering the library in a graceful sweep of movement and taking a seat next to me. His dark-blue professional attire was in stark contrast to the casualness of Kai's white shirt and dove-gray sweats.

I took a steadying breath. The large space was over-whelmed by magic.

"How is that different?" I asked.

"Ian is an old fae and believes that simply existing longer than most entitles him to rule. He and his acolytes were defeated during his first attempt at a coup in the Veil. He was ironbound and imprisoned for forty years as penalty. After his release he made a deal with a demon, and his immunity to iron is a result of demon magic and an ancient spell. Once the demon satisfied Ian's request, Ian rewarded the demon by killing it and thereby ending any means of finding a reversal."

The frisson of contempt in Mephisto's eyes gave me the impression he thought the punishment should have been more severe.

"It's not a natural immunity." Relief flooded me. Spells could be undone. Bindings could be unbound, and even curses could be lifted. I had options for defeating Ian.

"He's here. I'm not sure why he wants to go back or needs to be able to move between here and the realms," I said.

"Here he has the upper hand and options not available to him in the Veil. Here, shifters don't have an immunity to magic, so they can be controlled by his magic. He can't do that in the Veil. And it appears that the fae are much weaker on this side of the Veil." Kai frowned at the observation.

The more I learned of the Veil, the stronger my desire was to find a way to make sure no one passed through. The worlds should be kept separate, but I wasn't selfless enough to make it a priority. I would do it after I satisfied my agreement with Mephisto and had his magic.

Simeon had entered the library while Kai was talking, and I was highly aware of being surrounded on all sides by the "otherness" of their magic. Kai in front, Simeon to my right, and Mephisto to my left. The pages of the book I was searching creased under the pressure of my hold. Mephisto's hands covered mine and removed them from the pages. Then he smoothed the creases in the pages.

"Sorry," I whispered.

A look passed between the men, then Kai and Simeon left me and Mephisto alone. He slid the book he'd taken from me across the table. The extended silence became uncomfortable as I realized he was inching toward a conversation I didn't want to have.

"I need a way to send Ian back and make sure he never returns," I said. "The last thing we need is him here."

"No, the last thing we need is for him to join forces with the Immortalis. They also want to get back into the Veil. Ian wants the freedom to travel between the worlds, whereas they just want to free Malific."

"Even more reason to send him back as quickly as possible."

"Have you spoken with your parents?" Mephisto asked softly.

I busied myself pulling another book toward me and flipping through the pages. When he repeated the question, I shook my head without looking up from the book that wasn't nearly as interesting as the magic Mephisto was giving off. His long fingers were gentle as they hooked under my chin, guiding my face up to look at him.

"Is it because you already know the answer?"

"Because it doesn't matter," I disputed, although I knew that couldn't be further from the truth. Their confirmation would change things. Irreparably change my life. I would no longer be Vera and Gene's daughter but a god, or demigod, or whatever. And not just the daughter of any god but one so terrible she'd been locked away. "I don't care. I like my life as it is and I'm perfectly fine not having a psychotic god at the family reunion."

"It doesn't bother you to not know how they got you? Were you abducted from Malific, saved from her wrath, or kicked out?"

"Saved from her wrath?"

"You're her daughter. You share a blood bond."

I had her blood. In the magical world, familial blood—especially that of offspring—was just as valuable as having her blood.

Mephisto's dark eyes were pools of curiosity, and his concern wasn't selfless. I didn't know how to respond because he was asking the same questions I had posed to myself. What did this all mean? If released, would Malific come looking for me? If so, why?

He leaned in and asked, "Don't you wonder why you are her only one? The only child she has?"

This question disconcerted me the most. Stories of gods' children's blood being the only thing that could hurt them or, worse, the child's life being the only thing that could save them. Nature versus nurture filled my thoughts as well. Based on the stories, Malific was horrible—malicious, violent, and power hungry. She violated the basic rules of engagement, attacking shifters during their transition, drowning them and killing their allies because they dared reject her demand that they be her personal attack animals.

94

Ian was doing the same: forcing shifters to fight against their will. The anger that I'd managed to control blazed suddenly with a ferocity I couldn't control.

My business made me tolerant of a certain level of violence. It wasn't my first choice, although I was never categorically opposed to using it, but like most people, I adhered to the rules of engagement. Some behavior was beyond a display of power and strength and was sheer brutality and cruelty. Ian had crossed that line.

"I do," I admitted softly. "Most gods have more than one child, don't they?"

"They do. But Malific has always done things differently. Most gods do not exert their power on others. Living alongside fae, shifters, witches, and mages and knowing that their power is greater, but not their numbers, makes them vulnerable. Malific didn't share those beliefs. She believed in dominion and was willing to do whatever it took to achieve that. Which is why she created the Immortalis, an army that would give her that."

"She wanted to subjugate the other gods, too?"

"Her despotic nature made people cautious. And I do believe that if she had the ability to do it, she would have. She wanted to divide the Veil, taking the most desirable land and dividing it among the gods. The parts of the Veil I showed you is how most gods choose to live."

I cast my mind back to the scenic views of snowcapped mountains, clear blue water, animals coexisting unaware of which was predator and which was prey.

"It's a way of life that she doesn't understand. A way of life that she couldn't comprehend. Her thirst for domination and her refusal to be reasoned with is why she was imprisoned."

In desperate need of a topic change and a distraction, I pushed the hair that had uncoiled from my bun out of my face. The more I learned of Malific, the more I needed her not to be my mother and everyone's assumption to be wrong.

"Is it true that the magic in the Veil has been protected? A penalty for—" I didn't want to say murder. Thinking it, planning it, and even considering it as an option was one thing, but saying it aloud seemed crude.

He nodded. "The penalty for the murder of those who reside in the Veil is loss of magic."

"If the fae kill Ian, they lose their magic?"

"Only the person who kills him. The same would be true of Asher, if he did. He'd lose his ability to shift and ultimately, he'd lose his position as the Alpha. I think the price of Ian's demise would be too great." A small smile curled his lips. "I see you two are playing nice once again. How fortuitous for him that you're in his corner prepared to fight for his pack."

I ignored the speculation in his voice. "It's a job."

Murder was the nuclear option, one I hoped not to have to employ, but if this was just the beginning of Ian's terror on the city—on the shifters—he'd have to be stopped.

"A human could do it," I said.

"If a human could get close enough . . . but I assume they would lose something as well." The darkening of Mephisto's eyes exhibited what: their life.

Dammit. "But you all killed the Immortalis. They're from the Veil."

"Created by Malific. The same rules don't apply, and they can only be killed one way—with an Obitus blade."

I had a hard time believing that beheading a person wasn't the end. Vampires were nearly impossible to kill, but behead one and they're dead. True death unless you're foolish enough not to separate the head from their body. If you don't and they manage to feed, then you have an *almost* truly dead vampire with a vendetta that you won't survive. Rule number one with killing a vampire: Sever the head and take it down the road. But I guess that wasn't true with gods and the Immortalis.

Rubbing my temple, I attempted to ease the encroaching tension headache. This was a mess. Top priority: Ian. Stop him and worry about the Immortalis and Malific later.

Just as I was about to start questioning Mephisto about ways to stop Ian, the vibration from an incoming call caused my phone to rattle on the table. Asher's name came up. I quickly answered it and headed outside to give us some privacy.

"What do you know of Dante's Forest?" Asher asked.

"I've heard nothing good about it. It's easy to get in but not as easy to get out. But if you need strong magical objects, not widely available ingredients, or answers, it's the one place you might find them." I hadn't had a job where I'd needed to go to the Forest, but after learning of its existence, I found out as much as I could about it. My curiosity regarding rumors that surrounded it remained. I don't make it a practice to go places rumored to be unsafe just to satisfy my curiosity. I was an adrenaline junky—it helped with the magic cravings—but I didn't possess a death wish, despite what some may believe.

"Exactly. It's also where I heard we can find a Conparco Shield. Elizabeth believes that it, along with desisto root, will prevent Ian forcing us to change."

It was apparent that once you'd made a deal with Elizabeth, you earned the right to call her by her real name. But Woman in Black was more apropos and hinted at her dark disposition, her mercurial ways, and her reputation for dubious dealings. It also hinted at the inconspicuousness of her existence. I wasn't sure what type of supernatural she was. But her magical prowess exceeded anything I'd seen.

I could hear noise in the background and wondered if he was preparing to leave at that moment.

With Elizabeth's reputation being what it was, did Asher

really trust everything that came out of her mouth? He could determine lies, but what about the brand of deception for which she was known? She'd perform your requested spell and you'd be left with whatever trick she'd affixed to it.

"Do you trust her?"

"No. Well, up to a point. Limited at best. I've dealt with her enough that she's not able to get anything over on me. I'm very precise with my requests. Also with payments and the penalties if anything happens outside the agreement. Elizabeth challenges my negotiation skills at every turn."

"What are you paying her?"

Asher hesitated. "Nothing she can ask for will be too much to pay to ensure that Ian doesn't have control over me and my pack the way he does now."

"When are you leaving?"

"Tomorrow morning."

The noise in the background was probably him packing.

"Would you like an assist?"

He could pull people from his pack, probably even ask Sherrie to go, and I'd want a person who could shift to a lion with preternatural speed and heightened senses, but with Ian on the loose and causing mayhem, it was probably best if one of them stayed in the city, along with the strongest in his pack.

There was a long pregnant silence. The commotion in the background stopped and I could picture Asher's contemplative face. "Erin," he said, his voice deep and grave, "you getting the *Mystic Souls* and the release of Ian was just a coincidence, right?"

He was miles away; he couldn't hear any physiological signs or see my face.

"Uh-huh."

Another long pause. "I'll pick you up tomorrow morning at seven, at your place. I'll have a plane ready. Having a witch with us will probably be advantageous. Can Cory come?"

"Yes, he should be able to."

"Tomorrow then."

Nothing in his voice betrayed whether I had successfully lied to a shifter, but my gut was telling me I hadn't.

Mephisto was stretched out in a chair, his jacket laid across the back of it. With one hand clasped behind his head, his shirt molded to his body, showing off his defined physique usually hidden under his tailored suits.

"Asher calls and you leave. The war really is over." His expression was guarded as his midnight eyes tracked my every movement as I gathered my things. Magic snaked around me. *How the hell did he do that?*

"Stop it. Unless you plan on sharing, stop."

"Of course I plan on sharing. My conditions still stand."

I slung my bag over my shoulder. "That's not entirely true now, is it? You've suspended it." First, he wanted to find out the location of this infamous box before sending me in to retrieve it, instead of me just Veil-hopping to look for it. Now that he suspected Malific was my mother, he was reluctant for me to go into the Veil at all. My introduction to the Veil had been uneventful, even pleasurable, and I was more than willing to go again.

"I'd prefer to minimize the danger I put you in, so I'm being cautious. Are you faulting me for that?"

Agitation and frustration had me running my fingers through my hair and pulling it out of the bun. Mephisto stood and quickly moved toward me, taking my hands in his to stop my fidgeting. "I'm careful with your life, make sure that Asher is as well."

The muted energy of his magic was a subtle reminder of a weakness I couldn't fight. My teeth bit down hard on my lips, keeping the words of power in. I backed up several feet, slipping my hands from his.

"I'll be careful."

I powerwalked out of Simeon's home. Some might even describe it as a jog. My resolve wouldn't even allow me to slow down to give Simeon and Kai anything more than a quick wave. Once in my car, I opened all the windows and sat in the driveway soaking in the rich smell of pine, the robust scent of the surrounding earth, and the hints of floral. It took a few minutes but eventually Mephisto or his magic wasn't consuming my every thought. I started the car, and by the time I was at Cory's I was focused on the most pressing issue: stopping Ian.

The Conparco Shield and desisto root would only be a partial fix, just preventing him controlling the shifters, but it would significantly weaken his strategy.

"Someone better be chasing you," Cory grumbled from the other side of the door in response to me battering it. "What?" he demanded, opening it just a crack and keeping his body as a barrier.

"I tried to call but you didn't answer your phone or your texts."

"You have my attention, now what do you need?" he said, obviously eager for me to go away.

My eyes narrowed and I came to the tips of my toes trying to see over him. When that failed, I looked through the little gap and saw a figure behind him.

"You have a visitor?" I leaned into him. "Alex?"

His voice mirrored mine. "Yes, Alex, the shifter with the exceptional hearing so you can probably just keep your voice normal."

So I did. "Hi, Alex."

"Erin."

Cory stepped aside and I entered to find Alex at the kitchen table with a plate of pasta in front of him. Alex was pasta worthy, and I was a little jealous. I occasionally got in on one of Cory's cheat days, which consisted of a slice or two of pizza, leaving me to polish off the remainder and feel greedy.

"Chicken parmesan, that's my favorite."

Cory grabbed my shirt and kept me from advancing toward the table to make the heroic sacrifice of saving him from carb overload.

"Excuse me for a second, I have to retrain Jane the cave-woman here. No. Jane. No. You have to wait until you're invited. Nod your head if you understand."

I glared at him. "Me hungry. Me see food. Me eat food." I jabbed Cory in the chest. His teeth sank into his lips in his effort to not laugh.

I winked. "I was making the carb sacrifice for you and this is the thanks I get."

"There's plenty. I'm fine with her joining us," Alex offered, extending his hand to one of the vacant chairs. Alex's charis-matic smile was inviting, and his keen hazel eyes weren't cold or unwelcoming, but there was no sincerity in his invite. If that wasn't enough, I could feel Cory's death glare boring into the side of my face.

"Thank you, but I can't stay." I jerked my head toward the door and Cory followed me until we were well away from Alex's hearing distance. Even then, I still pulled him farther out until we were a good fifteen feet from the building. When a person can detect minor changes in heart rate, breathing, or intonation, you could never be too cautious.

"We have a trip planned tomorrow." My voice was brighter than it should have been, considering we were going to a forest into which some had ventured and never returned.

Cory knew me too well. His gaze narrowed. "Where?"

"Dante's Forest."

"No, we don't," he countered.

"We have to. Elizabeth believes she can nullify Ian's ability to control the shifters with a Conparco Shield and desisto root. She has the root, and we have to find the shield."

If this could be fixed, Cory would do it out of principle. The guilt tugged at me constantly; for him, it had to be an unbearable burden. I put a great deal of effort into the reassuring smile I gave him.

"I should have listened to you," he admitted.

"The past can't be changed. We can only do what we can to make it right. We're going with Asher. His ego won't let us do anything but get out of there unscathed."

Places that were great sources of rare objects, ingredients, and remedies were entrenched by warnings of great danger and foreboding tales. The warnings and tales were usually perpetuated by those who braved such places. They kept people from visiting and depleting the rare resources. I always remained skeptical of each story.

Cory was easing back to his apartment. I gave him the pick-up time and that Asher had already made the travel arrangements and then I started backing toward my car.

"When should I expect my nice dinner? You never make meals like that for me anymore."

"I don't take you to dangerous forests, so I think we're even."

"I bet it's not going to be nearly as dangerous as it sounds. A walk in the park. Easy peasy. We'll be in and out in minutes."

"Absolutely. Named after the nine circles of hell, it can't be anything but a cakewalk," Cory said, flashing me a grin.

CHAPTER 9

"We're not flying commercial, I suspect," Cory said as he watched me recheck what I was taking with me. I'd never get through TSA if we were.

"No, it's a short trip to South Dakota."

"Oh, just a short trip to South Dakota. Let's just hop on my plane and go. How do I become an Alpha?" Amusement curled Cory's lips into a roguish grin.

"It's not *his* plane, it's the Northwest Wolf Pack's plane. He only has access to it."

"Well, if he only has access to it, that's not impressive at all. What is he, a pauper, with his meager access to a company plane? We deserve better. There have to be people in higher places that we can rub elbows with."

"You know the STF and Mephisto have access to a plane?"

"Stop saying that like it's a thing!" he said. "We all have access to a plane, but very few people can just call one up and have it ready to go in a matter of hours. If you think that's normal, what is your life like?"

"It's not my life. I'm just pointing out that this is not as swanky a situation as you're making it out to be. We need to get to South Dakota. He has a plane. For the record, you can get a commercial plane with twenty-four-hour notice, too."

Eyes narrowed, Cory gave me a *"really"* look. I shrugged, but before I could respond I received a text from Asher notifying us he was downstairs.

Seeing me struggle with my bag, Asher started to get out of the car.

"I have it." I said.

"No, I have it. Last thing I need is for you to injure yourself on the way there."

He gave an exaggerated grunt while lifting the bag and putting it in the trunk. "Are you sure you need an entire trunkful of weapons?"

"It's better to have them and not need them," I offered, doing a fourth and final check of the bag's contents.

As Asher made his way back to the car, the studying gaze that he kept on Cory didn't go unnoticed by either one of us.

Cory looked at my bag. "I think I agree with Asher, you don't need a trunkful of weapons."

"I hope I don't need anything other than an amiable personality and a smile," I said with a beam.

"Please stop relying on that as a weapon in your quiver," he teased. "You're putting a lot of weight on its effectiveness. I fear that eventually you will find yourself disappointed."

"Hey!" I pushed him against the car and twisted his arm behind his back in a light hold he could easily break if he wanted. "I'm charming, fella."

He scoffed. "This is exactly as I imagined it would be. I'm butter in your hand. Enchanted, really. How could I not be?"

Laughing, I released his arm and flashed him a smile. "See, I'm delightful."

"So. *Very.* Delightful. I don't know how people stand it."

Cory relaxed back in the soft leather of the plane seat that Asher had suggested, sipping on the drink the flight attendant brought him. Asher's attention on Cory hadn't wavered. It wasn't hostile, but it did possess hints of ominous interest.

"Was it a spell in English or Latin that released Ian?" Asher finally asked Cory.

"What are you talking about?" Cory kept his face and voice neutral. He might not have answered the question, but he still gave Asher the information he needed. Asher knew that Cory did the spell.

Asher's eyes hardened. Cory sat taller, his hands moving in front of him, fingers spreading, his initial positioning before he performed defensive magic. Asher noticed the change and shifted forward in his chair.

"Come with me," I commanded Asher, unbuckling my seatbelt and standing to place myself between them. Shifter. Or Alpha. I wasn't sure which one made Asher an obstinate ass, but he didn't move. "Please," I pushed out through gritted teeth. Slowly he stood and followed me to the bedroom.

"What the hell is wrong with you?" I blurted as soon as he'd closed the door behind us.

Asher dropped into the chair near the door and blew out an exasperated breath. "I just wanted answers."

"Why? What does it change? Fine, you know Cory did the spell. So? He's here, on a very dangerous job. If that's not a demonstration of remorse and his desire to make this right, then what is?"

"It shouldn't have been done in the first place. Cory doesn't belong in the Veil and if he had adhered to the rules, Ian wouldn't be here." The pot/kettle platitude definitely was relevant here, but I refrained from pointing it out.

Kneeling to meet his eyes, I said, "You're right. Curiosity got the better of him, but just as you would do anything to protect your pack, I'm the same way with Cory. So, where does that leave us?" My voice was a whisper. "I'm trying to undo it."

"I hold you blameless."

"You shouldn't. Assign the blame to me. If I hadn't wanted the book, Cory wouldn't have been able to use it."

There was an attempt at a smile that didn't quite manifest. It was tight and missing his usual arrogance.

"What does it change, whether I'm upset with him or you?"

"True. But I don't care if you glare at me from across the plane. I'd just give it right back to you. And do some creative things with my hands to let you know exactly how I feel about it. I'm not above smacking the big bad wolf on the snout if he needs it."

That earned me a laugh, a deep sonorous rumble that filled the space. He leaned toward me, amusement etched on his face. "You say that because you've never felt the full intensity of it. It's quite cowering."

"I'll make sure to cower thusly," I quipped back as I met his challenging gaze. "Then I'll smack you on the nose and give you a 'bad doggie, bad doggie.'" It was a good threat, but calling some random wolf-shifter a dog would earn me more than a grin. I'd see teeth, but it would be him baring them right before he took my hand off.

A dry chuckle had Asher coming to his feet. He turned a little, shifting his gaze from me to the muted-colored walls. "I hate this," he admitted softly. The arrogance and overconfidence had fallen away. It was the most vulnerable I'd ever seen him and he quickly pulled himself taller, seemingly embarrassed that he allowed me to see that glimpse of it. I saw him as more than Asher the arrogant Alpha.

"I get it. You know what I am, how I get my magic. I'm at the mercy of others loaning me magic, me taking it—which never ends well—or being without. It's not exactly the same, but I understand what it's like not to have total control. It's not a good feeling."

"Yeah," he breathed out.

"I need to get back and work on a plan to get into Dante's."

When Asher gave me a rakish smirk, I knew he realized it was just an excuse to put some much-needed distance between us.

He shoved his hand through his tuft of thick hair and sighed. "I'm sorry, I was being an ass."

"Your words, not mine," I teased. I was so close to him that I could see the darker hues of gray in his eyes. Unnatural heat came off him, a reminder of how warm shifters ran. Maybe that was the reason they preferred to be naked after a change. Or maybe they just liked to be naked.

"We're going to get a Xios or its equivalent, send Ian's ass back where he belongs, and if I can lock down the Veil, I'll try to do that, too," I said confidently, knowing the latter part was contingent on me completing Mephisto's job. But there was enough truth to it that it got past Asher. After I had my own magic, locking the Veil down would be a priority.

Asher's finger lightly brushing against my cheek startled me. Not the touch, but me leaning into it and staying there for several moments.

"Are things good between you and Cory?" I finally asked.

Asher opened the door, his hand pressed to my back as he guided me out. His only answer to my question was his lips pursing into a tight line.

He didn't return to his seat but moved to another section of the plane. It made it harder to convince Cory that things were fine between them. I wasn't sure I believed they were.

"This is it," Cory said, pointing to the warded area that when viewed with nonmagical senses led the eyes to believe there were just mountains, small caves, sparse trees, and quiet serenity. The repulsion spell divested anyone of the desire to explore the area, urging them a few miles farther away.

Extremely perceptive humans and supernaturals could detect the seams of wards, unlike Mirras which were flawless in their construct. The tell on this one was the faint gold shimmer that appeared near the tree, easy to miss if you weren't looking for it.

Cory took longer working the ward, because he wasn't trying to break it but create a passage for us to slip through.

"Is it hard?" I asked after ten minutes had passed, far longer than it had ever taken him to bring down a ward before.

"Not hard, just fragile. We're not doing ourselves any favors by bringing down this witch's ward. This is a test. We enter without dismantling it and I guess we're proven worthy to go into the Forest," he speculated. "Why powerful people are so needlessly eccentric, I'll never know. How hard is it to have a power word that allows entrance, then hear the person out? Why make us go through this?" Cory frowned and blew out a breath.

Fifteen minutes later we were passing through a narrow opening that led us directly to the entrance of the cave. A stream of water forced us to the side, walking on the broken rocks following the path of the stream. The earthy dankness became overpowering the farther we advanced. Asher's lithe, silent movement over the uneven terrain made me nervous, making me grateful that Cory's and my steps echoing throughout the space were announcing our approach. No one wants to be startled by unexpected guests.

Our forehead lights illuminated the passageway. I could see Asher's face wrinkling at the strong smells. It wasn't unpleasant, but flowery scents coming from a cave was unexpected.

"Yes," a voice croaked in the darkness.

After the voice whispered an invocation, the cave illuminated. Scanning the area, I couldn't find the source of light. A broad man sat on what appeared to be a throne of rocks. The jowls on his round face moved ever so slightly with the slightest movement of his head as he surveyed each of us. The incongruous scent of ginger that wafted from him mingled with the floral, mineral, and dank odors that surrounded us. He didn't smell like a witch, but I remember being told that entry to the Forest was guarded by one. The ginger had to be masking the earthy scent that I associated with witch magic.

His cornhusk complexion had streaks of red along the bridge of his nose. Slouching on his throne of rocks and minerals made his stout body seem shorter and rounder.

"What do you need?" he inquired curtly. There wasn't going to be any idle pleasantries. Not too many people were trekking across the country to go to the forest affiliated with hell. It was a sign of desperation.

The cave guardian's hands were clasped over his stomach, and his disinterest was apparent. This wasn't a calling as much as an indentured servitude. I thought back to my research in Simeon's library. The guardian's family was responsible for a spell that destroyed the Forest hundreds of years ago. As punishment, a tree nymph bound their magic to the forest and its immediate environs. If the Forest was destroyed or in danger, so was their magic, therefore they protected it fiercely.

"Conparco Shield," I offered.

"Anything else?"

"Xios or its equivalent."

"I hope the person you plan to imprison with it deserves such punishment," he said, his voice taking on a sharper, colder edge, undoubtedly taking issue with it because of his current predicament. He allowed several moments to pass as he treated us to his judgmental and reprimanding gaze.

"I don't have one here," he finally said before quickly returning to his sedate mood.

Without further questioning, magic pulsed in the enclosed space. Embers floated through the air forming an arc of light that danced a chaotic allegro. Another wave of his hand and a sharp command made the stone wall behind him separate. The light zipped out of the opening.

"You need to follow it, that's your guide," he said, responding to our wide-eyed expressions.

"Thank you," Cory and I offered together. Something in me wanted to withhold my gratitude because this seemed too easy. Nothing about obtaining powerful magical objects was ever this easy. Asher must have shared the same sentiment because he didn't offer any words of appreciation, just a simple nod.

"I assure you, nothing about finding the Conparco Shield will make you thank me. I only lead you on the journey. I'm not responsible for any impediments you encounter during it." Hints of rue lingered in his voice. "Go," he ordered with a wave.

"It can't be this easy," Asher whispered as we did another quick check of our supplies in our bags. We'd prepared for a day of hiking: water, dried food and nuts, weapons that could fit in the bag, and ingredients for spells in Cory's. Asher had a change of clothes in his. I was glad he had negated Cory's potential need to have to clothe him. To most, seeing witches clothe someone was like witnessing a live action performance of a fairytale. A wave of their wand or hand and *bibbidi-bobbidi-boo*, the person is clothed. It wasn't that simple.

Witches had to pull clothing from the ether, which took strong magic. Cory once described it as searching an obscure closet where you had to be attuned to what you needed. It took more effort than it appeared to, which was the reason I had been fine with Asher staying in his birthday suit if he had to rip his clothing during a change. Now, I wouldn't have to decide between spending the rest of the journey looking at Asher's bare ass and naughty bits or sacrificing Cory's magical energy.

After the recheck, we followed the illumination over the rocks. The light seemed sentient, flickering impatiently while Cory and I climbed slowly over the jagged rocks of the mountainside. Asher's preternatural grace, speed, and agility became increasingly frustrating as the light beat in an impatient glow and Asher waited for us to catch up.

"I can do without the smirk," I told him the third time he had to wait. "And the show," I snipped as he effortlessly lingered on the edge of the mountain.

The inner debate of whether to release the silver spark of energy easing from Cory's finger in Asher's direction to unbalance him was clear on Cory's face. I shot him a warning look and he extinguished the spark.

The steady beat of the light was needed as we continued up a trail, the sun suddenly shadowing, taking away the light and leaving us in dusk. When the light zipped away, its glow nearly four hundred feet from us, I assumed it had gone to the location of the shield. The brilliant flicker continued as we made our way toward it, Asher taking the lead, his gaze sweeping the area, nose flaring to take in the scents. His ears twitched ever so slightly.

"There's movement," he declared, as he snatched an arrow out of the air just a few inches from my face.

"Fuck," Cory hissed, looking at the arrow in Asher's hand.

"I knew it was too easy," I admitted with the breath I'd been holding since Asher stopped me from being stabbed in the face.

Cory erected a magical field that would only offer

moments of reprieve. Magical fields protected against magic but not bullets and knives and, I was willing to bet, arrows either. That was humans' advantage against magic. Weapons of destruction weren't stopped by magical barriers.

"I'll go for the Conparco Shield and you cover me," I directed, looking at the trek of grass, bosky areas, and uneven terrain between me and my destination. Its harmless appearance didn't fool me. Double karambit in one hand and knife in the other, I nodded for Cory to drop the field.

Asher's attention immediately went to the blade he'd given me. His gift of the well-crafted weapon with a sturdy handle and good balance had me quickly discarding my plans to keep it in the pretty box it came in. Its function appealed to me more than its aesthetics. The hardness of the mother-of-pearl handle was useful.

The shift in Asher's eyes and the lamination that overtook them. With predatory interest, he took in the surroundings, his deft readiness showing that the man shell had been shelved. The moment the protective covering dropped, I darted toward the light, Asher to the left toward the direction the arrow had come from, and Cory covered the right. Running fast, I negotiated the uneven surfaces, changing direction sharply when an arrow whizzed by me. Zigging and zagging to prevent being an easy target, I continued toward the crowd of trees until the pain of an arrow grazing my shoulder made me halt. Blood trickled down my arm, but the injury wasn't deep. It could have been worse.

I kept racing toward the thicket of trees that would keep me shielded from the sniper, unless there were more waiting in the woods. The thump of a body landing hard on the ground and a deafening growl caused me to turn. Asher snatched someone, or something, out of a tree. It was surprising to see him still in human form when the sound he made wasn't anything a human could produce.

At the mouth of the forest, the guide light beat in a steady rhythm. I became wary of the odd movement of the trees. Some trunks were only partially rooted into the ground, the other part loose. Exceedingly long, wiry branches extended too far. The ones that looked like simple trees, interwoven between the strange ones, gave me a sense of foreboding.

I felt ridiculous waiting for a tree to attack me until something thrashed into my back. The sting lingered and I could feel the welt rising. The blade of my karambit ripped through the other branch that lashed out at me. Quickly, I started slicing through the branches striking out at me, vines punching from the ground and snaking around my legs, and the abnormal movement of trees bending to strike at my face. Bark was spat in my direction and wind violently hit me, obstructing my vision. I felt unexpected relief. If that was the best hell's forest had to offer, I was fine.

Minutes passed while I surveyed the mass of severed branches and vines, motionless in my path—the way they should be.

"Oh," whimpered a soft voice carried by the breeze. Spinning around, I looked for the owner of the melancholic voice. A few feet away, a slender, average-height woman slowly approached. Her hunter-green tunic and dark-brown leggings reminded me of the trees she seemed to be mourning. Her gaze dropped periodically from me to the limbs and vines littering the ground. Two knives were sheathed at the belt on her waist, and she had a bow in her hand and seven arrows in her quiver.

Molten chocolate eyes promised retribution. She advanced slowly but stopped. Lowering the bow she was carrying, she returned the arrows to her quiver. There was anguish in her eyes. She yanked both knives from their sheaths with the grace and precision of one who had done this before.

"The trees attacked me first, I was just defending myself." I couldn't believe that was a thing I had to say. But here I was, in Dante's Forest, defending my tree murder and dismemberment.

"They were just doing their job."

"And I was just defending myself."

Knives still gripped in her hands, she waved to the right at the pile of severed tree bodies, or whatever she would call it. I held my blade out and readied my karambit.

"You 'defended' yourself with the brutality of a common monster," she scoffed.

"Should I have let them beat me and whip me on the ground until I was unconscious?" I was seriously defending my right to keep from being assaulted by a tree. How is this my life?

Her advance was slow and her magic was strong. It complemented the oaky smell that mingled with cinnamon. Witch. Earth witch. Like Madison, the witch could draw from the earth for her magic. Based on her anguish over the brutalization of her trees, she didn't have to kill them to do so.

"Such brutality must be met with the same," she announced as she charged. A back flip allowed me to dodge her quicker-than-anticipated jab. The knife punched at empty air. I slashed out at her with the karambit, missing her by a fraction of an inch. A well-aimed spin kick slammed into my left shoulder, unbalancing me. Pain blazed through me when her blade sliced through my arm. Blood. The last thing I needed was to fight a witch while bleeding. Not knowing the extent of her blood magic ability left me at a disadvantage.

She simply smiled at the blood running down my arm. I shuffled back several feet and kept a careful eye on her lips. Relief flooded me when only a smile of satisfaction offered me some comfort that she wasn't going to use my blood for a spell.

"You were bold in your murder but timid in paying for your crimes."

Once again, I was being forced to defend myself against tree fighting. Before I could finish my defense, her knife flew at me. The blade of the karambit knocked it off course. As she took a furtive glance behind her, probably looking for her discarded bow, I exploded in her direction with all that I had and slammed into her. Her blade plunged into my leg. Ignoring the pain, I fixed her to the ground. Fear-widened eyes met mine when I held the blade of the karambit at her throat. She struggled under me until the words of power ended and she eased into the state of in-between, her face frozen in a peaceful rest.

Sucking in sharp breaths through clenched teeth, I pulled the witch's knife out of my leg and rested against the trunk of a tree. Responding to the padding behind me, I rolled from my position and aimed my karambit at the wolf.

"Asher," I whispered his name through a sigh of relief. An arrow had pierced his blood-matted fur. Scanning the area, I quickly found the knife I'd lost when I crashed into the witch. Asher shook his head, informing me that I had nothing to worry about. He gave a low rumble and jerked his head toward the arrow. Moving to him, I knelt next to him. He remained stoic as I yanked out the arrow, which was fine because I winced, shrieked, and groaned for the both of us. The moment the arrow was removed from the wolf, there was a naked man sprawled on the ground in front of me, next to the bag he'd dragged with him.

He stood and I looked at him as if he was fully dressed. Shifters being out seemed to produce the same effect that being on a nude beach does—make you indifferent about naked bodies. Even ones that featured defined lines separating their abs. Even one with sinewy pecs and bulging arms that contracted and relaxed with the slightest movement. I jerked my eyes up before they could travel below the modesty line, earning me a snort of laughter from Asher.

"Cory," Asher said, in a slightly raised voice, then he waited expectantly.

"He's not a shifter, he can't hear that," I reminded him. The annoyance that shifters and vamps had with others made sense. When you could just slightly raise your voice and people responded, running at a speed that would earn a gold medal, seeing unimpeded at nightfall, then it was a hassle dealing with the "normal," even if they possessed magic. Cory had tried on many occasions to replicate their gifts with magic. If he wanted to see better at night, he did a lighting spell. Moving faster involved Wynding, which Cory, like most witches, couldn't do without a powerful magical charm. Despite Cory's impressive physique, he couldn't effortlessly lift another human being, whereas shifters did it without significant exertion.

"I wish the trees would stop talking." Asher frowned as he continued to survey the area.

"What?"

He trained his eyes on the sleeping witch. "They're mourning her," he offered. Leaning toward the tree closest to me, I strained to hear something. Nothing.

Asher closed his eyes. While he listened intently, I focused on the rapidly healing wound on his side. Seeing a naked shifter gets old quickly, but watching injuries mend in fast motion was always entrancing. Tissue meshing and binding, healing itself. Witnessing something that occurs in a matter of weeks take place in a matter of minutes was something I'd never gotten used to.

"Cory's coming. His steps are heavy but I don't think he's injured. He walks like a Clydesdale." Asher's words echoed the derision on his face. "There were five protectors of the forest. They've all been disabled."

I hesitated but needed to know. "Disabled?"

116

"They're alive. Their duty to protect doesn't deserve a death sentence."

My gaze followed his as it moved to the dead-looking witch.

"I'll wake her," I told him.

"When?" Cory asked as he approached us.

"I don't have an iridium brace and when I wake her, she's going to want to retaliate."

Her magic pulsed through me, sating the emptiness that had deepened after the option of the *Mystic Souls* was taken from me and the option of Mephisto giving me his magic slipped away. Cory's soft brown eyes stayed on mine. He moved to stand directly in front of me, his eyes filling with empathy even as his lips dipped into a frown.

"Return her magic," he entreated.

"I'll do it on the way back." The magic high was consuming me. That feeling of wholeness was something I was reluctant to be divested of.

"And if we're delayed returning, then what?"

He knew what would happen: The witch would die and I'd have her magic. I dropped my eyes from his and kept them rooted to the ground, unable to hold his censuring gaze.

"Erin," he whispered.

"I'm doing it now," I blurted, irritated.

"Not yet, I need to do a slumber spell. Once she's awake there won't be time for me to prepare it."

Cory's movements were heavy. His shirt was ripped and dirt coated his pants. There were welts along his face and blood stained the left sleeve of his shirt. The adrenaline had worn off and the cut on my arm ached. The bruises from my fight were starting to throb and my leg hurt.

Pulling out small vials, Cory dropped a pewter-colored powder into his hand, mixed it with two other substances, and blended it in his hands while we watched, me exhibiting more patience than Asher. Cory and my movements were so synchronized it was like a choreographed dance. Kneeling down in front of the witch, I said the words of power. Her eyes opened with the typical euphoric haze, but she was only given seconds to enjoy it before Cory said the incantation. It had a soothing melodic cadence, like a lullaby. She didn't have time to react once she realized what was happening. The powder sprinkled over her face, the spell creating sparkles of color. Whoever found her would know that a sleep spell had been performed. It was one of the few easily identifiable spells. When the spell wore off, the dust would disappear.

"Ready?" Asher asked, advancing toward the faint blinking light guiding us to the Conparco Shield.

"Which one of us should tell him he's still naked?" Cory whispered behind Asher, who hadn't waited for an answer.

"He knows and I don't think he cares," I said.

"I don't." Asher's focus was on the pulsing light near a bridge almost sixty yards away. Asher quickly dressed in his spare clothes and moved again toward the suspension bridge.

The wooden slats of the bridge had gaps between them of about six inches. Asher moved along them with a steadiness that made it look easier than it was.

"Keep looking forward," Cory cautioned. If he'd told me to not look down, I would have, like most people. It didn't take seeing the drop to know it would be far. After all, we were in a forest named for the nine circles of hell. Would any of this be easy or safe?

Cool air whipped around me. The feeling of emptiness underfoot made me ever conscious that there wasn't anything but aged wooden slats between me and whatever lay beneath. Training my eyes ahead, I fought the urge to look down.

Any place other than Dante's Forest, I wouldn't worry about the bridge's weight capacity, but here, in a forest where they expected you to leave unsuccessful—or maybe not at all —I worried about it. Shifters were dense, weighing significantly more than their appearance would lead one to think, and Cory's muscled form weighed more than his slender frame would indicate. At the midway point, the bridge sagged more than expected. Heart pounding in my chest, I took several slow breaths.

"Erin, go back. I got it from here," Asher said. The way he moved over the slats was unnerving. There were definitely advantages to the lithe, predatory movements of a shifter.

"I'm fine."

"Tell your breathing and heart rate that."

Glaring at his back was a big enough distraction to refocus, or maybe it was just spite; both of them were great motivators. The guide light's brightening and erratic pulses drew our attention to it.

Midnight wings eclipsed part of the sky. Ian, hovering just a few inches from our luminous guide which was still blinking its lights of urgency. Asher, the closest to our destination, moved faster, but no amount of shifter agility would get him there in time.

Ian moved in and dipped away, taunting us with his victory. Cory had stopped moving and was leaning against the cable, his stance wide, eying Ian. His lips moved slowly, indecipherably. The energy that flowed from him was something I had rarely experienced. Telekinesis was difficult and required a lot of magic. Whereas witches excelled in spell weaving and casting, mages were better at telekinesis.

The pulsing guide jolted out of the way when the metallic-blue pentagonal prism steadily rose, inching its way to us. Neck muscles taut, face reddened, perspiration glistening on his face, Cory extended his arm, fingers curled, beckoning the object to him. He was panting ragged sharp breaths as it moved faster. Ian soared toward it but missed it when Cory let the shield drop out of reach before bobbing it up and moving it closer.

Come on, come on. Asher and I stilled, making sure we didn't distract him. I should have kept the forest witch's magic. But considering the time it took for us to make it to the bridge, it was good that I hadn't. The chances of getting back to her in time to return her magic and prevent her from going to the other side would have been slim.

Three times Cory was able to keep Ian from getting hold of the prism, but finally, Ian grabbed it and pinned it to his chest. Surges of energy came off Cory as he struggled to wrangle it from him. With a rough pull from Cory, the prism lurched Ian forward. Ian countered. Cory released the prism. A magic ball barreled into Ian's chest, sending him back hard, unable to decelerate, dropping down and out of view.

"Get off the bridge," I commanded. Moving as fast as the bridge would allow, we turned and made for the edge. Ian shot up, returning fire equivalent to the magic Cory had sent to him. One of the cables flamed. The right side of the bridge collapsed. Asher, who was farther out, grabbed the other side to keep from falling and pulled himself off it.

A cruel, vindictive smile curled Ian's lips. "It will be a better course of action to force Neri and Adalia's hand rather than mine." He made a display of slamming the prism against the side of the mountain, chips of it breaking away and falling, debris flittering in the air. Unable to completely destroy the prism, he damaged it enough to render it unusable before letting it slip from his hold and fall into the abyss.

He flew away, damage done.

Anger can be masked, fury can't. Asher's not at all. It radiated off him like heat from a fire. He paced the ground while Cory rested against a tree.

"There's no way that witch at the entrance didn't know he was here. I should've heard him, or at least smelled him."

"He could have come from a different direction," I suggested.

"Or the cave guardian cloaked him with magic so he wouldn't be discovered," Cory offered, drawing himself to his feet. It was obvious that he'd exhausted his magical reserve, so I followed him without mentioning my leg and cuts that I really needed healed.

"You think he would have done that?" Asher asked.

Cory shrugged, disappointment all over his face. "I don't see why not. He's forced to be here, why not amuse himself?"

That's what I thought as we made our way to the exit.

CHAPTER 10

"*A*sher." I kept my tone low, trying to reason with an angry shifter who had given over to his wolf side and was stalking toward the cave that led us to Dante's Forest. After the day we'd had, I felt like I had been through the nine circles of hell. "Asher," I called again, his longer legs and preternatural speed making it hard for us to keep up with him.

The third time I called him, I put steel and ice in my voice, which would either irritate the Alpha or speak to the man. He whipped around, his face calmer than I expected but his silver eyes granite hard. Knowing his anger was directed at the person who sent us on this fool's journey, I didn't take it personally.

"We should have been told there was someone else looking for the Conparco Shield."

I nodded. "But what exactly will you gain from wolfing out on the man? I'm pretty sure if you do, this is the last time you'll ever be allowed access. Are you prepared for that?"

"That will be for the next person who guards it to decide."

Looking over my shoulder, I saw Cory blanch. Asher was exhibiting the same ruthlessness and irrationality that Cory had anticipated when it came to protecting his pack. They can give them a fancy title, corporation status, private planes, tax breaks, and a staff of terrifying lawyers, but in the end, that's what they were—a pack. And Asher was the Alpha.

I ran until I was several feet directly in front of him. The determination of his gait made me second guess myself. He could easily bulldoze me, but he stopped abruptly and when he attempted to go around me, I moved to block him again.

"Just listen to me, okay?"

Mussing his hair with his fingers, he was starting to show the toll of their failure. "What, Erin?" he blew out with an exasperated breath.

"I'm angry, too, and to be honest, I kind of want to wolf out—"

"You're not a wolf," he pointed out, obviously slighted by my claim.

"I know, but I'm feeling pretty primal. It's not even my pack, and I want to protect them from Ian, too. But once this is over, you don't want an irreparable mess to deal with, do you?"

It took moments to inhale the breath he took and even more time to exhale it. Several more breaths were taken before he appeared to be calmer, although his irritation was palpable as we made our way back to the cave. The boulder to the entrance moved aside and the same man was seated in the same manner, but the layout of the cave had changed. He was off to the side of where we had entered. It was difficult to not fixate on the logistics, and Cory seemed to be having the same problem. If Asher wasn't preoccupied with shooting the throned greeter dagger glares, he might have been mystified as well.

"There was someone else looking for the Conparco Shield," I informed the man, despite knowing that he already knew.

"I'm aware."

"Why didn't you tell us?" Asher growled.

"Because it was irrelevant information. You said you were here to get the Conparco Shield. I directed you to it. I had no obligation to provide any more information than that."

"It would have changed things for us," Cory said.

"Perhaps. But it wouldn't have changed things for me." The dim cave light became a little brighter near the opening where we had entered—a less than subtle invitation to leave.

"It would have changed our approach if we knew someone else was looking for it."

"Would it have changed your failure into a victory?" His tone was rife with cool indifference.

Fury that felt like flames was coming off Asher. It wasn't just the greeter's smug twist of his lips but the miscreant shine to his eyes. Though his voice implied it was just another day at the office, he was amused.

"Until next time," the greeter said, waving us away. He slumped lower in the chair as he lazily palmed the armrest of his odd throne. Asher didn't move at first, planted in position while Cory and I made our way out. I called his name and moved to his side to urge him along. The greeter kept a careful eye on us. Either he wasn't watchful enough or it happened so fast, the sequence of events were just blurs of movement of Asher yanking the knife from my sheath, whizzing his way to the man, and plunging the blade into the man's thigh. Magic was a miraculous thing and often quick and adequate to defend, but sometimes it couldn't be executed with the swiftness necessary when dealing with a vampire or shifter.

Asher yanked out the knife and walked toward the exit without preamble or any apparent concern about retaliation. He wiped the blood off the knife on his pants and handed it to me.

"I didn't kill him," he noted.

He was right about that.

We showered on the plane and Cory slept in the bedroom. I was tired and wanted desperately to sleep in a bed rather than in the reclining seats, but when Cory was tired, he sounded like a car with an exhaust problem. After ten minutes in the cabin, Asher made a face and I figured it was at Cory's snoring.

Asher studied me, his gaze traveling along the lines of my face, the exposed skin under my ripped shirt, and to my tattered, painful-looking nails. We didn't look like we had experienced the same day.

"You're still bruised," Asher pointed out, taking a sip from his glass of wine. The alcohol wasn't easing the tension between us and our conversation had devolved to small talk as we avoided discussing our failure and his enraged reaction. I wanted to be furious with him, but recalling the smug look and wily eyes of the witch made it difficult.

I examined the bruises on my arm. "They're better than we were," I acknowledged weakly. I wasn't sure if it was the alcohol or fatigue getting the best of me.

Mending my wounds was Cory's final magical act before he nearly collapsed from exhaustion onto the bed. The cut was closed but the tree butt-kicking I received—something I never expected to say—left me bruised all over with minor cuts that I didn't want him to exert magical energy to fix. My leg ached whenever I put weight on it, but it was better than before. Post adrenaline rush, pain flooded me.

Asher was working on his fourth glass of wine and not showing any signs of being inebriated, which reminded me why a person should never drink with shifters. When the attendant refilled his glass, she poured a little more in mine. Asher would be fine; I would be a little drunk.

He took another sip from his glass. "What do you think is the penalty for killing someone from the Veil?" he asked.

"The loss of your magic," I informed him, relaying all the information that Mephisto had given me.

"Do you trust your source?"

I nodded. I trusted the information, but whether the source, Mephisto, could be trusted was debatable. Asher expelled a slow breath. He didn't look hopeful and I definitely could understand that. After the experience in Dante's Forest, I wasn't feeling particularly optimistic either.

His question was sobering. Placing my glass on the table, I clasped my hands together and considered him. Finishing off his wine, he put his glass next to mine, then reclined in the chair in silence. Several minutes ticked by before he spoke.

"I can't see this Veil. Even when they opened it in front of me, I couldn't see it." I'm sure it had to be difficult believing it existed, but the evidence was there. A person was there, and with a blink of the eye, they weren't and remained missing from the world we lived in.

Asher went on. "We don't have the Conparco Shield, and even if I thought Neri and Adalia would abdicate, I'm not sure it would be enough to satisfy Ian. I think he'd want more and won't stop using us to get it. We have nothing to bargain with." The anguish and sorrow in his voice had nothing to do with the alcohol and everything to do with what he was deciding to give up for his pack. If it were true that killing someone from the Veil was penalized by the loss of magic, would he be affected? Shifter magic was so different, there might be an exception.

If his ability to shift was lost, could it be reversed? Could he be changed again? This was where things got complicated for me. Maybe I was selfish or blinded by desire, but my perspective on death changed when it didn't involve me delivering the kiss and me gaining magic. It was compartmentalized. Was Ian deserving of death? This level of power-thirst should have some repercussions and punishment, but was it deserving of death?

"I can't imagine you without your wolf," I admitted.

"Me neither," he admitted softly.

"Then don't test it."

"I can't let this keep happening to my pack. Once a month, during the full moon, we have to change. Volition isn't our own. The only option we have is to change before the full moon and stay in animal form so we can feel like we have some modicum of control that night. We accept that; we are called by the moon. But having someone do it to you, losing that control, it's demoralizing."

"You won't lose your wolf, and you and Sherrie won't have anything to worry about." Asher raised an eyebrow at me. "I don't know how I'm going to do it—I just am."

Might as well admit it. If I made something up, he'd know I was lying.

"If you can do that, I will be in your debt."

I was racking up favors.

It was a lesson I should have learned years ago: Never drink with shifters. The polite thing to do was to allow your glass to be filled each time theirs was, but it wasn't the wisest thing to do. Alcohol languid and a little fuzzy, I slipped back in the chair, sipping on water after realizing my mistake.

"What is it with you and Mephisto?" Asher asked. His voice was warm and rich, but curiosity sparked in his eyes when he looked at me.

"What do you mean?"

"At his poker game. I saw the way he looked at you and how you responded to him. It seemed like more than a professional relationship. Did I misread something?"

"Yes, you misread it."

I wasn't ready to discuss the peculiarity of my situation with Mephisto, especially because I wasn't sure about it myself. Was it his magic that drew me to him, or was Cory right that Mephisto was my type and there wasn't anything more magical about the attraction than pheromones and lust? I wanted it to be more. To lay the responsibility and the cause at the feet of my addiction. My magic wanted his magic. Nothing more, nothing less.

"That's funny," I continued. "He seems to think the same about me and you." I decided to blame that confession on the four glasses of wine.

Me and Asher. Not likely. It's not that I hadn't thought about it, and seeing him naked on multiple occasions hadn't chased the idea away. The only thing that had resolved was a feeling of betrayal when he pilfered an object I had been hired to find. We were on a ceasefire, but I wasn't sure if I could ever truly trust him.

"I can see that," he admitted. A rakish look whisked over his face. "I tend to have chemistry with a lot of people. It's the nature of the beast."

"Which beast, the wolf or your bountiful arrogance?"

"Confidence is something that people are drawn to, and I have it. It's the reason you're good at your job and people gravitate to you. I guess in a way we're quite similar." He beamed. "I'm the prettier of the two of us."

"And I'm the more modest," I countered.

The low rumble of his chuckle filled the room. "Perhaps. Insecurity or self-effacement would not serve me well as Alpha, nor should it." Asher lifted his lips into a smile, his pale-gray eyes full of the undeniable Alpha intensity. "Do you believe my confidence is unearned?" he asked.

The question gave me a moment of pause. I could think what I wanted about Asher, but he did what was necessary to protect his pack. He built a network of contingencies to guard them in the event that humans or supernaturals turned against him. He never relied on the support or assistance of supernaturals because the shifters felt the supernaturals hadn't been advocates for them in the past.

Alphas shared the same qualities, toeing the imperceptible line between confidence and arrogance. They crossed it often. It was that confidence and dedication to succeeding and protecting their pack at all costs that earned them a loyalty I didn't see in other sects.

Neri and Adalia wanted to stop Ian, like Asher, but Asher went to Dante's Forest with me. They offered the service of their guards, those who were committed to protecting the king and queen, whereas Asher, the leader, protected those who were in his pack. There was a distinct difference in the way each group operated.

When Asher took over as Alpha of the Northwest Pack, it was his leadership and long-term thinking that led the pack to become a corporation, giving them a stake in society and more power. So, his confidence was earned. The arrogance, on the other hand, he could definitely benefit from bringing down a notch or two. Maybe by fifty percent. No, seventy-five would be good. A solid ninety would be perfect.

"I think you're a good Alpha," I admitted.

After several moments of companionable silence, he said, "And I think you're a great death mage. There's hardly ever any death around you," he teased. He just didn't know the struggle.

We shared a smile and as I sipped from my water glass I cast a furtive look in his direction, only to find him doing the same.

"Why didn't Sherrie come with us?" I asked, not only curious but desperate for the looks between us to stop. I wasn't sure how we'd gotten to that strange place, but I wanted to exit fast.

"We split duties." His silver eyes were steely and heavy. "She's following leads on the Xios and other things."

"Other things? Like what?"

There was a slight twitch in the muscles of his forearm. The companionable silence became weighted. After several moments of silence I finally said, "You can trust me, Asher, you know you can."

"If it were just my business to tell, I wouldn't have an issue discussing it. Our history has earned you that."

Had it? It was contemptuous for the past year. It wasn't mutual disdain, just me seething with anger at the very sight or mention of his name.

Awareness dawned. "Sherrie doesn't trust me," I said, shocked.

Doing a quick inventory of our interactions, I couldn't remember anything that warranted her distrust of me. "Did you tell her you suspect it was Cory who released Ian?"

His head barely moved into the nod.

"Why would you do that?" Despite my efforts, my tone was razor-sharp.

"She had the right to know who was responsible."

"You didn't know for sure. It was just speculation."

He took a long draw from his glass, taking a contemplative look into it, before he finally lifted his eyes to meet mine.

"I knew the moment I asked you. I could tell when you spoke. You were protecting someone. There are two people you would trust to be with you during that: Madison and Cory. Madison can't do spells. That left Cory. When I asked you yesterday, I wondered if you'd continue to lie to me."

"I wasn't lying to you, I was protecting Cory," I disputed. Although I did lie to him to protect Cory. "Telling Sherrie makes it seem like he did it on purpose and you know damn well he didn't mean to do it. It could just as easily have been me."

"Then you would have been culpable as well, and to her, your association with him makes you untrustworthy."

That was more sobering than the water I drank. Putting

130

the glass down on the table, I moved over to the chair directly in front of him. My eyes met his and held them, something very difficult to do with a shifter, even harder with an Alpha. No matter how warm they were, the moment the look seemed like a challenge, something dark, predacious, and vicious rose in their eyes. No amount of shoring of confidence adequately matched it. Eventually I gave up.

"You're being unfair and irrational. It wasn't intentional."

"Intentional or not, does it make him any less to blame?" he asked in earnest. I knew this was coming from a place of frustration, anger, insurmountable despair. Great tragedies often originate from those dark dwellings. Muscles around his neck bulged from him clenching his jaw.

"Intent always determines responsibility," I countered.

That earned me a glower of incredulity. "Really? 'Intent determines responsibility.' Hmm. I believe this is where we part regarding philosophy."

"Asher, how many times will we have this conversation?"

He and Sherrie could have their distorted views. If it didn't affect Cory, I'd mark them down as peculiar shifter policies and never think of it again. But this belief could have real-life consequences for Cory, and I had to do what I could to mitigate it.

Sighing, he ran his hands through his hair, disheveling it. "I don't hold anything against Cory. Him coming here has satisfied his debt to me and my pack, but I can't speak for Sherrie or make her trust you. Magic should be handled responsibly, and he didn't. He did a spell that released Ian from the Veil. Why would Cory want him here?"

"It wasn't to release Ian. It was to see the Veil and possibly visit it. He was curious after I told him about my experience there."

"You're able to go through the Veil?"

"It's a long story," I said dismissively.

"We have time."

I glanced at my phone on the table. It seemed like we had been in the air longer, but it had only been an hour.

"Just as I keep your confidences, I must keep those of others. But I'll tell you what I can, if you make a promise to me."

"What's that?"

Shifters have many flaws, but loyalty and honoring their promises wasn't one of them. They weren't tricksters either, wording things in a way that would allow verbal gymnastics to avoid compliance. They were a direct bunch and expected the same from others.

"You have some influence. Cory isn't responsible for this and no one can retaliate against him. None of the shifters. No friends of shifters, allies. No one. Do we understand each other?"

White-hot anger had entered my voice, which had the opposite of my intended effect. It sounded like I had challenged Asher. Bad move.

"Erin, that hardly sounds like a request but a demand. I would go as far as to say a threat."

My voice softened, losing the edge and heat. "I'm trying to make an arrangement with you. Do we have a deal?"

He nodded once.

"There are some people I can borrow magic from without any consequences. As I thought it would be with you."

"And you can see the Veil?"

I nodded. "And travel through it."

"The people you are borrowing magic from are . . .?"

"A confidence I must keep."

Mephisto was strangely secretive about his magic to the point of practicing discretion when using it because magic left a fingerprint that often could be linked to the user.

Another nod showed understanding. I would keep his secrets as I would keep others. The shared information eased the tension in him. I relaxed in the chair and decided I

132

wanted more wine. I was confident that Cory was safe from shifter retaliation, but I still felt as if I had an unspoken debt to the shifters that I must satisfy. Perhaps it was guilt, but I had to find a way to break the magical hold Ian had over the shifters.

CHAPTER 11

as Asher being irrational? He had every right to be upset, but with the situation, not Cory. Needing a distraction, I repositioned the cold pack on my shoulder and leg and started flipping through my spell books, going over the same spells as if they would change. There wasn't anything that worked as well as the Xios to send Ian back. I hadn't found a spell to remove his immunity to iron either, and that had become my primary focus.

Frustrated with my unsuccessful search, it seemed like the only option was to make a deal with a demon, and I wasn't *that* desperate. Yet. It was a demon spell that led to Ian's immunity to iron. Demons don't usually reward until they've enjoyed living in your body throughout the agreed-upon time. Once summoned, they are limited to staying in the summoning circle. Once the payment is decided upon, your agreement and blood—because all dark magic begins with blood—allows them to become corporeal to inhabit the host. Ian killed the demon after he was rewarded. Hosting a demon is taxing on the body, but Ian was still strong enough to brave the demon circle where the demon was corporeal, and kill him.

A wave of panic flooded me. I'd never been without options. Scrolling through the pictures on my phone, I looked over all the objects Asher had, then I went to the pictures of the dragons' collection, whom I'd met after I was hired to retrieve items stolen during a poker game. The dragons and I had a strained relationship built on mistrust— needless to say, it wasn't a thriving or healthy one. They were a source. Sort of.

Like me, the dragons found things too. Unfortunately, they found things in a person's home, and they helped the person lose the things. They had stolen from the wrong people, which was when I was brought in. When I needed to find a D'Siren for Victoria, the dragons saved me a trip across the country by having one in their possession. On the first job, I had taken a picture of their hoard of treasures; that was weeks ago, and I was positive they would have more by now. The pictures were taken so quickly, I wasn't sure if it adequately showed their inventory.

Finding rogues was always easier than finding magical objects. People are just snitches by nature—not out of malice but because they assumed that if a bounty hunter, which most people considered me to be, was looking for someone, that person had done something wrong and should be off the streets and made to answer for their wrongdoing.

Magical objects were different. If one was being sought after, most people assumed the object was worth something and they'd wait for the highest bidder. If it wasn't money they wanted, they were inquisitive about why I was searching for it. It became a delicate dance where some people only cared about the money and were good leads and some, well, let's just say, "found" objects. I'd pay for the object, add my surplus to my client, and get paid.

The pictures didn't show a Conparco Shield, but that's not to say the dragons didn't have one. Grabbing my phone, I prepared for the unnecessarily impertinent witch who was romantically linked to one of the dragons and apparently their spokesperson.

"What?" the discourteous witch asked after my second attempt to contact them.

Hello, Sunshine.

"Hello, Lexi," I greeted her in a cloying voice, refusing to give her the satisfaction of letting her rudeness get to me. Or that's what I'd tell anyone to make myself look like the bigger person. My bright ebullient voice irritated the hell out of her.

"What do you want, Erin?" I could just picture her pixie face pinched into a scowl.

"How are you, Lexi?" I was going to kill her with kindness. My cloying voice didn't get the expected results. I thought the worst thing she'd do was voice her discontent, grumble something rude, or insult me. *But* the call disconnected.

Erin, don't yell at the tetchy little witch. Don't say "bitchy, much," no matter how appropriate it is.

I ushered the frown off my face, soothed my irritation, and made a vow not to use any of the four-letter words and creative eight-letter ones that were coming to my mind too quickly.

A deep voice answered the second call. Maddox, the younger and more mercurial of the two dragons. I had managed to ingratiate myself to him after gifting him a Glanin's claw. He didn't hate me. And using him to shield me against Lexi's magical attack seemed to have earned me a soft spot with him.

"Maddox?"

"Yeah."

"I need your help, please." I gave him the highly edited and condensed version of what was happening, leaving out that Ian had escaped from the Veil, and explaining that the Conparco Shield was needed to stop Ian controlling the shifters. Being a shifter himself, I knew he would be more agreeable to help.

"What does it look like?"

"I don't think I'll be able to send it to this phone." The number I had for them was a burner phone, given to me by Lexi.

His voice dropped. "Give me a minute." When he came back on, the background noise had changed. I could hear the rustle of trees. He gave another number to send the picture and after receiving it, he got back on.

"We don't have anything like that," he told me.

"Thank you. If you find it or anything that looks similar, will you let me know? I'm sending you another pic. If you have one, I'd really appreciate it." I wasn't ready to tell him what the Xios was for. If he knew how important it was, whatever he wanted for it would increase significantly.

"We don't have anything like that, either." He paused for a moment. "Erin, if you want to continue to work with us, don't antagonize Lexi, okay?"

"Greeting her and asking how she's doing is antagonizing her? I had no idea it would irritate her, please extend my apologies." There had to be an Academy award in my future.

"Obviously you think I'm naïve, Erin." His affable tone turned stiff. I guess my performance wasn't as believable as I thought. "We can work together, but if Lexi dislikes you, it's not going to happen."

It was time to make amends. These people weren't a resource I wanted to lose, especially not because of my inability to stop antagonizing the woman who might be the leader of their little group.

"Maddox, I really appreciate your help. Have you been to Kelsey's?"

"Once, when it first opened, but it's so hard to get reservations."

It wasn't. During my bodyguarding detail, I figured out

quickly that Victoria turned people away to give the place the illusion of exclusivity.

"I do work for the owner and I'm sure I can get reservations. Maybe we all can have dinner," I offered.

"Lexi won't come and Zack won't go without her."

Great. I didn't want to spend an evening with her sneering and me trying to indulge the prickly witch. "Maybe the two of us?" I suggested.

"It's a date." I could hear the grin in his voice. Maddox was back on Team Erin. I'd correct him on it being a date—more like a business dinner—but for now, he could think what he wanted.

I had never considered Mephisto a resource, and as I walked up to his door, feeling the aches and pains in my body with each step, I wasn't convinced he was, but I was desperate. The worst he could say was no. I couldn't look at his collection of objects. Come to think of it, the worst he could say is that he had the Xios and the Conparco Shield and had no intention of giving either to me.

"He's in his office," Benton offered after answering the door. He made the strenuous effort of pointing his finger before returning to his spot in the room near the door where he kept a cup of coffee and a book which he enjoyed reading while relaxing in a leather wingback chair. I thought his job consisted of being the answerer of the door and escort through the house. It seemed like the latter was no longer part of his job description.

Don't strain yourself with all the effort, Mr. answerer of the door, pointer of the finger.

In a particularly mischievous mood, I pretended a momentary directional lapse. "Is it that way?" I asked.

Benton wasn't having any of it. His lips moved from the

resting amiable small smile to a tight flat line. It became overwhelmingly obvious that he was content with letting me roam the mini-mansion until I stumbled upon Mephisto's office.

"No." With that terse response he returned to his book. I was committed to the scene, so I stood, seemingly flummoxed about which direction to go. He read a page of the tattered paperback, slowly. Then for several beats his eyes looked forward in deep contemplation. From my angle, I couldn't see the title, but I really wanted to give whatever held his attention a try. He dragged his eyes in my direction. I expected irritation but there was a hint of amusement in his eyes that spoke volumes: "I have all day, you're the one who needs to speak with Mephisto."

Jabbing my finger in the correct direction, I said, "I guess it's that way."

"Very good, Ms. Jensen." He let out a light chuckle before biting it into silence.

Touché, Benton. You win this round.

"Come in, Erin," Mephisto directed before I could announce my arrival by knocking on the slightly ajar door. His back remained turned to the door, his attention on the picturesque view. From my position, I took in the breathtaking sight, from the floor-to-ceiling window to the flourish of trees, exotic colorful flowers, clear blue sky. The lure of the outdoors intrigued me but not as much as it did Mephisto, who seemed to have a peculiar fascination with it. Was it because he was without it? Or was this just a general appreciation for nature's beauty?

The light walls were a stark contrast to his head-to-toe midnight attire.

"You needed to see me?"

His stolid appearance didn't belie the whetted curiosity in his eyes. Were my parents really Vera and Gene? Was I The Raven? Most importantly, not only could I navigate between the worlds in the Veil, but I could bring things out—the thing he wanted.

"I need a favor," I said.

"Favor? Based on the urgency in your voice when you called, I'm assuming it's a big one." He took a seat at his desk and pointed at the chair across from it.

I started walking toward him when he stood. "You're injured." His movement, perceived by my eyes as just a blur, had me stopping mid-step. It was not quite a blur of movement but preternatural in speed, something I'd expect when dealing with vampires.

"A tree tried to beat me up yesterday," I said, flippantly. Mephisto didn't respond as I'd expected. He simply nodded, as if he'd heard that reason before.

How often did people get beat up by a tree?

Taking my hand in his, he examined my fingers.

"Then an enraged earth witch attacked me," I admitted as his eyes trailed to the cuts on my hand.

"Ah, Dante's Forest is full of many little surprises."

"You've been before?"

He nodded. His hand touched my back gently, coaxing me to sit on his desk. The day after a fight was always the worst. No longer flooded with adrenaline, the soft tissue had been given ample time to discover its mistreatment, sending pain with a vengeance. My jaw clenched in an effort not to show any discomfort as I lifted myself onto the desk.

"To get . . ." I let my question linger, raising my brow and waiting for him to complete the sentence. Ignoring me, he continued to assess my injuries. They were minor, but based on the rigid frown on his face, they looked worse to him than they did to me.

"To get something I wanted," he finally offered. A devious smirk tugged at the corners of his lips.

What answer did I expect from a man who guarded his name like a trade secret?

"Remember you said we needed to trust each other. That's hard to do if you never reveal anything about yourself. I don't trust strangers."

"Ah, but as you've pointed out on many occasions, we aren't strangers. We've known each other for over three years. You've eaten at my table, slept in my bed, showered in my home." His liquid coal eyes were suggesting far more than what actually occurred.

"No matter how naughty you attempt to make that sound, it was all innocent."

"And the kiss?"

"What kiss?" I tried to say it with a straight face, but my lips twisted.

"You didn't forget the kiss," he whispered. From his position between my legs, it made his examination of my wounds seem far more salacious. He leaned in, the warmth of his breath brushing my lips. "Neither have I."

"What did you get from Dante's Forest?" I pressed.

He released my hand, his expression pensive as he considered me, or the question, for a while. So much time lapsed, I considered repeating the question. "Amber Crocus," he finally admitted, taking my hand in his again. The tips of my fingers were still inflamed and red and the nails had been ripped down past the edges. They weren't tender unless I brushed up against something.

"Plan on slaying some vampires?" I asked. He was responsible for my recent discovery that a weapon laced with the plant could kill a vampire as fast and efficiently as beheading them.

A lazy smile formed and vanished. "Beheading is such a nasty way to kill a vampire. Amber Crocus works as a suitable warning when they aren't being amenable."

"The forest was a bust," I admitted in a tight voice.

"It was for me as well. It wasn't Amber Crocus they had but a poor imitation. It was a good thing I knew what it actually looked like. Others probably found out the hard way."

A shudder pushed through me at the thought of what a person would endure after a failed assassination attempt on a vampire—especially an old vampire.

"What other injuries do you have?" Mephisto's frown had deepened at the state of my hands. Cory had repaired the knife cut. I showed him the spot on my arm discolored by bruising.

"My back has a few welts, but they should go away soon. My arms are the worst. I'm just sore and some areas are tender."

He enclosed the tips of the fingers of my right hand in his hands, and a cooling breeze enveloped them, similar to menthol or a topical analgesic. Interlacing his fingers with mine, he looked at the result of his magic. The redness had retreated, and buffed nails with a light sheen stretched out past the edges as if they hadn't been ripped to the nub.

"Better," he whispered. My nails only received a fraction of my attention. Scrutinizing him, I tried to see past the glamor I was sure existed. This wasn't his face, or it was just a variation of it. At least that was what I was convinced of, especially after our visit to the Woman in Black. Despite their familiar relationship, she had looked at him and his three friends as if it was the first time seeing them, guessing at their names.

As he repaired my left hand, I leaned into him, feeling his magic pulse against me. I fought the urge to whisper the power words and taste his magic once again. He remained close without a hint of distress. He knew that he wouldn't die if I borrowed his magic and he could combat me taking it, if he wanted.

"What are you?" I asked.

"I thought I was Satan," he teased, putting some space between us.

142

"Mephisto—"

"Let me see your back."

He wouldn't give me an answer. I stood and lifted my shirt, exposing the marks that I was sure were raised, red, and angry looking. His fingers tracing along my skin were a delicate wisp. The cool menthol suffused over my skin, easing it. The nagging ache was diminished but the magic that ensorcelled me was strong and intoxicating. A gasp caught in my throat.

When I turned, he offered me a smile. "Perfect," he whispered.

He instructed me again to return to my seat on the desk. He rested a hand on each leg, his lips moved slightly, and heat inched over me. I relaxed into the warmth.

"How do you feel?" he asked.

"Fine." I shifted my weight forward. The need to be closer to him was overtaking me. It was the pull of magic, the thrall of it. I was ensnared. Longing for his magic, I would accept being close to him as a consolation. It was like being chilled and taking the comfort of a flimsy blanket rather than the soothing warmth of hot chocolate that warms you from within. It was a superficial satisfaction. A comfort that paled in comparison. But it was what I had.

Mephisto's finger traced along the line of my jaw, and his weight shifted too. We were just a hairsbreadth away. If either one of us moved, our lips would have touched.

My eyes slipped to the door and for a brief moment I considered saying the words of power and seeing if I could make it out the door. It was a morbid thought. Horrendous. As if he read my thoughts or felt my impulse he increased the distance between us, removing the temptation. It felt like a repudiation.

I immediately missed the warmth of his body. The blanket left emptiness that I wanted desperately to fill.

Sometimes I allowed myself to forget that the desire

for magic existed. But when I was around Mephisto there was a keen awareness of the lack, especially because I was so close to having it without repercussions. Part of me wanted to despise him for giving me a glimpse into a life that I could see but not have. When I realized I was glaring at him, I dropped my eyes to the floor.

"How did you know we went to Dante's Forest?" I blurted. It wasn't my intended question, but it dawned on me that he knew. Maybe he was affected.

"Asher's plane went to South Dakota, so I figured that's where he was going. Based on the urgency with which you left, I guessed it was to meet him and that you would go with him."

"Are you keeping tabs on me or him?"

"I like to know Asher's whereabouts. We tend to have the same interests." Amusement flitted across his face. "We both are collectors and on more than one occasion he has procured items of interest to me. We travel in the same circles and often are invited to the same auctions." He regarded me with curious eyes. "What's the favor, Erin?"

The reality of what I was about to ask hit me hard. Going through Asher's vault wasn't as big a deal because Ian's presence directly affected him, but it didn't affect Mephisto. I wasn't sure it ever would.

"I need to see what objects you have. I need a Xios or Conparco Shield." I hopped down from the table, forgetting to do it gingerly. "Hey, no pain." I shifted my weight from one leg to another, feeling like I could go another round with whatever Dante's Forest had to offer.

I approached Mephisto with my phone out, prepared to show him pictures of the objects.

He shook his head. "I know what they look like, but I don't have them."

"May I check?"

His eyes narrowed; I felt the full weight of them on me. "You don't want to take me at my word?"

No, not at all. But instead I said, "Sometimes magical objects have more than one name. It's happened before."

He ran a finger lazily over his bottom lip. Had I offended him?

"Have you spoken to your parents?"

"What? That has nothing to do with this."

"No, it doesn't. I find you to be quite the quandary, Ms. Erin Katherine Jensen," he admitted. He'd swallowed up the distance he'd put between us in moments. He wasn't hiding his otherness as much, or else this was another lure, reminding me that he was the person standing between me and magic. His magic. This type of magic. "You'll go to Dante's Forest, fight a rogue fae in a park, come to me to ask for a favor I'm not likely to agree to, but finding out if you are The Raven is something you won't brave. Why?"

"There's no why. It will have no effect on my life. So what? If I am, it doesn't change anything."

"But it does. Malific was bound to her prison using her magic and blood. She won't be released until her death."

"What does that have to do with me?"

"You're her daughter—"

"I'm not her daughter," I asserted.

He took a breath and held it before giving me a conciliatory nod. "*If* you are her daughter, you are the only one. You share a common bloodline. She is bound to the ward. If she dies, the Omni ward falls. I suspect it's not just her death that will break the ward, but yours as well. Ms. Jensen, it is very important that you know whether you are The Raven, because it's the difference between your life and death."

Blood rushed from my face and I blindly put a hand on the desk to hold me steady. Mephisto eased closer. Several beats of silence passed before he spoke.

"Ignoring the problem doesn't make it go away, it only

leaves you vulnerable. If I've come to this theory, don't you think the Immortalis will have as well? Do not think for one minute that they have given up their objective to be with Malific again. Her army was created solely for this purpose. Right now, you are a means to an end."

I was starting to understand why Mephisto lived with such anonymity and guarded his secrets with such ferocity. It was the best defense.

The list of things I had to do was becoming longer and longer. But I could not be bogged down by wondering whether Malific was my mother. It was fear that allowed me to put the issue on the back burner so easily, I knew that, but I would have to address it eventually. What was tugging at me now and had ever since Mephisto gave me the information about my alleged mother was the apprehension on his face and the obvious distance that had come between us. A tear in the tapestry of our alliance.

I wondered what had changed between him delivering the information at my apartment and seeing me in Simeon's library.

"You were apprehensive when you told me that I might be Malific's daughter," I reminded him. "Yet you want me to approach this head on."

He nodded. "I will admit, I was taken aback."

Why can't you just say I was shocked, like everyone else?

"I thought you were unique to the Raven Cursed, but as a god, your abilities are as expected."

I hadn't taken a breath for some time and was in desperate need of one. When I did, it reminded me of the way vampires tried to breathe around humans to be less off-putting. It sounded mechanical and rough.

"When you do have access to magic, it's concentrated and strong. Massive amounts of magic, probably boundless. It brings up many questions, not just why you aren't with your mother. But did whoever took you restrict your magic in an

146

effort to prevent another Malific? If they believe you to be like her, why let you live at all? Finally, is it irresponsible of me to allow you into the Veil, knowing you could be used to release Malific?"

"I don't know, but is what you want not important enough to take the risk?" Once again, I was seeing the hope of me having my own magic slip away. Would he give up on me and continue his search for someone who could move through the Veil but who didn't have the baggage of a psychotic god for a mother?

"Was Malific always like this? At some point she had to be just a typical god, gliding around in her glory being worshipped. How did she become that person I read about? A person who lacked mercy and craved power—"

I stopped abruptly, suddenly seeing the small parallel between her power and my thirst for magic. I looked down at my hand, my thoughts racing. Nature versus nurture. No less than fifteen times had the thought of taking Mephisto's magic crossed my mind. Even for a brief moment, I thought of keeping Cory's magic, the only thing stopping me being my feelings for him. I've only ever had magic for short periods of time and never considered what type of person I'd be if I had limitless access to it. My ability with magic surpassed so much of what anyone else could do. Godlike power.

"I'm curious as to what's on your mind," Mephisto asked after several moments of uncomfortable silence.

"Nothing," I lied. "If what you want in the Veil is important, I don't think me going to retrieve it should be a problem. The question isn't whether I should go, it's how important the box is to you. I'm risking my life going in there, how much are you willing to risk?"

I wanted my own magic. Limitless use. In those few seconds I'd decided that my desire to obtain his magic was stronger than any potential problems. Fine, I might be Malific's daughter, but I was raised by parents who were nothing like her. There was nothing wrong with having a great deal of magical power: Cory and Madison were powerful. Flashes of Ian came to mind, but I brushed them aside. He wanted to rule. I had no desire to do that or have dominance over anyone.

"May I see your collection?" I asked again.

A lazy smirk lifted the corners of Mephisto's lips. "Ms. Jensen, you do realize that this has nothing to do with me? The warring between the shifters, fae, and Ian will not affect me in any way." His head tilted as he examined me more closely. There was so much intensity in his scrutiny I felt exposed, naked. "This is important to you, isn't it? You have no stake in this and yet I can see it's important to you. Why?" he inquired, intently searching my face for answers I assumed he expected me not to give.

"It's the right thing to do," I said. It wasn't a lie. It was the right thing to do in order to correct a wrong.

Doubt sparked in the depths of his coal-black eyes. His lips curled into a frustrated moue. I felt a bit of satisfaction at his aggravation. People who use information as if it's scarce currency hate when the tables are turned. The glower and tick in his jaw proved that.

His jaw clenched. "What are you doing here?" His voice no longer had that honeyed sweetness and dark allure that I now realized he reserved for me. It wasn't quite cold, but it had an edge.

Jarred by the sudden change in his mood and his voice, I blinked. The answer to the change entered the room. Clayton. Even with a large duffel bag on his shoulder he moved with the lissome grace of a person trained in martial arts. An easy smile spread over his lips, seemingly finding gratification in Mephisto's irritation.

"M," he greeted. Ignoring the surges of magic in the room was getting more difficult and I wanted to stop his advance, warn him not to come any closer. But it was too late.

Clayton's locs, which had been tied back before, were loose. The shoulder-length mass of hair draped over his shoulders and fell over his face. He shoved his fingers through it, pushing the tight locs back. Several feet away, I felt crowded. Clayton's brows inched together and I realized I was staring.

Hitching his bag further up his shoulder, he said, "I didn't think you were going to be here."

"I had to reschedule my meeting," Mephisto informed.

Clayton glanced between Mephisto and me and then settled his attention on me.

"Ah, did The Raven need you?" He was teasing but I didn't miss the edge of ridicule.

"Why are you here?" Mephisto asked again.

"I wanted to use your pool."

Mephisto blew out an irritated breath. "And there aren't any public pools you can use?"

Clayton looked disgusted at the idea. "You know how I feel about public pools."

"Yet," Mephisto pushed through his teeth, "you won't have your own installed."

Clayton's smirk could not be described as anything other than devilish. "I can't do that, then I'm 'that guy' with the indoor pool. Who wants to be him?" And then he shot Mephisto a look.

Mephisto's jaw clenched even harder. I was trying to understand the dynamics between them. Between them all. There was a familiarity as if they were brothers, but their varying ethnicities made that doubtful. Their magic was so similar but had subtle differences I could pick up on. They moved with the stealth and gracefulness of men who knew how to fight. Warriors.

"The Raven," Clayton greeted.

"It's Erin," I corrected.

He nodded. "Erin, what can we do for you?"

We? Okay?

"She would like to see my collection. She's looking for a Xios and Conparco Shield," Mephisto said. The two men exchanged a look but their faces remained as emotionless as Mephisto's voice. Maybe my request was unusual? Rude? Ballsy? Uncouth? Even within the Supernatural Task Force, special clearance was needed to view the collected supernatural objects.

"Oh, is that so?" Clayton finally said. "We don't have those." He looked at Mephisto for confirmation, as if he'd missed a new acquisition.

Hmmm. "We" again.

Clayton's gaze flicked to Mephisto and studied him for a moment. The look of neutrality vanished. His lips pressed into a rictus line.

"Ms. Jensen is quite thorough with her searches and would like to determine this for herself," Mephisto offered.

"I see." Clayton jerked his head toward the door. "I'm going that way, let me take you there." Before Mephisto could object, I followed him out the door.

Mephisto had returned to his favorite position at the window, his hands shoved in his pockets, his attention outside.

"Erin," he said, just as we made it past the threshold. "This is done for you. I need there to be trust between us."

"Okay, give me a name."

After waiting for a few moments, I realized his deep chuckle was the only response I would get.

Clayton pressed his finger to the reader and opened the door.

"Do you live near here?" I asked, following him into the vast room that made Asher's vault pale in comparison.

Like Mephisto's library, there was wall-to-wall, glass-fronted dark-wood shelving. Lighting in each one. Mephisto wasn't just stashing these objects, he was a collector, displaying his impressive, expensive, and from a quick perusal, illegal objects for easy access and view.

"Not too far. I prefer a less ostentatious community."

"You just like to partake in it without owning it, right?" I teased.

"Of course. There's nothing like pseudo-humility." He flashed me a smile and let his duffel bag slip to the floor. He leaned against the wall, arms folded over his chest, and watched as I looked over the assortment of objects.

"So you just come over for the pool?"

"And dinner. His cook is very talented."

"Since he's already here, you might as well take part in the feast, but you'd never be so brazen as to have your own cook."

"Exactly, who wants to be that person?" Humor was in his voice and his face was genial, but he was watching me keenly as I moved from display to display.

"How long have elves been extinct?" I asked, feigning disinterest as I took an orb from a shelf to examine it.

"Over fifty years, I do believe. I haven't seen one in that time."

I glanced over my shoulder to get a look at him: flawless dusk-brown skin, defined jaw, full lips, warm chestnut-colored eyes. Nothing about his features would have placed him near the age of fifty. I'd guessed early thirties. Slightly younger than Mephisto. But he'd been around for longer than fifty years. But how much longer?

Clayton approached me and slipped the orb from my grasp and returned it to its spot. "This isn't what you're looking for."

151

He stayed close to me as I perused the collection. His presence kept becoming a distraction, and I found myself weeding through the intricacies of their magic.

"Why is it so important to keep your anonymity?" I asked.

Instead of answering, he moved from me. Languidly walking around the room, he looked at the objects as if seeing them for the first time and realizing the magnitude of what the collection represented.

They had access to so much magic, and objects that could undo or create catastrophic things. And the fact that they had it meant they could use it. Or maybe not. I thought about Asher, who collected magical objects that he couldn't directly use. But I wasn't positive that he was collecting them indiscriminately. I believed that each one of them was somehow linked to his pack; I just didn't know how.

Clayton watched me carefully as I moved to another shelf. When I opened one display case and found an object I'd never seen before, I took out my phone to take a picture.

"No," he said firmly. The speed at which he reached me and closed his hands over mine shocked me. He guided my hand back so that I could return my phone to my pocket.

"Sorry, I haven't seen anything like this before. I wanted to look it up."

"But that's not what you're here for, is it, Raven?" he asked in an even voice. The closeness of his body made me stand taller and lean in, basking in his magic for a moment before I came to my senses. But instead of backing away, I inched closer. He dropped his head so that his eyes met mine.

"Are you immortal?" I asked.

His lips pinched and he withdrew into his thoughts. I was familiar with that look. He was deciding what information to give me. His eyes roved over me, then swept over the room. "I'm confident that you will best Ian."

What the hell? That answered no part of my question.

"A simple 'I don't want to answer' would have sufficed."

"You will best Ian because you know what he is and all his magical abilities. You know that his tolerance of iron was created by a demon spell. It might be difficult to find and perform, but all spells can be reversed. That is why anonymity is important."

One question out of two isn't bad.

I should have moved, increased the distance, and removed the temptation. But I didn't, and during that small window when desire overcame logic, the words slipped out. The wall he erected doubled me over, my head throbbing so hard it brought tears to my eyes. I braced against the shelving to stay upright. When it passed, I found Clayton's reproachful eyes on me.

"May I have your phone, please?" His voice was cool and monotone, losing the effortless ease and mesmeric lilt.

"Clayton—"

"Phone. Please."

Pulling it out of my pocket, I handed it to him.

"I'm removing the enticement. M will have it." With that he exited, leaving me with the weight of my guilt. What if he hadn't been able to stop me from taking his magic? I was positive that, like Mephisto, the effect wouldn't be the same. But I'd attempted to steal his magic, because I couldn't control my desire.

Dammit.

I finished going through Mephisto's collection. Neither the Xios nor the Conparco Shield was there. Exiting the room, I considered searching for Clayton to apologize but decided against it. Instead, I returned to Mephisto's office where I found him at his desk, perusing a book. He looked up and slid my phone to the edge of the table at my approach.

"I'm familiar with the many names that objects go by. In the future, take me at my word."

I was sure Clayton had told him what happened, but how Mephisto felt about it was carefully hidden.

"Okay." I grabbed my phone, slipped it into my pocket, and turned for the door. Mephisto called me before I could leave. At his approach, I was reminded of the numinous way he moved. His finger brushed lightly along my hand and he moved so close to me it was as if he was oblivious to what I'd done to Clayton. Or perhaps this was a test. Another magical seduction?

"I don't like to be taunted," I said in a raw, raspy whisper.

"I'm not."

When he brushed the back of his hands against me, I leaned into his touch, into him, our lips brushing against each other. I inhaled him, bathed in his energy, and desired him in a way that felt torturous.

"Say them," he whispered against my lips. My heart pounded in my chest; my breathing hitched. Was he serious? He wouldn't be so cruel as to offer it only to wrench it away. I hesitated.

His tongue brushed against my lips when he moistened his lips. "Go ahead."

Before he could change his mind, I said the words quickly, pulling the magic from him. It poured into me like warm chocolate, filling the part of me that felt constantly void. The hunger sated, cautiously I stepped away, fully aware that he was able to take the magic away from me. I kept inching back, step by step, until my back was pressed against the wall closest to the door.

"I said before there are consequences for me as well, just not death."

Pressing my fingers against my lips, I could still feel the tingle of his lips pressed against mine.

"Why?" I asked.

He shrugged and moved to his favorite spot. With his

back to me, I realized he had no intention of taking his magic back. Or at least not at that moment.

"You seem to need it. It's just for today. I'll come to you around this time tomorrow for its return."

Although he didn't voice it, I could hear the tacit request not to disappoint him by trying to keep it.

"Okay," I croaked out. "Tomorrow."

CHAPTER 12

$\mathcal{M}$y fluffy furred paws padded softly over my floor to my bedroom to get a look at what I'd done. I was an ash brown Maine Coon cat, definitely not the lion I was aiming for. It failed despite the changes I made to the transformation spell. The only other time I'd shapeshifted, I hadn't even used a spell. I was trying to Wynd but instead I ended up a cat. I'd figured a deliberate transformation spell would allow me to shapeshift to any animal. I was wrong. I was a cat. Just a big cat. Not a Big Cat.

Three hours with Mephisto's magic and I had expected to be able to do more, because his magic was intense. When I borrowed magic from someone, their abilities, whatever they were, came easier. Simeon said that Mephisto had strong defensive magic and could Wynd. Maybe if I tried to Wynd, I'd turn into a lion.

Whispering the spell, I shifted back to human. My hair was a disheveled mess, face flushed pink, and perspiration glistened on my skin. What did I expect; I'd changed to a cat three times. Now I knew that I changed into a cat well. Three different changes and the only thing I managed was to transform into three different breeds of cat. Maybe that would come in handy at some point.

Showering and quickly getting dressed, I knew why Cory was always ready before me. When you had access to magic, a move of your hand and your clothes could dance from your drawer or closet and be neatly placed on your bed, ready to wear. My clothes were doing a choreographed performance as they swooped through the air. Effortlessly, I made my towel soar across the room and dive into the hamper. With limitless access to magic, would doing something like that become mundane?

Back in my living room, Mephisto's strong magic strummed through me as I scanned over the magic books sprawled on the sofa. The spells in them didn't appeal to me as much as trying to Wynd. Making a last-ditch effort, I shored in the magic and concentrated. Hand extended in front of me, I shuddered and watched it become translucent for over a minute and then return to solid. It was on my third attempt that my stomach clenched with pain.

Shoving the books aside, I plopped on the sofa. Cory couldn't be used as a resource because he wasn't able to Wynd. I considered calling Tetchy Lexi, who had managed to do it and bring someone with her. I glanced at the clock and decided against it. There was something else I wanted to do.

The building was dark, the solitary light illuminating the battered metal door the only source of light in the darkened alley. The few windows that faced it were covered by privacy glass. With a flick of a switch, you couldn't see through them. Tonight, it was set so no one could see in. During the day, it looked like nothing more than an abandoned warehouse. It was around ten, when the things that needed to be hidden were.

At the doorway, I could just imagine the windblast of energy and magic that would meet me once the door was opened. One knock, that's all I did. Anything more would go ignored.

"Erin?" the tall vampire said. He smiled. His teeth had a red tint to them. Most vampires were attractive, or at the very least average but charismatic enough to convince a person to be their dinner. They learned to tamp down the ominous mien that surrounded them. They lured you into their trap by pretending to be innocuous. This vampire either couldn't or chose not to, which meant he was getting his meals from people who loved the danger of it. Grups, humans drawn to badly behaved supernatural beings. Despite his dark and foreboding countenance, his appearance was the opposite. Pale skin, jaw-length platinum-blond hair.

Leaning against the doorframe, he gave me a long inquiring look. "It's been a long time." He looked over his shoulder at the clock. "You almost didn't make it." He extended his hand to me. "Two."

"Kane, it's up to two hundred dollars now!" I exclaimed, glad I'd stopped coming here to get my fix. Magic fighting was like UFC but with magic. That made it sound classier than what it was. It was magical street fighting. The STF spin job painted magical beings as people who used their magic sparingly and only when necessary. Most of that was accurate. But there were supes who loved their magic, wanted to push it to the limits, revel in the raw, unrestrained depths of it. Fight with it, with minimal rules or restrictions. This was the place to do it.

"I'm not here to watch," I informed him.

Brow raised, the corner of his lips lifted to expose his fangs. "Do you need to go first? Where are you parked?" He knew the deal with me; I'd only come one time to fight using Cory's magic. Cory rarely gave in to my needs like that, but he had sensed something in me needed a release. I didn't want to use magic for a spell or for a job. I wanted to be reckless and push my abilities to the limit.

Not to give anything away, I nodded.

"Welcome back to the Dome," Kane said, moving aside and letting me in. It hadn't changed. He was definitely making a profit from his setup because he put zero effort into making it look nice. It was a large open space. The walls were painted plum with variations in the color from where it had been patched and he hadn't bothered to color match the repair. The exposed ceiling added to the industrial feel. There weren't any benches or cushy seating, just chairs—folding chairs. He hadn't even sprung for cushioned folding chairs.

The fighting area, or "presentation" area, as Kane liked to call it, wasn't any better. There wasn't an octagon or walls to protect the spectators from injuries, which was why most people stood. There weren't even padded floors to cushion falls.

I suspected that was the draw of the place; it was just dangerous. Magic and adrenaline filled the air. People didn't participate for the meager cash prize but for the same reason people spar. The rush and the ability to dominate another person with your skill and power.

From my quick glance at the audience, thirty had come for the show.

Phone in hand, Kane's mouth twisted as he looked at it. "You'll be paired with a witch, Wendy, but she calls herself the Maestro."

Rolling my eyes, I said, "Let me guess, the Maestro of Magic."

With a spark of amusement in his eyes, Kane nodded. "No one wants to be paired with her. She was going to sit this one out but since you're here . . . Are you good with that?"

Did I have a choice? Entering last minute, I was lucky he let me participate.

"Yeah, I am."

"Good. Most people don't last more than a few minutes with her. You'll be out in no time."

"Thanks for the vote of confidence."

He grinned, treating me to his stained fangs. "I didn't say you'd be the loser, I just said you'd be done in no time." The look he gave me bordered on charming before he extinguished it like an unruly fire. "But if past performance is an indicator . . ." He left the remainder to my imagination.

He placed a red band around my wrist, to be thrown into the center of the room if you were in a position where you wanted to concede. The magic battles weren't violent—well, they weren't supposed to be. But when dealing with displays of magic where one wielder is attempting to overpower another, the situation tended to invite some level of violence.

Kane placed a reassuring hand on my arm as he entered the center of the room to announce us. I received lukewarm applause—purely obligatory so that my entrance wouldn't be met with uncomfortable silence. Announcing Wendy sent the crowd into a roar. The gust of smoke that obscured her disappeared. Standing several feet from me was a woman dressed in blue slacks and a black wizard robe. I craned my neck to look at Kane. I knew my face showed exactly what I was thinking.

Really?

His smirk and arched brow seemed to urge me not to judge a book by its cover.

But I couldn't help it. I was a proponent of letting your weird flag fly. Put it right out there for the neighbors to see. But there had to be a line. And that line was a woman in her thirties rocking a wizard robe. How was I supposed to take her seriously?

As I approached the center of the room, my eyes widened.

Dear fates, she had a wand. Witches didn't need a wand. No one needed a wand. How was this the opponent that people feared? I ignored the black round glasses. Shrugged off the shaggy long dark hair. But the wand that she waved with exaggerated flair just made everything about her laughable.

She didn't belong in the Dome. This wasn't fight club material. The robe-wearing wizard with the haughty sneer commanding a certain level of veneration belonged on stage, performing for children. My mind quickly went to Claire, who didn't look like she belonged anywhere near a government agency, but there she was, one of the best agents they had.

Wendy's confidence made me stand taller and assume a defensive stance.

The Dome fights weren't formal and there were minimal rules. Kane intervened when things got out of control.

"Present" was the only indicator that we were to fight. The spark that came from the wand wasn't impressive, just a thin line. I expected it to be a little shock, but instead it wracked through my body and I folded over in pain. Her brow cocked, her way of telling me not to underestimate her. And I didn't.

I retaliated with a wave. There wasn't anything harmless looking about the colorful thrum I pushed in her direction. It hit against the protective wall she erected. The next wave of magic that I sent shattered the field. Eyes widened, she looked at the remnants of it, sediment floating in the air around her.

A look of appreciation moved over her face. "Impressive. No one breaks my walls."

"Thanks." I knew that her compliment was a precursor to her showing me exactly how impressive she was.

A flick of her wand caused sparks to crackle at my feet. One singed my pant leg. Focused on putting it out, I looked up in time to see another blast from her wand, larger than the previous one. She had me dancing back as she kept them coming, putting me on the defensive. One of them pelted me in my chest, pushing my breath out.

This should have been discouraging. I was getting a magical ass kicking. But I felt invigorated. I returned fire with my magic. With a wave of her wand, she froze the spool of magic midair. Distracted by her own talent and cleverness, she missed the one I sent into her leg, dropping her to the floor with a crash. Her wand rolled out of her hand and she became entangled in her silly robe.

She rolled toward her wand, but I sent it to the opposite end of the room with a wave of my hand. Fury in her eyes, she came to her feet. With her hands spread wide, magic smacked me hard, sending me back several feet and crashing to the ground.

Her robe that I'd thought so derisively about slipped from her body and became a black eclipsing sheath of fabric. It blocked my vision, wrapping around me and entangling me. My struggling to get untangled provided the distraction she needed to get her wand, which she had in her hand when the robe, acting like it was sentient, unraveled, spinning me. Disoriented, I erected a protective wall while I got my bearings.

The world stopped spinning and she lifted her arms dramatically, the robe dancing in the air in a choreographed move to slip back over her. It was an extension of her, doing her bidding. How strong was she to have such meticulous control of it while distracted by looking for her wand?

Arrogance and cynicism curled her lips. I looked back at Kane, expecting him to disqualify her. We weren't allowed to use outside gadgets. Magical ingredients could be used, and clothing. Not too many people could use a shirt or pants in the same manner she'd used her robe.

Kane said nothing. So despite how ridiculous I thought she looked, I scanned the spectators only to find that her robe show was a crowd-pleaser. He wouldn't disqualify her on that alone, because it brought him more money. People would return to see Wendy, the Magical Maestro and her stupid balletic robe.

"Cute trick," I said.

"Not a trick, a skill, love."

Ugh, now she's doing a fake English accent?

I focused on the red glow on the tip of the wand aimed in my direction. She cut through the air, and I flinched at the searing pain in my arm. Another air strike and my other arm received the same treatment. Arms throbbing, I didn't chance looking at them. Instead, I opened my hands, concentrating, taking slow controlled breaths, using the same level of concentration it took to shift to the cat. I'd wielded fire before, when I had an elemental mage's magic. It was simpler with his magic. A spark singed the bottom of her robe. It was equivalent to my electric pellets: a much-needed distraction. As she attempted to put it out, I pelted her with a rapid fire of magic, sending her crashing to the ground onto her robe, where she manually patted out the flames.

Darkness cast over her face, anger blazed in her eyes, and her lips moved rapidly as she slowly approached me. My lips were pressed into a tight line, unable to perform any spells, and my arms were bound to my sides. Her first push secured me to the wall. I tried to fight against it. Mind clouded, I figured she was doing a distraction spell. I searched for a spell to release me, a weaker one that required cognitive execution. Everything was a fog. Releasing me just a smidge, she pushed me even harder against the wall. She inched closer until she was directly in front of me.

Her face relaxed. It didn't look as if she was wielding the level of magic to perform the combination of spells. Her fingers traced along the red bracelet, a nonverbal request as to whether I was to concede.

"Blink twice to concede," she said, her voice raised

163

slightly to ensure Kane would hear. He was a vamp; she could have whispered it and he'd have heard. Pride made it take longer for me to do so. Several minutes passed as I unsuccessfully tried to weave through the fog. Two blinks and she removed the band from my arm and tossed it to the middle of the floor and then released me from my position on the wall. The crowd erupted in applause and jeered. She'd be rewarded for winning and, based on the buzz from the audience, probably receive a bonus for being the crowd's favorite.

Defeat left a dank taste in my mouth, despite not having anything to feel bad about. I held my own against a person who had access to magic continuously. She should be more skilled than me.

I concentrated on the red band in the middle of the floor, making it dance in front of me in a steady beat. Discarded paper on the ground joined in the movement. Having access to magic for such a short period of time made it difficult to let any time go by without using it even for something as frivolous as this.

Every moment I had use of it, I wanted to do more. Practice, perform a spell, battle with it. Despite being drained from earlier activities, I couldn't bring myself to stop indulging in my borrowed magic. I binged whenever I had access to it. How could I not?

I slowly made my way to my car, my shoulders drooping from fatigue. Finally, I stopped the performance of dancing objects around me. I was weighed down by more than just tiredness; it was the knowledge that I wouldn't have my own magic for a while. Savoring every moment of it wasn't enough. I wanted to keep it, and by the time I'd made it to my car, I'd come up with several scenarios on how to achieve it, one being just leaving town. It was an extreme and unreasonable idea that I quickly dismissed when I saw Cory's car parked in front of mine.

"Why are you here?"

"I could ask you the same question," he responded wryly, scrutinizing my appearance. Using a light touch he brushed the perspiration-matted hair from my forehead. He took my hand in his and assessed my arms that were now trembling. He looked pensively at my state. His hands were cool against my warmed skin.

"How did you know I was here?"

"I didn't, Madison did." His contemplative look remained. "She got word that you were here from an unlikely source."

"River."

He nodded. "We really should be leaving. He's convinced he's going to be the first on "the scene" of another *incident*." The Dome wasn't technically illegal. It was just people getting together to demonstrate their magical prowess, but because of its very nature, things happened.

While I looked up the empty street, expecting to see River's car, I could feel Cory's eyes on me. "How many escape scenarios have you come up with in order to keep his magic?"

I didn't bother asking how he knew. Of course he knew I'd borrowed it from Mephisto.

"About four, each one more ridiculous than the previous one."

He forced out a laugh, rough and mirthless. Giving me a narrow-eyed evaluation, he asked, "I thought you two had a deal regarding the magic exchange. What changed?"

"Nothing," I responded quickly. "It was just a loan." Based on the way he looked at me, I knew he wasn't buying my response and that there was more to it. I appreciated him for not pushing.

"So who did you duel?"

I rolled my eyes. "The Maestro of Magic. A wizard robe–wearing magical savant."

"Ah, Wendy." He grinned but managed to keep his

165

opinion of her to himself. The miscreant twinkle in his eyes and tightly pressed lips convinced me that it wasn't kind.

Cory walked me to my car and once I was in, leaned in. "I met with Harrison today," he admitted. Now I knew why he hadn't pressed me on the Mephisto issue.

"Why are you meeting someone who was kicked out of your coven for performing dark magic?"

"Because he's the only person I know who would deal with demons. We need to stop Ian, and the best way to do that is to remove his magic immunity. I thought he could help."

"By summoning a demon!" I snapped, immediately regretting it. With all the things I'd done in my past, I had no right to chastise him.

"Relax, I wasn't going to have him summon demons. I wanted to confirm what you said about reversing Ian's immunity. You're right, only the demon who cast the spell can reverse it." Raking his hands through his hair, he blew out a frustrated breath. "I have no idea what else to do."

Me neither. "We'll figure something out." Each time I said it, I sounded more confident than I felt.

"I think we should go," Cory suggested, seeing a car creep down the street. "Don't skip town with Mephisto's magic," he teased while backing away.

"That was on my list of ridiculous things to try."

CHAPTER 13

*M*ephisto's midnight eyes were imperceptible as they reflected back at me when I finally answered the door. Did I think he would forget about his magical loan and just go away?

"I don't know if I did you any favors by doing this," he admitted, his gaze trailing over me. When I returned home, I did several more spells and more attempts to Wynd and I was positive I looked as exhausted as I felt.

"I don't know either," I said, chewing on my lip. I was afraid if I bit any harder I'd draw blood.

"Just for a few more days. You can work on finding your box. I know you want it and it is so important for you to find it. That couldn't have changed. Not in such a short time." Everything rushed out in a long string of words as I floundered to come up with a justifiable reason to keep his magic.

"As I said, there is always a penalty for loaning my magic. I can't search for the box without my full strength."

He stepped closer and I moved an equal distance back.

He sighed. "You're not like the other Raven Cursed and you know why—because you're not the same. Theirs is a lust that can't be ignored, but with discipline it can be controlled.

Yours is a need that has to be satisfied because your magic is restricted differently. You have to know this, Erin."

"I don't know that!" I snapped, fully aware of the direction he was going with this conversation. I was clinging ever so desperately to the fact I was just a terrible death mage, the worst of the worst, which was why I lacked control. My parents were mine and I wasn't related to Malific, let alone her daughter. All the denial in the world couldn't make me forget the raven that showed up on my arm. That had to have meaning. And maybe someone did put a restriction on my magic, hoping I wouldn't turn out to be like Malific.

Covering my face with my hands, I took a moment. Once again faced with the creation of another liminal period in my life. Before and after I confirmed that I was Malific's daughter.

Mephisto's hands were gentle as they enclosed my wrists, pulling them away from my face. His eyes tracked mine as I attempted to avoid the sincerity in them.

"Talk to your parents," he urged.

As if that was an implied contingency of keeping his magic, I nodded and stepped away.

Okay, I'll talk to my parents. Bye-eee.

Me backing away made him chuckle as he grabbed my arm and tugged me to him. "Erin," he entreated.

I leaned in and pressed my lips to his, my tongue languidly running against his lips, making his breath come harder. My fingers traced the curves of his jaw, down his neck, where my mouth soon followed. Fisting his hair, I placed soft kisses on his neck. The warmth of our attraction enveloped us and his desire for me was very obvious. I pressed my body even closer to him.

"Give me time to talk to my parents," I whispered in his ear. My tongue eased out to caress his lobe. "And you'll leave and return later to retrieve your magic. Okay?"

He lifted me and my legs curled around his waist.

Turning around, he backed me to the wall until I was firmly pressed against it. Eyes heavy lidded with lust, he regarded me for a few moments, then he leaned in and kissed me, his tongue exploring mine before tracing the outline of my jaw with soft kisses. He nipped lightly and teased the fragile skin of my neck. Soft pants escaped me as I held him tighter, digging my nails into his back.

"You little seductress. If only you knew how much I would love to fall for this."

Then his lips were over mine, pulling his magic from me. He released my legs, allowing them to touch the ground before giving me a chastising look.

Then he straightened his clothes and ran his thumb over my lips.

He backed away to the door, keeping his eyes on me. "Erin Katherine Jensen, you are quite the temptress, and I'm so easily tempted when it comes to you."

Not enough because he was gone and I had been divested of his magic.

I ignored the faux look of exasperation my mother gave me whenever she answered the door because I'd rung the doorbell instead of using my key. It only took me once seeing my parents' affection for each other on full display on the kitchen island to discourage me from ever just walking in again. The key was for emergency purposes only.

"Use your key," my mother admonished before pressing a kiss to my forehead.

You get an eyeful of your dad's ass and your mom's boobs and see how willing you'd be to "use your key."

"It's rude. I don't live here anymore. I need to give you the courtesy of deciding whether you want company or not." And time to put on some clothes.

As soon as I entered the house, she pulled me into a hug. I held her tight, taking in the scent of her perfume. There wasn't a pulse of magic coming from her; before, I thought I couldn't perceive it because it was too weak, but with my new knowledge, it made sense. When she pulled away and studied me, new lines appeared around her mouth and the crease between her brows became more pronounced. Seeing her through unfiltered eyes made me question how I hadn't seen this before. Round face, wide eyes, and a fair complexion no amount of sun could tan was in contrast to my olive tones. Strawberry-blonde hair with hints of gray with natural waves couldn't explain my brunette hair, even taking into consideration my father's deep caramel-colored hair.

In the living room, I stared at them both as if seeing them for the first time, examining our differences, searching for our similarities.

My dad's discerning gaze stayed on me. "Erin, good to see you. Are you staying for dinner?" He gave me his typical quick casual hug. He wasn't as affectionate as my mother, whose hugs were so tight they pushed the breath out of you.

I forced the tension out of me. So damn what if they weren't my real parents? That wasn't what bothered me; it wasn't blood that made them my parents, it was their love and caring that did. People who cared for me all my life, worried about my inability to control my magic, did everything in their power to protect me. My mouth dried to the point I could barely speak.

"Water," I squeaked and went to the kitchen to get some. I was on my second glass when my parents slipped onto the barstools at the island and turned the same concentrated look on me that I had given them.

"Do you know who my real parents are?"

Great, Erin. Real smooth. Not fucking tacky at all. I felt even worse when my mom's eyes became glassy with unshed tears. To their credit, neither one looked shocked. My dad seemed relieved, my mother sad. No one said anything for a while.

"No. Sophie doesn't know either."

Sophie? Why would Madison's mother know anything about it?

"What does she have to do with it?"

"She found you . . . or rather, you found her." My mother's voice was tight, losing the battle with the tears she'd been fighting back.

My dad pressed a kiss to her temple. "Vera, it's okay." Then he directed his attention to me. "You were left at her door and they had Maddie—" He stopped, chewed on the words. "And we were trying and couldn't. She gave us you. Her gift to us." And now he was having a hard time speaking. His voice was rough and low.

It explained how he was so accepting of my mother and Sophie's weird relationship—and no one looking from the outside would consider it anything but freakishly weird. They raised Madison and me as sisters because we were supposed to be.

We'd moved twice and each time, it was close to Madison's family. Either on the same street or a block away of their home. Now my parent's home was three houses from theirs. Madison and I often teased them about how we lived in a commune. Dinner together at least three times a week, and it wasn't unusual to come down and find Madison and her parents at the table for breakfast.

"You have no idea who my real parents are?"

"No," my mother whispered. "When we saw what you could do with magic, I wondered. You nearly killed Sophie." New tears glistened in her eyes and I vaguely remember them telling me about how they discovered what I was. As a toddler sitting in Sophie's lap, I had pulled the magic from her. I had to be coaxed into returning it. My magic was so instinctual, I knew what needed to be done. Well, that's the version they told me.

"How did you all know what to do?"

"We didn't. You saw her there lying lifeless. We thought she'd had a heart attack, stroke, or fainted or something. But she wasn't breathing, and her face had a peculiar expression of peace. We panicked. Administered CPR. Did whatever we could to save her. You simply walked over to her and . . . then you started moving things around the room from where you were next to her on the floor." My mother gulped in air as tears streamed down her face. I blinked back mine. She swallowed hard. "We couldn't get you to stop. It was like you felt our panic, innately knew something was wrong. You told her to wake up and she came to life."

I used words of power in Latin, which were translated into "mine" and "wake up." Something I started to do in magic school. They were just words, focusing the intent. I could draw the magic just thinking it, but just as it was easier to take the magic with contact, it was easier with power words.

"We hated having you wear that damn iridium bracelet, but we had no choice until you were able to control it," my father explained, shaking off the memory.

Should I remember nearly killing my mother's best friend? I didn't remember it, and Sophie never treated me as if I was someone to fear even when she saw me struggling with managing my magic as a child and even more as a teenager. The bracelet stopped me from taking people's magic; it did nothing for the urge. Nothing other than having magic staved that off.

"How did you find out?" My mother's question was a strained whisper that broke the tension-filled silence.

I couldn't tell them the truth and have them worry. I was still clinging to the hope that Malific wasn't my mother. And my father? Who was he? Was he human?

172

"You had no intention of ever telling me?" I asked, evading the question.

"No." My mother's response was terse. "How did you find out?"

I shrugged. "I guess I always knew. For the first time, I opened my eyes to it." This wasn't a lie. Mephisto reading off my list of peculiarities did open my eyes to something that on some level I had suspected. "If Grandma is Raven Cursed, she controls it better than I do."

Both of my parents' mouths were pressed into tight lines, like they were fighting the words threatening to come out.

Giving them a wry smile, I saved them the effort. "Grandma's just human, too, right?"

Flushed cheeks provided the answer. The strain on their faces and their sorrow-filled eyes were heartbreaking. I'm sure they expected anger or frustration, but I didn't feel either—just fear of who my real parents were.

My mother gave me a look that spoke volumes. It said: "We'll talk about this when you're ready."

I answered with a weak smile.

The rest of the visit was a performance as we tried to pretend that a veil of deceit hadn't been lifted and our lives irreparably changed.

I stayed for dinner. I needed to. Being with my parents that day was what I needed most.

CHAPTER 14

*T*he royals' French Provincial, being the official home for the king and queen, reflected their modern elegance, sophistication, and regality in its beautiful tan brick, large stately windows, and ornate balustrades. If Ian could convince them to abdicate, he'd never embody the home the way Neri and Adalia did. But if Ian had his way, they'd step down and this would be his residence.

In the past when I drove past the gates made of intricately woven iron flowers onto the estate, I found myself taken in by the elegant beauty of the home. Groves of oversized trees flanked the driveway. To most, the trees would have seemed there simply for the aesthetics, a beautiful landscape befitting of a stunning home. But they weren't. The large trees allowed the guards to inconspicuously protect the home and its occupants.

Closer to the home, I got a glimpse of the exquisite statues that decorated the verdant lawn; I assumed magic was involved to get such vibrant color. The manicured bushes around the home had been trampled. Glass and splinters of wood littered the grass.

I jerked the car into park when a dingo stumbled in front

of it and collapsed. Snatching my karambit off the passenger seat, I jumped out and approached the animal blocking my way. There was a cacophony of noise: arrows whooshing, knives and swords hissing, growls, roars, howls, and groans. Ignoring the sounds, I focused on the dingo lying on its side. Blood pooled around the arrow protruding from its flank. He struggled to lift his head. A whimper escaped him before he dropped back to the ground. He had the desire to move but not the ability. He made several attempts to roll to his feet, collapsing with each effort.

"I'll have to remove the arrow," I said, keeping my voice soft and reassuring. The arrow had to be silver. Bullets, arrows, knives all worked to weaken and prevent healing if they penetrated the skin. Anything else would hurt but wouldn't weaken them like this.

"Count of three, okay?"

Another rough whimper escaped.

Counting aloud, I yanked hard and pulled it out. To my surprise, he made a soft noise of pain. Instead of reverting to human, he stayed in animal form, exhausted from trying to heal with silver imbedded in him.

When I came to my feet, so did he, aggressively growling at me. He snapped at me and I jumped back just in time to keep my arm from being chomped.

"Stop!" I growled, putting the same command into it that I heard in Asher, but it didn't have the same effect. Not even a pause. He lunged. The blade of my karambit went into the dingo's side. He howled in pain but stayed on his feet.

The dingo lunged again, knocking me to the ground. I hammered hard into his nose with my free hand, thrashing with full force until he retreated. I rolled into a crouch, adrenaline not enough to stave off the pain. I ached. Gripping my karambit tighter, I backed away, waiting for him to attack again.

This time he tackled me to the ground and sank his teeth

into my arm. Pain shot through me. Trails of blood ran down my arm. Tears blurred my eyes. The dingo loosened his grip only to bite down with a better grip. Side-bending, I angled my body to get a better aim at my target, the Achilles, then slashed into his left side. The dingo collapsed lopsided and howled in pain. I delivered the same treatment to the right side, forcing him down on his hind legs. Only then did he release his hold on my arm. He'd be helpless for a few minutes until it healed.

I took that time to look for the arrow I had pulled out of him. My heart ached at what I had to do. The dingo was a victim too.

"I'm sorry," I whispered, shoving the arrow back into him. He wouldn't heal until the silver was no longer in contact. My simple apology wouldn't absolve me of the guilt that ached just as much as my arm.

I'd learned it was better not to look at an injury during a job because everything always looked worse covered in fresh blood. Resisting the urge to peek, I pushed aside the long-held misconception that a shifter bite changed you into one during the full moon. The falsehood continued to exist despite being disproven. Even statements by the Wolf and Lion packs hadn't worked to dispel it among certain groups of people who were determined to see shifters as more menacing than they were. During a press conference, a particularly cantankerous reporter with ties to anti-supernatural organizations asked about it again and Asher suggested biting him to let him find out for himself.

I opened the trunk of my car, slipped on my holster, grabbed my Ruger, and changed out the magazine, loading it with the more expensive silver bullets. I'd shoot to injure, not to kill, but the idea still left a dank taste in my mouth.

"You'll pay for this," I made a promise to Ian as I shrugged on a vest outfitted with places to stash four silver blades, push knives, three shuriken—made of silver, of course—and another magazine. I sheathed a knife to my right leg and an iron knife to my left and ran for the royal couple's home.

I got quick glances of the uniformed guards: white prince–styled tunics with silver embroidery decorating the necks and edges of the quarter-length sleeves. Simple midnight slacks. The royals may be pretentious in their own dress and mannerisms, but their guards were functional.

I only saw twelve of the usual twenty. I had thought twenty was far more than was needed, but apparently I was wrong. Nine animals: three wolves, a panther, a lynx. Lying on the ground with arrows sticking out of them were another wolf, a coyote, and I couldn't make out the others.

The royals had to be protected, and with Ian around there wasn't anything I could do to help the shifters.

I scanned the sky for Ian and caught a glimpse of his midnight wings as bronze and copper spiraled together and crashed into its target in a tree. A body fell. I quickened my pace to get to them, arrows whizzing past me in Ian's direction. They missed him. Ian retaliated by sending a hellstorm of magic toward the coppice of trees where the arrows came from. A fae guard fell from it.

The wolves changed direction, teeth bared, eyes thirsty for violence. Before the fae could lift his hand to evoke defensive magic, one wolf bit into his arm, dragging him forward. Another was about to pounce from behind. The fae likely wouldn't survive. Quickening my pace, I shot the wolf mid-pounce. He dropped to the ground with a thud. A second shot grazed the other and he continued to bite and claw at the fae. It took two shots to stop him.

Advancing closer, I could see they were both still breathing.

The lynx and panther were waiting for an opening into the home, one I knew they would never get. They weren't an immediate threat and I was confident from scanning the surrounding area that there was a guard prepared with a silver arrow or magic to stop them if they did. I holstered my gun.

I needed to get to Ian. An unconscious man can't do magic, and I wanted to beat him into that condition.

As I continued to search the sky for him, he spotted me. Soaring upward, he darted over the trees at a speed that made it difficult to track him. Whipping around at the sound of footfalls behind me, I slashed the karambit in his direction. Shock covered Ian's face as he looked down at the knife that had missed him by a fraction of an inch. He flitted away, but not before I was able to get one shot off, into his leg. Rage hotter than any fire burned on his face. I waited for the opportunity to do it again.

"The emissary," he ground out with contempt. His midnight wings drank up the light and would have been considered glorious, an image of beauty, if they weren't attached to the likes of Ian.

A coil of magic twined around his fingers and I leapt out of the way just as he lobbed it at me. The next one came faster, throwing me off balance and crashing me to the ground. I kept rolling, missing each bolt as they slammed into the ground, kicking up dirt and grass from the power of their impact.

I scrambled to my knees, grabbing my gun and shooting at him rapid fire. Pain blurred my vision. I squeezed off two more shots that missed him by a large margin.

He soared even higher, so high that I couldn't make out his expression, but the tension in his body told me he was angry. His movements weren't the relaxed winnowing of before. He stayed in my line of sight, probably seething with self-righteous anger. Good, because I had my own and I enjoyed the company.

While his attention was focused on me, a similar coil of magic flew at him from one of the fae on my right. It knocked him back several feet but not out of the air. I needed him grounded.

Ian was strategic and fast in flight, with the precision of an eagle. Like a bullet, he flew out of sight. Gun trained on the sky, I waited.

When I came to my feet, I was surrounded by ten guards, some holding bows and arrows, magic skating across the fingers of the others.

For several minutes we scanned the sky, looking for the menacing winged fae. Nothing. They retreated but I remained, waiting for one more chance to ground him.

Finally giving up, I took in the violence-wrecked area. Blood stained the grass, broken ceramics littered the ground, injured shifters and fae were trying to ease their wounds. Fae weren't able to do healing spells, but they healed fast if they weren't bound by iron.

"Can someone please call Asher and Sherrie?" I instructed, but no one moved until Neri came outside. He took in the damage, the injured shifters and guards, his face becoming flushed with barely contained rage.

"Her instructions are to be followed," he said simply, frowning at something on the ground. It looked like a note. A card. A bloodstained card.

I began giving instructions. "Call Asher, tell him to bring their physician. There are two shifters who were shot with silver bullets that will have to be removed. Any shifters with arrows in them, remove them."

Then I made my way to my car to help the dingo. Violence wasn't a problem for me, and if a person was irreparably damaged or injured when attacking me, I had no sympathy to give. But I wouldn't have been attacked if it weren't for Ian. This felt worse.

After my third apology, the fourth probably sounded hollow to the dingo's ears. My consolatory words were probably worse. I pulled out the arrow and positioned his feet to allow the Achilles to heal in the correct position. Moving out of his way, I sat back awestruck by the speed of the healing. Minutes later, a slender man stood before me. I covered him with a blanket from my car.

"Asher will be here soon," I told him. Asher wasn't his Alpha, but just the mention of his name seemed to relax the man.

The bloodstained card lay on the middle of the coffee table taunting us with its threat: *Last Warning.*

The blood on it was a reminder that more would be shed if Neri and Adalia didn't abdicate. Their faces showed their restrained rage and dismay. Asher was right: A person like Ian wouldn't just stop with his coup here. This would be just the beginning.

Asher scowled as he dragged his gaze from Neri to Adalia.

Ian's approach to taking over the court would lead to more bloodshed. Each denizen had their own way of getting power. The Master of the vampires usually controlled the family. When they no longer wanted a public presence, they appointed a representative. Most recently that was Landon, who had been sired by the city's Master, so it was only fitting that he would take on that role.

Shifter rule was based on dominance. It was to submission now rather than death, but the Alpha was always the strongest of the pack.

Witch covens and mage consortiums both had smaller units and were often headed by the strongest and most knowledgeable. The transition of power was often seamless. It was more of a communal relationship.

The fae were the most democratic of them all. They petitioned for their position and leadership was determined by the fae and chosen every half century. Adalia and Neri were strong, but they weren't the strongest fae in the area.

"Have you found anything that can stop him?" Neri inquired. Telling him nothing had changed since we spoke yesterday would only make things worse and invoke hostility I didn't need.

"No. I've exhausted my sources for finding the Xios and Conparco Shield."

He didn't hide his disinterest at the mention of the latter.

Asher's dark expression mirrored Sherrie's as they approached, their clothing bloodstained.

"It's time for you to abdicate," Asher announced. The galvanized edge to his voice didn't invite a debate although Neri and Adalia were rearing up for one.

His steadfast demeanor didn't falter even with both Neri and Adalia giving him varying looks of reproach. Neri's throat bobbed as he swallowed his intended words. The tightened muscles of his face and neck made his narrow features look gaunt. Adalia eased her frown, making a valiant effort at a smile, but her eyes held displeasure at Asher's proposal.

"You know very well you never reward behavior such as this with placation. If that's your answer, then why don't you submit to him so your wolves won't be forced into compliance but do it willingly?" Neri said.

"Is that what you want, for me to align my pack with him to take your position? Right now, I don't see too much of a difference. I've lost two people today in a fight that we didn't ask to be part of—"

"We, too have sustained loss and—"

"We don't care," Sherrie pronounced, looking past them as if looking directly at them would prevent her controlling her emotions. "Step down, appease him, and give us a chance to find a way to either send him back, subdue him, or at the very least contain him." Before either of the royals could speak, she added, "This isn't up for debate. Do it or he won't have to worry about you stepping down."

She directed her withering scowl in my direction, turned on her heels, and left. I wasn't sure if that was the way Asher felt too, but he left with her.

Negotiations between denizens was my least favorite thing to do. I didn't have the temperament for it, and suggesting a time-out never went over as the lighthearted suggestion it was intended to be. Before Asher and Sherrie could make it to their cars, I called out to Asher. He didn't immediately respond. The glower from earlier had eased but not by much. He advanced toward me and stopped, looking at my ripped sleeve and mangled arm.

"You're injured."

"It looks worse than it is."

"Lie."

Yeah, we both knew I was lying. A dingo chomped on my arm. Of course it hurt as bad as it looked. I wanted to ask if anyone had died from a bullet wound but I couldn't. That extra burden wouldn't help. Pressing my lips into a tight line, I suppressed the question.

"One died from injuries from an arrow, another from the injuries sustained from a silver bullet," he offered in an even voice, as if he knew what I wanted to ask.

"I'm sorry," I said. I might have confessed then, because there wasn't any way to hide my guilt and I wasn't sure I wanted to. Playing over and over in my mind was the moment when I shot. Could I have handled things differently?

The silence between us spoke volumes. Asher gave me a small, mirthless, forced smile and went to his car.

Thirty minutes with Neri and Adalia and I was sure even if I spent thirty hours it wouldn't be enough to convince them to concede their position to Ian. I wasn't one hundred percent confident that they should. I left, not answering their pressing question of whether I thought Sherrie would follow through.

I knew the answer and they did, too.

CHAPTER 15

I'd quickly accepted that the set expression on Cory's face wasn't going to ease. I widened my tight-lipped smile, hoping he'd mirror it. Or at least relax the rictus. His thumb ran absently over my magically healed arm. Cory's touch was light enough not to be painful, but it was a reminder of the event.

"It can be done," I said. "Asher has already confirmed it with Elizabeth. She was going to use a Conparco Shield to prevent the shifters from being changed by binding his pack to him, allowing them to benefit from the strength of the Alpha. Then she could bind a shifter to another shifter, making them immune to magic."

The idea had come to me during my drive home. It wouldn't solve the problem of getting Ian back to the Veil, but it would take away his ability to use shifters as his army. Beat a person from the Veil by using magic from the Veil. I was surprised when Asher answered my call. More surprising was how reluctant he was to me doing it. I had expected the hesitation and debate from Cory but not Asher.

"It's the best chance we have. I've put out some calls to get some leads." Picking up a magic reference book, I'd searched through earlier, I showed him an object that looked like an infinity circle enclosed in a bronze circle. "This will undo the demon magic and remove Ian's immunity to iron if used with a Salem Stone, which Asher has." Mentioning the stone that Asher had stolen right from under my nose didn't evoke the same rage that it had less than a week ago. I reached under my sofa and pulled out the shuriken with Ian's blood on it.

"You only have two of the three items you need," Dudley Downer pointed out.

"I know. While I try to find the third, this is the best option."

Cory made a face. "You can't get into the Veil without Mephisto. Are you sure he'll agree to it? He doesn't seem to be enthusiastic about you returning to it or getting involved."

Peter Pessimist was making things worse. It wasn't going to be an easy task. The thing I was most confident about was taking away Ian's animancy ability. "I'll have to convince him."

Cory chewed on his bottom lip, worry putting painful looking creases on his face. He stood and grabbed the small wastebasket from the corner and began discarding the supplies used to clean up the dingo bite.

"You think you can walk up to a shifter and say, 'Hey, I need to use you as a test subject to make shifters on the other side of the Veil immune to magic, because we aren't positive it will work'?"

"What do we have to lose?"

His eyes widened and he turned away from me. "Are you drinking or smoking the good stuff when you come up with these ideas?"

He finished cleaning up and went to the kitchen to get a bottle of water from the fridge. He refilled it and took another drink, probably to give him time to come up with an argument. Before he could speak, his text notification beeped. He looked at it and his frown deepened.

"What's wrong?"

"Nothing. My plans for this evening were canceled." His attempt to sound indifferent failed.

"With Alex, right?"

This would have been their third date or "hanging out" since Cory wasn't describing it as dating.

"Did he give a reason?" I asked.

He shook his head. "I don't think you should do this," he asserted. "It's too dangerous. I know you sometimes manage the impossible, but this is too risky. You aren't even familiar with the Veil."

"Not as dangerous as you think. You know shifters have preferences about where they live. I'm sure Mephisto will be able to get me there. After all, he did live there." The confidence that I intentionally put into my voice should have swayed him.

"For Asher! Are you serious? Let them handle this. I have to agree with Mephisto, this isn't your fight."

"I'm not just doing it for Asher or the shifters. I'm doing it for us. For me and you."

"What?"

"Alex is the Northwest Pack's fourth. Him canceling isn't because he doesn't want to see you. You brought Ian here. Asher knew and so did Sherrie. Asher promised to keep the secret, but Sherrie didn't commit that to me. Nor do I believe she plans to keep it a secret. I'm sure Alex knows. Right now, you are a pariah among the shifters and possibly an enemy."

"I can take care of myself." Cory's face was alight with anger, and his fists balled at his sides as magic pulsed off him. "It was an accident and I'll be damned if they make me an enemy over it!"

Cory liked to believe he was the logical one, but he absolutely wasn't when he felt he was being falsely accused, his honor was at stake, or someone was accusing him of being reckless with his magic, the very tenets he lived by. I grabbed his arm before he could charge out the door and go find Asher and Sherrie.

"Asher knows it was unintentional, but that doesn't change the fact that we have a rogue fae who doesn't seem to have any weaknesses. I want to take away one of his strengths so he won't have a pack of shifters at his beck and call."

"Do you understand the magnitude of what you're doing? If you bind them to the shifters in the Veil, they'll be immune to all magic, not just Ian's."

"I know."

"Essentially making them shifter versions of Ian."

"No, they'll still be vulnerable to silver. They will have weaknesses. And they're still ruled by the full moon." I didn't say what I was thinking: Worst-case scenario, if they needed to be reined in, it could be done during that time.

"Both Asher and the royals tried iron on him. It doesn't work."

"Have we tried runed manacles?"

My lips pressed into a thin line at Cory's irrational suggestion. Perhaps runed cuffs would work, but they were always placed on metal that weakened the wearer. Ian didn't have a metal weakness, and his ability to fly made things especially difficult.

I was used to supernaturals flexing their power; it didn't bother me. Showy displays of magic was just another day at the office. Ian, though, was a menace. I needed to stop him.

"Erin, I think this is a terrible idea. Find another option."

"I killed one of Asher's wolves today." I blinked back the tears welling in my eyes and looked away.

He cursed under his breath. Washing his hands over his face, he blew out a breath. Moving close to me, he pressed his hand gently against my cheek, but I found no comfort in it.

187

Because his face spoke volumes when his words would not. It said: *You've killed before.*

"Is it the shifter's death you're trying to atone for?" he asked in a low voice. I couldn't meet his eyes. It seemed like my life was a series of contradictions and I couldn't get people to understand that every day I was fighting a battle that I seemed to be losing constantly. I wanted magic. I needed it the way people needed to breathe. The way an alcoholic needed that next drink, and an addict needed that next fix. I battled every day with a body that wanted to betray me. My conscience was in a never-ending struggle between right and wrong, trying desperately to do the right thing.

Did Cory realize that as much as I loved him, at moments I thought about taking his magic and walking away from it all? So, yes. I was in perpetual need of atonement because I knew my thoughts and I suspected that one day, if I didn't get a handle on things, I'd kill again.

"I don't think it's atonement. Maybe I'm trying to get karma points," I said, giving him a weak smile.

"There are no points for sacrificing your life for them."

"What's that from, the Book of Cory?"

A bark of laughter filled the room, and when it eased, he placed his hand on my shoulder.

"I don't want you to keep taking unnecessary risks in a search for some arbitrary feeling of atonement to right something in your past that can't be fixed. It's your past. Let it go."

As I debated whether to tell him about what Dr. Sumner suspected, he grumbled a curse under his breath at the knock on my door. I opened it to a pursed-lipped, scowling Madison. She slipped past me without an invitation. Cory was holding his hands out in front of him as if trying to ward off an animal readying to attack. He seemed to believe I was the animal.

"In my defense, I contacted her when I thought your plan was poorly planned, problematic, and dangerous. Now, I only think it's dangerous and not well planned. Not much has changed, but I'm feeling ten percent better."

"A whole ten percent. Great."

That explained his need for the bathroom immediately after I told him what I was considering. Madison was his nuclear weapon that he employed far too often for my taste.

"How much do you know?"

Taking out her phone, Madison read Cory's texts as he found any and everything else to focus on while I glared at him.

"Good, you know everything," I said drily. "You can't talk me out of it."

She gave Cory an apologetic look. "I wasn't planning on it. If you can do this, then that's one less thing working in Ian's favor."

Wariness of the situation showed in her face. Her responsibility to the royals and her responsibility for dealing with the fragile and tenuous relationship between humans and supernaturals was starting to show.

"River is really making a case for his 'riotous and unpredictable shifters and over-powered supernaturals that can't be managed by STF' claims. If he finds out about the Veil, I don't know if I can prevent the fallout." Making her way to my kitchen, Madison looked at my selection of alcohol and turned up her pert nose.

Hey, beggars can't be judgy. I guess if my sister was going to drink on a workday before 5:00 p.m. it wasn't going to be with cheap whiskey and bottom-shelf wine. I went to the pantry and handed her one of the three bottles of wine Mephisto had sent me, the wine I'd had at his home.

Her eyes widened when she looked at the label. "Chateau Leoville-Las Cases. When did you get this? How do you even know about this?"

"She didn't know about it. Erin has no problem going into the Veil to convince strange shifters to follow her back here, but she takes gifts from strangers, too."

"Mephisto is hardly a stranger." Reflexively I brought my finger to my lips, remembering the gentle brush of his lips against mine. The feelings it invoked didn't have anything to do with his magic.

"Not a stranger. What's tall, dark, and mysterious's real name?" Cory asked, bemused.

"Bob." I flashed a grin.

"Mephisto is okay with doing this?" Madison inquired.

"I have to ask him."

"So, Cory was right. It's not quite a plan, yet." She took a sip from her glass. When she relaxed back against the counter, she smiled and took another appreciative sip. She might have been enjoying the wine, but she had the same look on her face that she had when she was dealing with *the incident.*

"I have a meeting with the mayor tomorrow," Madison told us, refilling her glass. There weren't a lot of similarities between us, but not adhering to the proper serving size of alcohol was one.

I didn't know what to say. What do you say? *Good luck.*

"I really hope it will work. It will make my life infinitely easier." She put a hand up to her hair to fidget with it, then stopped, remembering the mane was gone.

"Are we sure this will work? The shifters in the Veil are immune to magic, so will Elizabeth be able to cast a spell on them?" Madison asked.

Cory sidled up next to her and poured himself a half glass of wine then lifted the bottle to ask me if I wanted any.

I shook my head. If all went as planned with Mephisto, I'd be going into the Veil later.

After sipping from his glass, Cory finally spoke. "They're binding shifter magic to shifter magic. Maybe it will work like a software upgrade and repair the patches." Cory laughed at the absurdity.

"Can't be too far off," Madison offered, but a small smile had settled on her lips as she gave him a sidelong look. "So we'll be patching the shifters on this side of the Veil."

"Oh, that's what's wrong with Asher," Cory said. "His software isn't quite up to standard." He narrowed his eyes as he paused to take another sip. "A spell from *Mystic Souls* brought Ian here, do you think—"

"Don't even think about it," I said, cutting him off.

By the time Cory left, he still wasn't fully onboard with me going to the Veil, and no argument was going to change his mind. Doing it without his full support wasn't going to be easy, but it had to be done.

Madison closed the door behind him and turned to me.

"Erin," she started in a slow voice, "you don't mind danger. We both know this doesn't have anything to do with you being fearless." She gave me a weak smile. "I'm proud of how you've been handling things. Do you really see this working or is this . . . you know . . ."

My history of being reckless was reasonable cause for concern. It was more than being an adrenaline junkie; it fed a need. Lately, I'd been able to control it more than in the past, if you ignored me having to lock my legs around a chair to stay away from Kai, or that weird moment between me and Clayton, or me trying to seduce Mephisto so I could keep his magic. Okay, I wasn't handling this well at all, but I wasn't a total failure either.

"I'm dealing with things fine. I'm better. Dr. Sumner's really helping a lot."

The Sumner lie was a step too far. Madison's lips pressed into a tight line. "Erin?"

Shrugging, I said, "Madison, what do you want me to say? I want magic and I know the cost and it doesn't subdue the desire. I'd never put you through what I did using the spell from *Mystic Souls*, but I'll go to the Veil for Mephisto and get whatever he wants to do it."

There was a debate brewing in her and she was working hard to keep it to herself. I didn't need any lectures, warning, or requests for caution.

"Okay," she finally breathed out in concession. "Be safe. I'll be there when you go, if you want."

I nodded. She started to head out the door and stopped. "I know you found out about your parents," she whispered, keeping her back to me as if she couldn't stand to see my look of anger or disappointment, or both. Madison finally turned and pulled me into a tight hug. It reminded me of one of my mother's hugs. "I should have told you, but I was sworn to secrecy."

"It's okay." I had to be okay with it, because I was keeping a lot of things from her too.

CHAPTER 16

*M*ephisto met me with an inquiring look. Peering out into the darkness, he opened the door wider, inviting me in.

"Two visits in two days. One could get used to this," he drawled in a deep, silky voice.

"The gate, is it really necessary?"

"Of course it's necessary, Ms. Jensen. What proves to be a minor inconvenience to you is invaluable to me." Mephisto stayed close, despite the expansive entryway. "You wanted to see me. Is it safe to assume it's business? Perhaps you've considered what we discussed."

"My parents aren't my real parents." Although the words came out casually, it felt like an elephant had decided to hop on my chest. I thought each time I said it, or thought it, the shock would wear off. The bandage-ripping pain would ease and I'd become used to it. But each time opened the wound anew.

"Oh," he whispered. His finger brushing against my hand was a feather touch. I looked down when he took hold of my hand. I took a step back. He was right, there was more between us than magic. Much more. I wasn't going to explore it.

Generally, I sucked at impulse control, but with him I would exercise restraint. There was more to him than met the eyes—so much more—and I needed to know what. In a world of horrific gods, of people who survive deals with demons, possess powerful magic, and travel between this world and the Veil, it was smart to learn more about him.

"I need a favor."

"Ah, more favors." His irritation was apparent. "How may I help you this time?"

"Technically, you let me see your collection, but I didn't take anything. So, was that really a favor?"

He looked at me with marked incredulity. Eh, it was worth trying.

Without answering, he started down the hall and I just stood there. *Am I supposed to follow? Who does that?* My clients, that's who. With the people I dealt with, I was used to eccentric behavior and variations of power moves like this. They walked and expected to be followed without question. My obstinance had its benefits and at times like this was worth its weight in gold. Planted at the entryway, I stayed, as I did with my clients, until he returned.

"Ms. Jensen, please join me in the Conversation Room."

"That's not a thing, no matter how many of you have it," I mumbled, joining him in his study. Like all his rooms, this one didn't lack a breathtaking view of the outdoors. A large bay window offered an enchanting view of illuminated greenery against the backdrop of the dark sky with just a crest of light coming from the moon.

A small bar was in one corner. A built-in bookcase took up one wall. Smaller than the other rooms in the house, the room felt warm, quaint, and inviting. I wasn't sure what I'd expected. Something like a war room maybe.

I'd prefer the office. That would remind me that I was dealing with Mephisto and our interactions were transactional. He invited me to sit and I dropped into a dove-gray club chair that contrasted with the steel-gray walls. Walls that were very similar in color to the gray of Mephisto's slacks and shirt.

He sat across from me with a round table of reclaimed wood between us. I admired the beauty of the craft and the intricacies of the wood and coloring.

"Kai?" I asked, touching the table.

He nodded, looking at the table, and showing an appreciation for it in the same manner I had. Concern flashed across his face but was quickly smoothed into a neutral expression.

Was he concerned that Kai wasn't adapting to this world? They had similar magic, but Kai's energy was frenetic, unmoored, raw. Was it because they had to practice restraint to avoid being discovered? Mephisto had magic, but the only time he'd ever used it was in his home, when he repaired my wounds, and in my home, when I borrowed it to go into the Veil. It was obvious that they subdued their magic, masked it when necessary, because I'd felt the full power of it.

Relaxed in his chair, elbows on the armrests, fingers steepled, Mephisto commanded the room as if he were in his office about to make a deal.

"What do you need, Erin?" he asked.

"To go into the Veil. I need to convince a shifter to come to this side so Elizabeth can bind his magic to the shifters here, making them immune to Ian so he can no longer use them in his quest to claim the royals' position." I spilled it out as quickly as I could as if that would make it sound less absurd or dangerous.

Nodding his head slowly, his tongue moved languidly over his lips. I waited patiently for him to speak. The first minute passed quickly; the rest of the time dragged. How long did he need to consider? Was it good that he was taking so much time? At the five-minute mark, irritation flared. I was convinced that he'd given up his right to say no. The justification didn't make any sense, but it made me feel better to think it.

"You're accumulating a lot of debt on Asher's behalf. Is it worth it?" he finally asked.

"I have a large debt to repay."

Mephisto's brows raised. "Debt? Do tell."

"I'll show you mine if you show me yours. Give me your name. Your real name."

"Mephisto," he said, slowly enunciating every syllable. Dark amusement curled the edges of his lips into a smirk.

"My debts are my business," I responded with the same slow enunciation. *I'll play your game.* I flashed him a wide smile when he narrowed his dark eyes on me.

"I will say, Erin Katherine Jensen, I find your audacity both fascinating and frustrating," he said, a hitch still in the corners of his lips.

"Are you going to do it?" I asked, becoming increasingly impatient as the conversation devolved into our typical banter.

More beats of silence passed.

"I don't know. I'm curious as to why you're so entrenched in a battle that is not your own. Is it the debt? I wonder how you became so indebted to Asher when I was under the impression that you're *friends*, since you claim there's nothing more, were having a spat that wasn't able to be resolved."

"There isn't anything between me and Asher. I'm not going to tell you why I'm so invested in this. It's my business to tell and my secrets to keep, just like yours."

Confessing the why would give Mephisto too much information. One, he'd know I was trying to find an alternative way to get magic to negate my need to do his job. Two, I had access to *Mystic Souls*. I had a feeling the book was probably on his list of collectibles. I wasn't sure I wanted him to have it, or anyone for that matter. Three, telling him would mean one more person knew about Cory's mistake. I wanted to insulate Cory as much as I could. If River found out, I'd rather it came back on me—he already had a vendetta against me and it couldn't get any worse.

"Are you sure the shifters can cross between the Veil?"

"I don't know. Do you have any reason to believe they can't?"

Mephisto had said there were many who could cross the Veil but chose not to. It could work for or against them. Magic that allowed others to cross between the worlds restricted them from seeing it, as was the case with so many on this side. Or the very magic that kept the Veil hidden didn't work on them. I was hoping it was the latter.

"Say that they can, then what?"

"We do the binding spell and . . ." I ended with a shrug as if the other things were inconsequential. I didn't want to have the debate about me making the shifters invincible.

The intensity of Mephisto's face made it apparent he was already thinking about that.

"The very thing that makes shifters fierce warriors and welcome allies is their immunity to magic."

I held my breath and started thinking of alternatives. I hadn't considered that the shifters couldn't cross. I had only considered that immunity to the magic would allow them to cross the Veil.

"But they would still have their weaknesses. They are still moon called and have an aversion to silver. If bound to the Veil shifters, the shifters here would have the same weaknesses," he said slowly. Despite saying he didn't have an investment in the outcome, it was a relief that he didn't want to leave things worse off. He cared about consequences, although I was fairly confident he was concerned about them in relation to him.

"Will you help me?" I pressed.

He stood and paced, his face inscrutable. "I have not decided. I think I'd like to discuss this with Kai, Simeon, and Clayton."

Can we leave Clayton out? I thought, recalling the look he gave me. I didn't want to see that look again.

"I didn't realize that your decisions were made by committee." Frustration had gotten the best of me and I immediately regretted it. "I shouldn't have said that. I apologize."

He nodded and took a seat on the wooden table, leaving just a few inches of space between us. "The wisest thing a person can do is know his weaknesses. The most foolish is to believe he has none. I think when it comes to you, I suffer some lapses in judgment. The others have noticed." He pulled his eyes from me and looked at the abstract canvases on the wall.

When he drew his attention back to me, there was a wanton intensity in his gaze that made it difficult to hold. "I wish I was as good at denying what's between us as you are," he said softly.

I wasn't in denial; I just refused to act on it.

"I don't have time to wait on a consult. I need a decision now."

"If that's your position, then the answer is no." He stood and went to the bar. "Would you care for a drink?" he asked, taking a bottle of scotch off the shelf. From the small ice maker next to it, he dropped two cubes into the glass. After taking a sip, he raised his glass to me in another offer.

I wasn't sure what shade of red I'd turned, but I could feel the flush of anger warming my neck and cheeks.

"You're an ass," I blurted.

He threw his head back in a deep throaty laughter that filled the room. "I'd like to make sure I've fully grasped this situation. You come here after being allowed to go through my collection to find a Xios or Conparco Shield, which I told you I didn't have. During that time you attempted to photograph items in a secured room where, other than Kai, Simeon, and Clayton, no one has ever entered. When prevented by Clayton, you rewarded his intervention by attempting to take his magic. You ask for the favor of borrowing my magic but refuse to tell me why you are so invested in this. But by seeking counsel to make sure I'm making a decision not influenced by my obvious enchantment with you, a woman who has more gall than one person should ever possess, somehow I'm the ass."

"Sometimes you just have to lean into your weaknesses. Give in to them."

"What a peculiar invitation to your bed," he said.

"How did you get that from what I said? I'm suggesting you just give me what I want. It would make my life so much easier."

"Ah, another proposal. I'd love to, but you're still in a state of denial over what you want."

I didn't dignify that statement with a response.

"Erin, they'll be here in fifteen minutes. There might be an alternative. Something safer. It might not satisfy what clearly is a taste for danger you possess that I don't quite understand, but an alternative plan might remedy the situation without changing the balance of this world. Something you haven't considered. I do not do this to irritate you or make this more difficult for you."

"That was rude of me," I admitted.

He placed a glass of what he was drinking in front of me. I was becoming increasingly embarrassed by my outburst. It's not that Mephisto was above pulling power plays—no one I've ever worked with was above that—but this wasn't one of them.

"I'm the reason Ian's here," I confessed quietly, picking up the glass and taking a sip. Enough to relax me but not inhibit my ability to function in the Veil. It wasn't the complete truth, but it was close enough.

He made a sound, took a sip, and pressed his lips into a line. His dark eyes were like flaming coals as they fixed on me.

"We can have our secrets but not lies. I'd rather you keep a secret than tell me a half truth."

I remembered he'd said he could read me. I'd negotiated with people. I'd told my share of embellishments. And I had an expressive face, but when necessary, I could keep a stolid expression just as I'd done with him. Or at least I thought I had. What about me was giving things away? I wanted to ask but doubted I'd get an answer.

"Some of it I won't tell you," I said, conceding. "But we found a spell that we thought would allow us into the Veil. Cory was curious. He did the spell, but it didn't open the Veil to him. What it did do was let Ian out. Neri, Adalia, and Asher were responsible for sending Ian back and restricting his ability to return."

"Ah, now I see the investment. It's not Asher, it's Cory." That information seemed to relax him, or maybe it was the drink he'd just finished.

"Kai, you got here fast," Mephisto said without even looking back at the man standing at the door. No one needed to announce his presence with the magic bounding off him like the town crier declaring his arrival. If that was Kai subduing his magic, I wondered what he was like when he wasn't.

"It's a table not a chair," Kai pointed out to Mephisto, who simply smiled.

"The others should be here soon."

I scanned Mephisto and the room, looking for a means of contact. When I didn't see any obvious way that Mephisto could have called them, my interest about their means of communication piqued even more.

Simeon arrived next, nodding in Mephisto's direction, who then stood and left the room, Kai right behind him. Simeon lingered.

"How is Pearl?" he asked.

"Victoria's Pearl?" I asked, baffled by the worry in his voice.

Nodding, he said, "Is she okay?"

Yes, Simeon, the hundred-pound apex predator is just fine. Not only does she have her predator instincts but she is also guarded now. She's more guarded than we are.

Instead of expressing those thoughts, I smiled, forcing as much authenticity into it as I could muster. "She's fine. Victoria has a guard for her." I was quite impressed that I was able to keep the sarcasm and derision out of my voice.

Looking down at his feet, he hesitated before speaking. "I'd like to see her again to check on her. Just to see how she's doing."

"What?" I couldn't suppress my shock. I blinked several times when I realized he was serious. As a person who communicated with animals, he had a connection that I couldn't understand. But I really didn't get his fondness for the snow leopard.

"I'll contact Victoria and see if she wouldn't mind. I don't think she'll have a problem. In fact, I bet she'd like it," I offered. *Then both of you weirdos can fawn over the murder kitty.*

A look of appreciation spread over his face.

"I should know something in a few days."

It wouldn't be long before I received my occasional reminder from Victoria that I was doing a crap job at guarding her. Sending Simeon to check on her dear Pearl might appease her, especially if she knew that he could speak with the animal. But would he disclose that to her? Probably better that he didn't. She probably wouldn't be pleased to find out that her precious cat would eat her if there wasn't any kibble around.

Added to the list of things I already had to do: Set up playdate with animal-whispering magical being and Pearl, the apex predator under the illusion that she's a house cat. My life was anything but boring.

Simeon's attention snapped from me to something to his left.

"Clayton." He welcomed him with a nod and left.

I didn't wait for Clayton to greet me. I doubted he would, but I was hopeful that he'd at least poke his head into the room, even if it were just to glare. That would give me an opportunity to apologize. He didn't.

Their deliberation took longer than I expected. Fifty minutes longer than I expected. Something that should have taken fifteen minutes took over an hour and Mephisto returned alone, his face indecipherable, making the tension in me rise. Depending on others frustrated me. But depending on Simeon, Kai, and Clayton to rule in my favor was a different kind of frustration and lack of control. I couldn't just borrow Cory's magic to see the Veil, nor could I use it for the length of time I needed to search for a shifter.

"I'm from the Veil," Mephisto said as a reminder that he could kill Ian without consequences. It was a tempting offer, because the more I dealt with Ian, the less I felt like his life was worth preserving. This situation felt like a test in redemption and I didn't want to fail.

My mouth worked to form the words "do it" but nothing came out. An assassination, that was exactly what that would be. It would end the problem, but it would be a fix that couldn't be undone. Swallowing the words of assent, I shook my head.

"He wants to move between the two worlds for a reason.

Maybe for a person. If he's killed, then you leave mourners, people ready to avenge him. Just because we don't see him as a person worthy of avenging doesn't mean others won't. There needs to be an alternative, but for now, I need to stop Ian using the shifters."

"Okay."

"You'll help?"

Mephisto nodded. "What happens now?" he asked, taking a seat in the chair next to me, allowing him to view the garden.

"I need to pack up and prepare to go to the Veil. Tomorrow, I'll go. If I'm successful, then we just worry about sending Ian back."

"I'm going to another auction. I'll pull some strings to get you an invitation as my guest. Perhaps they will have a Xios or something just as useful."

Mephisto not only dealt with the darker aspects of the city, he tended to wrap them up in great packaging complete with a pretty bow. You weren't a thief but a retrieval specialist. There wasn't such thing as a threat but simply opening dialogue for negotiation. I was curious about his "auctions," the ones that only a person like him could get invited to. I hadn't earned such an invitation, probably because I couldn't afford it.

"When is it?"

"In two days."

"Thank you. I'd love to go." Feeling mildly unburdened, I looked at the options that had opened up. Mephisto presented another option—a less desirable option, but an option nonetheless. It was the nuclear option and would only be used after I'd tried everything, including negotiating the royals' removal. Considering it still left a dank taste.

Mephisto was quiet as he led me to the door. "Your visit to Dante's Forest didn't yield the desired outcome. Ian has terrorized the shifters and made them accomplices in his

goal to take over the throne. I'm surprised he is still alive."
Mephisto frowned. "People treasure their powers and magic, but I'm shocked that there isn't a shifter willing to give up that part of them to stop him—to protect their pack."

There was. Asher. But it wasn't my information to tell.

No, Mephisto, you aren't the first to come up with that option.

CHAPTER 17

I lumbered to the door to answer the pounding. Eyes half closed, I looked at the time on the microwave: Two-freaking-thirteen in the morning. Blinking several times, I tried to clear my vision before looking through the peephole. Asher.

"You have to be fucking kidding me," I growled under my breath.

"You know I can hear you, right?"

"Good, then you know exactly how irritated I am." I yanked open the door. "What do you want?"

It was the most casual I'd ever seen him. His black v-neck t-shirt stretched over the sinewy muscles of his chest. Exposed arms displayed impressive biceps. Loose-fitting jeans hung off his narrow waist. He looked just as good in a t-shirt and jeans as he did in an expensive tailored suit. It annoyed me that I noticed and it annoyed me even more that he knew how good he looked as well.

"I couldn't sleep," he admitted softly.

"For most people, pills, liquor, sex, or exercise works," I snarked back. "Try those. Thank you for joining my TED talk." I started easing the door closed, but he placed his hand on the jamb to stop me.

He offered me a lazy smile but it lacked the Asher brand of allure. "My body metabolizes pills and liquor too fast for either to be any use. If you're offering sex, that would cover me for exercise, too. Unfortunately, I have to decline your offer."

I scoffed. "Goodnight, Asher."

"Erin, please, can I talk to you?" His tone was low and reticent. His entreaty gave me pause. If I didn't know any better, I'd assume he was timid and unsure, two things that he definitely wasn't.

Stepping aside, I let him in. He ran his fingers through a tuft of loose waves, his eyes drifting to the floor. He slid them from there to look at me. "Your text said you're going into the Veil tomorrow."

"It's two o'clock in the morning. It's today. I told you to be on standby so when I return we can do the spell. The sooner the better."

"I know. Is it safe?"

"As safe as it can be going into a foreign land to find a shapeshifter and ask them to return with me. Easy peasy. Preferably I'd like an Alpha—so, I might get arrogant-ed to death." I flashed a grin but it didn't ease the tension in his face. "I'll be fine. I can take care of myself."

"If something happens, I'll feel responsible because you're doing it for me."

"No worries. The only thing I'm in danger of is finding an Alpha who thinks way too highly of themselves."

"Erin. I saw your face at Neri and Adalia's home. I smelled the sorrow and fear and I smell it now."

"First, gross. Stop doing that. Smelling people is undoubtedly the grossest thing you and the vampires do. So, just stop it. Second, how do you think this is going to end? Someone is going to have to do something that's not safe in order to stop

Ian. No one who helps is going to have it easy, whether in the search or the execution."

"I've been thinking about it since you told me your plan. Debating whether I'd let you."

I barked out a sharp laugh that surely would have ended in a snort if I hadn't cut it off after seeing the serious expression on his face.

"Do you want to rephrase that?" I sat on the sofa and crossed my arms over my chest.

He considered my request as laughter played over the sharp lines of his features. Crossing his arms to match mine, he said, "No, I'm good."

I blew out an exasperated breath. "I'm not part of your pack. You don't *let* me do something. If there were another option, I'd take it. But this is where we are now. And I hope it works."

We lapsed into an uncomfortable silence. Eventually he dropped into the chair. The arrant confidence muted; gentle gray eyes fixed on mine.

"What's your plan?" he finally asked. Concern punctuated his words.

I shrugged. "I imagine the Veil is similar to here and people live in communities. I'll go find some shifters and ask them to take me to their leader . . . or something like that." I started chuckling at the shock that he quickly schooled off his face. "My plan is fluid and it's not comforting to me either. I can plan all night and enter the Veil and everything might still fall apart."

"Shifters have community homes, and if you find that, more than likely the Omega will be there. They're typically there to help the pack and typically the most reasonable."

For nearly an hour he went over information about shifters that I already knew. If there's a forest, they're more likely to be there. Don't hold eye contact, it can be considered a challenge. Don't wear silver, especially bracelets. Don't conceal weapons, it's considered hostile.

In silence I sat listening to a comically overly concerned Alpha reiterate basic information that most people knew. They weren't shy about telling people what they found offensive. It seemed like something Asher needed to do. That it would bring him a level of comfort.

He was boring himself with the information because he suppressed two yawns. I stood after the second and stretched.

"Got it. The first shifter I see, I should punch him in the face to show dominance. Then whip out my concealed blade and show off my cool hand work."

Asher's scowl was a blend of amusement and frustration. I knelt down in front of him, breaking the first cardinal rule of dealing with shifters, and met his eyes and held his gaze. Something that took more effort than anyone should. I got submerged in the raw intensity of his eyes, equally captivating and repelling. An odd dichotomy.

"It's the only option we have. I got this. This is not the first time I've entered unfamiliar areas and it won't be the last. I'm still here."

"You get hurt, often."

"Every cut, bruise, and scar is a reminder I survived." Standing, I stretched again, positive that I was going to have a restful sleep. "If you don't want to drive home, you're welcome to stay."

"I'd like that," he whispered, standing and heading for the opposite end of the apartment.

"Not in my bedroom! The sofa. I'll get you a blanket or you can change and wolf it."

"The sofa's fine." His disappointment was clear.

The next morning, I awoke to the smell of coffee and food. Inhaling the enticing aromas, I quickly brushed my teeth and showered. My shirts clung to me where I hadn't efficiently dried off. I towel dried my hair and pulled it back in a pony-tail and made my way to the small kitchen, where I was accustomed to smell food that had browned a little too much or stayed in the oven a little longer than recommended.

Today, the kitchen was filled with the robust smells of coffee, bacon, fruit, mushrooms, peppers, and onions. As of last night, I had only bacon and coffee.

"Did you go grocery shopping?" I asked Asher, pouring myself a cup of coffee. At some point, he'd showered and dressed in different clothes, probably the set of clothing that most shifters kept in their cars. I assumed, like me, he kept an overnight bag in his car.

"Sort of. I borrowed a few things from Ms. Harp. I've already called for someone to bring her more groceries."

"She must like you if she opened the door for you."

He shrugged. "We talk often and I had someone bring her groceries yesterday. I explained that while Ian's around, I'd rather reduce her chances of running into him."

"You think he can make her change?"

"No. I suspect he would try to force her into a change, but she can't and it might do something to her body she might not survive." With a heavy sigh, he ran his hand through his hair. "She's such an anomaly I don't know what to expect, but it's better to consider the worst-case scenario. A shifter has never procreated with anyone and the baby not become a shifter. I don't know how she is possible. I'm not ready to find out what would happen. I'd like to be careful with her." There was concern in his voice. If her existence vexed him, it would vex anyone who found out about her, but they might not be as concerned with her safety and well-being.

He clenched his teeth and moved toward my door in quick, lithe movements. "I might care about her safety, but she doesn't seem to have the same attitude." He yanked open the door. "Ms. Harp, didn't I ask you to call me if you were planning to leave?"

I moved ever so slightly, so I could watch what I was sure would be the unfolding of an amusing encounter. Asher was so used to people following his orders and Ms. Harp, who cared very little about anyone or anything, was cantankerous enough to tell him just that. She might like him but she didn't care about his status as Alpha. She was going to do what she wanted.

"I decided not to. I need to go to the store."

"Someone's bringing you groceries. They should be here soon."

"I need cream for my coffee."

"Which flavor?" Asher asked, his voice tight but kind.

Huffing out a breath, she said, "I like my privacy and don't care much for answering to anyone."

"You're not answering to me. I explained this to you several times. There's a situation and it might adversely affect you. I just need you to be careful for a few more days." He sighed. "Please."

That could not have tasted good.

"Then you can go with me," she chirped back in a compromise.

Asher craned his neck in my direction and gave me a withering look. One of Ms. Harp's fists was pressed into her hip while the other held the cane. Rather, she had the cane hooked on her arm. I still wasn't convinced she needed it.

"Give me a minute," he said.

My new goal in life: Be Ms. Harp.

"Give me your keys, I'll meet you in the car," she told him.

"No, I'll meet you in your apartment." The command in his voice left no room for her to object and she was warring to do just that. She looked between her cane and him several times and I wondered if she was considering whacking him with it.

He ducked back into my apartment and gathered his phone and wallet. "I'll watch a few episodes of Judge Judy with her and maybe she'll forget about cream," he said with a shake of his head.

I couldn't figure out if he was more dismayed by Ms. Harp's noncompliance or her desire for cream. It came to me why they preferred to keep things in the pack. There were rules and a chain of command. The Alpha tells you to be careful and call. You do it. There was a simplicity in it.

"She won't." I opened a lower cabinet and pulled out a bottle of Kahlua. "This is the cream she's determined to get. Once I helped her bring in her groceries and noticed it next to her coffee pot. I suspect she enjoys her 'cream' with her coffee when she's hanging out with Judy."

He shook his head, blowing out a frustrated breath, then thanked me as he took the bottle from me. Before leaving, he hesitated for a long moment, his face indecipherable. Leaning into me, his lips pressed against my cheek in a feather-light touch that still managed to warm my skin.

"I'll see you later today when you return from the Veil. Hopefully unscathed."

Giving me a small appreciative smile, he left. My finger pressed against where his lips were. My life was getting too complicated.

CHAPTER 18

*M*ephisto's face was impassive as he approached me. His dark expressionless eyes traced every inch of my face. When we were just inches apart, he dropped his eyes and a pained look flashed across his face. With great effort he brought his eyes back to mine before allowing them to drift over to the others. I turned to look at Cory, whose attention on me only wavered long enough to look at the others in the room. He probably wondered, as I did, why they were there. I expected Madison and, of course, Cory and Mephisto. I hadn't been expecting Kai, Simeon, and Clayton.

The powerful energy and unyielding confidence of people who possessed great magic and were even greater warriors filled the space. Cedar, smoke, waterfalls, and earth were a mélange of magical smells. It was different than being in a room with just witches, mages, fae, and shifters. *But why wouldn't it be*, I thought. These people were wholly different, and my living room couldn't hold the sheer volume of magic. Kai commanded the lion's share of my intrigue; he reverberated with energy even when he wasn't in motion. I dragged my eyes from him when he caught me staring for the third time.

"Do you think it's a good idea for everyone to be here? Can you imagine the shifters coming through the Veil and seeing you all?"

"Have you any idea how unwise it would be to not have anyone here when you come back?" There was an unspoken *if* in Mephisto's voice.

"If they agree to come with me, do you think they're going to be hostile? Seeing you magical brutes is what's going to make them hostile."

Mephisto considered it for a while, creases of concern and apprehension forming on his face. He went over everything again, for me to guide myself through the Veil in the event he wasn't able to help with navigation. It was like adding coordinates to a spell to change location. Simplistic in theory, harder in execution. But that was how it was with most magic. People thought that it was just spouting out spells, but it was the wrangling of it once it was in motion and directing it like steering a boat through turbulent waters.

"Are you afraid?" Mephisto asked in a voice for my ears only.

"Whether I am or not won't really change things."

"Do you at least have a plan?"

I shrugged. "It's rather fluid at this point. I'm going to find a shifter and ask him to take me to their leader." Similar to what I told Asher. I grinned. "Like any other alien."

It wasn't arrogance at the root of my response but the bravado and breezy confidence I needed to display to put everyone at ease. If I showed even a hint of fear, an iota of self-doubt, I'd leave Cory and Madison worrying or, worse, Cory reigniting his attempts to convince me not to go. So I donned an armor of overconfidence for their sake, but it didn't chase away my own doubt. Madison was onboard but her unease was palpable. She had slipped into the background, observing the Others with a level of interest that mirrored mine. She'd fought with them, seen the Immortalis's magic have no effect on them, and for some reason, they had now relaxed into their magic. Whatever they had been doing to mask or subdue it, they had abandoned.

Kai, Simeon, and Mephisto ignored her intense scrutiny; Clayton found it amusing. His eyes shone with a casual mischief each time their eyes met. His melodious laughter drifted throughout the room when she tore her eyes away, making more attempts at furtive glances.

"I'm okay with you looking," he finally said. "I'm rather flattered by it."

That's definitely not a color she'd be happy about, I thought as rose tinted the bridge of her nose and cheeks. It gave her a look that she hated to be called: cute.

She mastered her expression into one of professional calm and fixed her eyes on me and Mephisto, which only earned her a chuckle from him.

Mephisto leaned even closer to me. "You are so authentically you," he pronounced. What? Was I supposed to be someone else? "Quite interesting," he said in a deep lazy drawl. "Be careful."

With an audience, we attempted to make the exchange of magic clinical and impassive, but it was a daunting task. I was painfully aware that the Others were watching us, assessing our chemistry and connection, looking for evidence in support of their accusations of Mephisto being compromised when it came to me. I didn't want to add fodder to the flames of their concerns. I had the same apprehension, confusion, and curiosity about us that they had.

We stepped apart and I whispered the words of power, just a few words, but they dragged and dragged, and I realized at the end that I was in front of Mephisto, swept up in the tapestry of his magic. It coursed through me, the gnawing need sated. His lips brushed lightly against mine. A wisp of a touch. At Cory clearing his throat, I attempted to step back, but Mephisto's hands were at my waist.

"Be careful," he repeated in a whisper.

"Nah, I think I'll be reckless," I shot back, wishing he knew how much I hated it when people said that tautology. Most people check the "be careful" box whenever possible.

"Erin," he whispered. "So very Erin."

I backed away even farther, evoked the spell to open the Veil, and looked over my shoulder once before entering. It was the look on the Others' faces that gave me a moment of pause. Sadness? Worry? No, *yearning*.

This section of the Veil wasn't picturesque like the places I'd seen on my first visit. Before, I was treated to a world where predators and prey lived in harmony, surrounded by lush forestry and vivid flowering trees, unaware of their hierarchal positions. Despite having spent only moments there, the memories stayed with me. I thought constantly of the vibrant sky and snowcapped mountains where winged people soared through the sky. The serenity was something I hoped to experience again.

This part of the Veil was not unlike what I could see if I drove just fifteen minutes from my apartment to the nearest subdivision, although it didn't consist of the varying models of different trim, siding, and brick. Each home here had its own personality, and if I were to guess, I'd be able to tell which were the Felidae and Canidae homes. Interspersed between the houses were large stretches of forestry. The leaves were gold, brown, and orange, as expected for autumn, which it clearly was. I zipped my jacket and continued to walk.

There weren't cerulean-blue skies, beautiful arboreta, breathtaking landscapes, or winged humans. Or any animals, living harmoniously or otherwise. I was supposed to be in the land of shifters and I hadn't seen a single animal, period. I hadn't seen anything. Had I done the spell wrong? If I had, I'd expect Mephisto to link in like he had before and guide me to a new area.

Warily, I passed another forest that at first glance seemed empty. I moved deeper into the thicket of trees, still wondering how it was possible that I hadn't yet seen an animal. Beyond the Veil, I was used to seeing shifters in animal form strolling around as if it was normal for cheetahs, lions, cougars, dingoes, or others to be traipsing through the city. It was typical to see a human walk into a wooded area, leaving a trail of clothing in their wake, and moments later to catch sight of an animal sprinting through the woods. Or sitting in the park, a wolf or coyote might poke its head out from the trees to let you know it was there. They did it as a courtesy, but no matter how meekly they attempted to warn you of their presence, seeing an apex predator poke its head out was alarming. Plus, shifters didn't really do meek, so it was even more off-putting.

I hadn't gotten any of that here. A few cars passed by, heads turning and eyes regarding me with suspicion.

If I knew their politics here, it would make it easier. Did the shifters have a common retreat like the shifters at home? Were the buildings where they conducted their business taller than any in the area?

I decided to just knock on a door and see what happened; a modified version of "take me to your leader" seemed to be the way to go. Then an eagle flew close, its wing brushing the side of my head. It wasn't until it landed a few feet away and made a "follow me" movement with its head, that I was sure the wing-brush was intentional.

As I inched cautiously toward the Harpy Eagle, it became obvious it was a shifter. There was the telltale human awareness combined with a predatory alertness that put you on edge, glints of gold in the eyes that let you know they straddled the worlds between human and animal.

Following the eagle farther, I realized that the woods were denser and larger than I'd thought. The eagle stopped in a patch crowded by more trees. A gray wolf trotted by. Then a reddish-gray wolf padded closer to me. The jaguar advancing made me put my hand on my gun. I'd tried to follow shifter decorum and make sure none of my weapons were concealed: two guns and a knife were in plain sight.

Cloaked by the dense trees were two more wolves and another jaguar. Sounds of branches being broken and padding feet let me know there were more around me. *Breathe. No fear.*

I didn't move and neither did they. The eagle flew at me, its talon bit into my skin, then it retreated. It did it again, only to retreat again. When it pecked at my shoulder, I went for my knife.

"Brayden," a gentle but commanding voice spoke from behind me. At the mere sound of the cool, raspy voice, the eagle moved away and landed on the ground. Then it shuffled back several more paces from me.

Turning, I saw a tall woman, her jet-brown hair in a choppy short cut. A modern look on classic features. Intense emerald-colored eyes were set deep, and a slight flush of color swept along the cheeks of her fawn-colored skin. Her expression didn't give anything away, causing me to remain still under her scrutiny.

"Change," she demanded, keeping her eyes on me but directing her instruction to Brayden. The Harpy flew deeper into the forest. No one moved or said anything until minutes later a teenager emerged from the woods in an oversized t-shirt and leggings. Were they able to clothe themselves with shifter magic, or did they have clothes lying around the forest? I wished our shifters would extend such courtesies so we could stop seeing naked asses all the time.

If I'd seen Brayden in human form, I would have guessed a fox based on her vulpine features. Small, round, unusually flat black eyes, long brownish-red hair, and a long sharp nose gave her a dangerous cuteness.

"She smells," she announced with indignation. "I don't like it." Then she shot me a look. "Or her."

I tried to guess her age because I thought it was entirely appropriate to tell a child sixteen or older to fuck off when they were being rude. It wasn't just teenage angst that made her insolent, it was her training wheels. In adulthood, when they were removed, I suspected she was going to be a terror.

The tight but amiable smile I put on my face was hard-earned and remained, knowing that I was in a new land and needed their help.

"I know. It's fear that you smell," the short-haired woman informed Brayden. "But it wasn't right for you to attack her. You should issue an apology."

Tightly pursed lips refused to let the words past until the woman gave her a stern look. Brayden huffed. "Sorry your smell made me want to attack you."

What age is too old to get a time-out? Can she be grounded? Teenager is old enough for throat punches, right?

Smile still in place, I simply nodded.

"You're from outside the Veil," the short-haired woman provided, walking around me, examining me with a combination of disdain and curiosity.

I nodded. "Yes, I'm here on behalf of the shifters."

That got her attention. She stopped circling and stood directly in front of me. I lowered my head and eyes, making sure not to seem challenging in any way. I *hated* shifter etiquette. I wasn't a shifter but a person in need of a favor so I shouldn't have to play their little shifter games. But I did, because I needed them.

"They sent a human on their behalf." Clearly she felt like they had sent an inferior being to do their job.

"They can't go through the Veil. They don't even see it."

"That's why I've never seen one from the other side. We don't cross the Veil, but I'm sure you can understand why. It's nicer here, fewer humans, and not as many"—she leaned forward—"smells."

That's not fear, that's me five seconds from going total bitch mode if you don't stop insulting me.

But instead of saying that, I demurred, hating every moment of it. "I'm in a strange place in need of a favor that might be denied and get my friend killed."

"Shifter?" She responded to the emotion in my voice. I was surprised by it myself. It was a very conflicting feeling. If shifters had usable magic, I had to stave off the impulse to take their magic and possibly kill them. But here, in this moment, I wanted to save their lives.

I nodded. Her mood noticeably eased.

"What's your name?" she asked.

"Erin Jensen."

"I'm Tabitha." That was the extent of her greeting. She didn't even extend her hand for a shake.

"What color is your hair?"

What? Before she would listen to anything, she needed a baseline. A way to determine if I was lying. Human lie detectors. They do more than just tell people they stink of fear and anxiety.

"Brown. I'm a brunette," I said.

"The color of your pants?"

"Black, leather."

"How many weapons do you have?"

"Two guns with silver bullets and a knife. The blade is silver too. All my weapons are visible to you. I was told not to bring them by the Alpha, but as you noted, I was afraid to go to a strange place without any means to protect myself."

A smile crept onto her lips. "Are you good with them?"

"Very. If you all were to attack, even if I died, several of you would go with me." I kept my face neutral so it wouldn't come off as a threat but rather a statement of fact.

"Confidence. I like it." Her smile widened and with a nod she urged me to continue.

Careful with the telling of my story, I explained that a fae had escaped from the Veil who had the ability to control shifters and was using them to force the royals to step down.

"Fae. Is it Ian Carden?"

"Ian. I don't know his last name."

"No one knows a fae's true name, but that's the name he goes by."

Names were important in magic, as Cory reminded me often. Knowing a fae's true name gave another fae power over them, in the same manner as a vampire compulsion with humans. To prevent being servant to another fae command, they hid their true name carefully. I didn't know Madison's true name, nor those of her parents, and neither did my mother.

With a nod of Tabitha's head, the shifters retreated into the thickets. Moments later, one returned in human form. I didn't need him to tell me which one he was; it was quite apparent that he was the jaguar. The sleek agile movement, deep-olive skin, cinnamon eyes, and slim lithe build. He was exceptionally tall, close to seven feet, and had the same level of command as Tabitha. It was bad form to ask if a shifter was the Alpha because somehow we were supposed to instinctively know. Fates, dealing with them was exhausting.

"They should have never allowed him to live after his first attempt. The forty years of imprisonment clearly didn't quench his thirst for power. He will always possess that thirst, and nothing but subjugation of his betters will satisfy it," Mr. Jaguar noted. His anger-laden words implied he agreed with Tabitha about a more permanent answer.

His gaze trailed from my feet up the rest of me until he came to my eyes where he held my gaze. Intense inquiring eyes scrutinized me with interest. *I've already endeared myself to Tabitha. I don't have the time to win over another shifter. Move along.*

"What are you guilty of?" he queried, moving closer. His light, swift movements had me reaching for my gun. I quickly dropped my hand from it but kept it positioned at the ready.

"What do you mean?"

"It's not fear. You're here to atone?"

Ugh, go back to the woods, Kitty. Damn, damn, damn. I didn't know if this would help or hurt things.

"I accidentally killed a shifter when I was trying to prevent an attack. I don't want another one to die for something he had no control over."

Rage is a powerful emotion that's hard to miss, and you don't have to be very attuned to emotions to feel it and want to get as far from it as possible. Rage toward Ian was a good thing, so I laid it on thick, going into great detail about how he attempted to use an Alpha to attack me, the incident in the park, and how he was using them as his little army by taking away their free will.

Shifters can be annoying and the laundry list of pack particulars made navigating their world difficult. Everything from their rules, secrets, pack loyalty that dictated unwavering fealty and hierarchy that required unquestioning obedience. But despite all the things I deemed as problematic with dealing with them, I admired the level of camaraderie and sense of duty that was absent in the other denizens. For that reason, part of me knew that the shifters in the Veil would help, because it's exactly what Asher would do for another shifter. It was the very reason he saw to Ms. Harp being taken care of, despite her not being a true shifter.

"He's using them as attack dogs," Tabitha ground out. I could understand her indignation; Ian was treating shifters as though they were true animals. Petting a domesticated wolf might get a nuzzle at your hand, perhaps an affectionate cuddle at the neck, but do it to a wolf shifter and you're probably going to pull back nubs and have them going for your throat.

Tabitha and the jaguar were seething. One point for indignant arrogance. I'd take it. I went into more detail, adding dramatics for effect.

"Will you help them?" I was shocked at the wistful urgency in my voice.

With their faces still twisted into scowls, I had my answer. Shifters aren't to be controlled by anyone that isn't a shifter. It's an arrogant, self-indulgent, and somewhat narcissistic belief, but hey, *yay for self-indulgence, narcissism, and arrogance!*

Preparing for departure didn't take long. Mr. Jaguar—or rather, Ezekiel, a name he provided after becoming irritated with me calling him Mr. Jaguar one too many times—offered to accompany Tabitha. Two shifters were better than one and I was pretty sure I had the Alphas, or at least ones who ranked pretty damn high in the pack. Ms. Petty couldn't wait to rub it in Cory's face. I might even have to give Asher an "I told you so. I got this" nod.

Ready to depart the Veil, I could hear the light padding of feet as someone ran toward us. We turned to find the mouthy teen heading our way. She'd changed into a pair of jeans and t-shirt and was carrying a slingover bag.

"Aunt Tabby, Dad said I could go."

"Aunty Tabby" raised a brow. "I don't recall asking him if you could. I just informed him of where I was going and with whom." A sly look in my direction let me know that if anything happened to her, I'd be dealing with her brother. I wondered if her mother was an eagle or she was taken in.

"I saw it in the way you looked," Brayden touted. "You looked like you wanted company. And"—she slid her eyes at me—"it's better if you have backup."

Tabitha didn't bother to entertain the comment, her eyes narrowed on her niece, then shifted in my direction in a silent command and stipulation.

Brayden's eyes nearly rolled to the back of her head. "Erin, I'm sorry I pecked you." Her voice sounded just as disingenuous as her apology.

Raising my arm, I showed her the scratched skin from her talons. *Hmm, maybe I'm an ass too.* I contributed my response to teaching the youth of tomorrow to be better people. Yes, that's it. I'm a mentor.

"Fine," she huffed out. "I'm sorry I scratched you and told you the truth about your smell."

I'm going to trip her.

A tight-lipped smile was all she got by way of acceptance. You issue an insincere apology, you get an insincere response.

CHAPTER 19

*T*raveling through the Veil alone was simple and painless. Just a slight movement, a whisper of the spell, and a seamless transition. Traveling with three shifters was cumbersome because we quickly discovered shifters can move through the Veil but not without a guide who can actually navigate it. Being the guide, I had them clinging awkwardly to my extremities.

When I returned to my apartment with the shifters in tow, only Cory, Mephisto, and Madison were still there. The greetings were sparse, nearly nonexistent. The Veil shifters looked disinterested in introductions. They only cared about meeting Elizabeth. Despite their rude directness, it made things go quickly and Madison tried not to show her offense when her introduction and extended hand earned her a perfunctory nod from Tabitha.

The limited view outside the Veil left the shifters unimpressed, except for Elizabeth's elaborate forest that served no purpose other than to frustrate the person navigating the labyrinthine twists and turns that landed you in the very place you had been minutes before. Greeting us at the exit was the persnickety imp, dressed in a dark-blue vest and slacks and a white shirt with one open button—more casual than our first meeting, I noted. His glasses perched on the edge of his sharp nose allowed the four-foot-tall red creature to look down his nose at anyone he addressed.

During one of our visits to Elizabeth, he had shifted to a massive creature and tossed us out of the forest. I had no desire to experience that again.

His imperious gaze swung from me then to Cory before baring his teeth in a mocking grin. He then swiftly moved his attention to the shifters. Bowing in greeting, he said, "On behalf of the mistress, I welcome you and your offerings. The others are waiting for you." Extending his hand, he invited them to the house. We remained uninvited. Mephisto, standing off to the side a great distance from the Veil shifters, didn't look as if he was expecting the snub. Madison and Cory were incensed by it.

I'd expected the shifters to at least hesitate and wonder why we weren't invited along. Or at least request that I follow. Nothing. Did they not consider that this might be a trap? Perhaps they would have if Asher and Sherrie weren't outside the home waiting for them.

From afar, I watched their greeting, which was more cordial than their greeting with Cory and Madison. Mephisto made no attempt at an introduction.

I was too far away to hear anything. Even if I were closer, with their heightened hearing, I'd only hear what they wanted me to. When I took a step past the imp, he placed a firm hand on me and nudged me back, a suggestion I ignored until I felt a sharp prick. I stepped back several inches away from the pain, and looked down at the hole in my leathers. It didn't stain my pants, but I knew the injury was there. The imp looked at his sword and pulled out a handkerchief to clean it off. Where on earth did he store it?

On our first nightmare of a meeting, I had every intention of punting him across the forest. I never got the opportunity, but it seemed like a new one was about to present itself. Cory, reading my intent, looped his arm around my waist and tried to ease me back. When I didn't move easily, he lifted me several feet back.

"We don't need his big mean friend visiting us," he whispered against my ear.

"I'm just going to kick him once. Just let me do it once," I hissed in a low voice.

"Not a good idea, Erin."

The curve came to the imp's lips. "Riddle me this."

"I'm not doing any of your riddles," I told him.

"Hear him out," Madison suggested, placing what was intended to be a soothing hand on my shoulder, but I was too riled for it to have any effect on me. I felt jilted out of an experience that was rightfully mine. I had magic; currents of it formed on my hand, but I extinguished it. Messing with Elizabeth's imp might mean she'd refuse to do the binding. And I didn't want to draw attention to still having Mephisto's magic, on the off chance he had forgotten. It was highly unlikely, but I was going for the glass half full perspective.

"What's the riddle?" Madison asked.

"Riddle me this: What does the mistress need with an earth fae, an embittered witch, the cursed raven"—he looked at Mephisto, brow raised in a manner that led me to believe he had an idea what he was but wasn't going to say— "and a warrior, to do a spell she's done before?"

Cory glared at the imp, who simply lifted his nose in a haughty show of ridicule.

"I would like to see it done," I explained.

"Which is why you won't."

"Arius," Mephisto intoned in a deep, silky, entreating voice that I'm sure opened many opportunities to him, "I'm sure Elizabeth would not mind the audience. She loves to put on a show."

"There are five shifters there. She has an audience," the

imp responded curtly. Backing away, he smiled. "*But,* if you insist." He mouthed a few words and the area erupted in the same flames Elizabeth forced us to walk through to get to her on our last visit. It was through those flames that I was marked with a raven and the Others with intricate markings similar to each other's. Mephisto, as he did on rare occasions, was wearing dark jeans and a t-shirt, the fabric molding to his form and showing off defined arms, a muscled chest, and, what I knew from memory and touch, finely delineated abs.

If he walked through the fire and the marks appeared, they would be there for all to see. Before, it was just me and the Others. From his glower, I had a feeling he wasn't going through the fire and suspected he didn't want the shifters from the Veil to see his markings. Would they know what they meant? Curiosity spiked in me. Could I convince him to go? From the rigid set of his jaw, it was doubtful.

I didn't care if the raven marking showed up again.

"Nothing's burning. The grass and the trees aren't affected," Cory said.

"It won't." It was a Mirra, which looks so similar to that which it mimics. "We can go through it, but I warn you, it's painful."

"I can't do binding spells so there isn't any need for me to see one done," Madison said quickly.

"How painful?" Cory asked.

"You're walking through fire. You won't have any lasting injuries, but it duplicates the sensation."

Giving the blaze another look, he said, "That's a pass for me."

"Aren't you even a little interested in how she's going to do it?"

I pressed my hand toward the flames and recalled Mephisto trying unsuccessfully to bring it down when we encountered it the first time. Close to the fire, the warmth licked at my skin, heating my face, bringing back the excruciating pain that folded me over, wracked me, and was only eased by Mephisto. But I had his magic; I could ease my own pain.

Committing to the chasm of pain that would accompany me, I heard Mephisto call me just before I stepped into the fire. The flames kissed my skin, pain and heat consumed me. Choking on the searing feeling that rampaged through me, I tried to take calming breaths but it just wouldn't ease. It wasn't like before; it seemed deeper, an arduous walk that I just couldn't make. I stumbled backward, eyes closed. I called on the magic, its coolness, pulling it to me to ease the scorching feeling of my skin. My breathing eased from torturous to something tolerable, and I opened my eyes to find Cory, Mephisto, and Madison standing over me and the fire gone.

In unison, we started toward the house. Madison tugged me to her, where she held me.

"I'm going to rip you a new one," she threatened through clenched teeth.

"The fire kind of took care of that," I yowled in response to her tight grip. "I see you've been working out."

"Erin, stop making light of this. How could you do that to us? You were screaming and we were about to go in after you, then it stopped and you came back. Why would you do that?"

"I've been through that fire before. I knew what to expect. It looked worse than it was," I lied.

"That's doubtful." She plodded away and Cory gave her an appreciative look, living vicariously through her as he glared back at me. Their annoyance wrenched through me. Madison of all people I hated putting through unnecessary grief. Storing it with the rest of my guilt baggage that was becoming heavier to carry, I rushed to the house.

The magic that met me at the door was dark, baleful, and foreboding. Elizabeth wasn't hiding trade secrets but rather

her use of dark magic. I'd penned Elizabeth as a fae, and I was still convinced that she was part fae, but there was something more. Intermingled with her distinctive arcane magic with the hints of freesia and dark chocolate I associated with the fae, there was now the putrid scent of darker magic. I knew she peddled in it. Something reeked, like the blackest of black magic.

If I could sense it, the shifters certainly could, but perhaps they had dismissed it as a necessary evil.

Asher and Sherrie were on one side of the room leaning against the wall, glancing at the cuts on their arms. I thought they should have been healed, but perhaps not if there had been multiple cuts or a spell done to keep them from healing as quickly. Blood still pooled in a bowl on the table. Tabitha and Ezekiel weren't looking at their cuts but looked in need of a seat.

"Are you all okay?" I asked the room but went to Asher whose head had bobbed down. He jerked to keep it up. Sherrie looked equally lethargic.

On our first encounter with Elizabeth, she had been dressed in a shirt and yoga pants. Sensing my disappointment that she didn't look as I'd imagined or her moniker led me to believe, with a simple wave of her hand, she was donned in a different outfit, with a bracelet of an open-mouthed serpent. Now she wore a Victorian era–inspired outfit. Layers of black satin and lace made up the skirt of her dress. Eyes lined by thick liner and wine-colored lips made her look every bit the title she was known by. But it extended to more than her clothing. The serpent she wore as a bracelet before was now coiling and making sinuous movements on the table. It was the same length as the bracelet and had the exact same red eyes.

The Woman in Black had access to magic that most people didn't have.

"It is done," she announced.

"Did you check?" I asked.

She wore the insult of my inquiry heavily in the turn of her frown. "My work doesn't need to be checked." Then she looked at Asher and said with a stern voice, "I've met the requirements of our agreement. I know you will honor yours."

Asher nodded and they pushed themselves from the wall. "It will be delivered tomorrow."

"I trust that it will."

Falling into step with Asher, I asked, "What was the payment?"

"The vault."

"Everything in it." I stared at him.

He beamed. "Yes, everything she saw in it, which was about half of what you did."

Even half seemed like an extraordinary payment, but then again, the shifters were now immune to magic.

"Did she check to make sure you're immune?"

He nodded.

With plenty of experience of deceptive practices, I wasn't keen on not testing it. Cory must have felt similarly because magic swirled in the air and a silver ball of magic whizzed past my ear and drove right into Asher. It spread over him like a cloud of confetti before disappearing.

"Would you like me to change?" Asher asked once we were in the wooded area at the exit to our car.

I nodded and he and Sherrie undressed and shifted to their animal. Cory and Madison spent several minutes using aggressive offensive magic, earth magic, and disarming spells without avail. I decided to use elemental magic. Fire was fire, but did magical fire have the same effect? Sherrie wasn't in a hurry to come near it, although her curiosity got the best of her. Seeing the inquiring looks of the Veil shifters, I got the impression they were similarly curious. Flames danced along my fingertips, but I hesitated, remembering what it felt like to go through the Mirra; I wasn't in a rush to inflict that pain on someone else. Slowly Asher approached me. Steeling himself, he gave me a slow nod. I flicked the fire toward him, and orange-blue heat ran along his leg, leaving the fur unaffected. We decided then that cold and wind tests weren't necessary.

Once they changed back, the shifters distanced themselves from us, although I made every effort to listen to their conversation. While they spoke, it was hard to ignore the acuity of the glances Ezekiel and Tabitha made in Mephisto's direction. He made them uneasy. Tabitha's eyes settled on him like a predator determining the hierarchal status of another predator.

When Mephisto's dark eyes finally lifted to meet hers, she held his gaze but directed her words to me.

"Take us back," she commanded.

Ezekiel and Tabitha looked pleased to be home, although the teenager with the bad attitude looked agitated after giving her unsolicited opinion about her trip to the land of the "boring" where she only got to meet unimpressive shifters and a "steampunk fae-elf hybrid." I ignored most of her complaints but packed away the elf part to explore later. Could Elizabeth be a fae-elf hybrid? Being part of a powerful creature believed to be extinct would explain her magical ability.

Aunt Tabitha, who should have been canonized for being patient with Brayden, kissed her on the forehead, implicitly letting her know that her tirade was over. "Zeke" would take her home.

Once they were out of sight and, I assumed, what she really wanted—out of earshot—Tabitha turned a severe face to me. If she'd shown me that harsh a face when we first met,

I would have thought twice about approaching her, let alone asking for a favor of such magnitude.

She regarded me with an acuity that hinted at her realizing there was more to me than met the eye, and I suspected it was because of the company I kept. Mephisto.

"I did what I agreed to do," she said eventually, "and am satisfied with the outcome and the newfound relationship I have with shifters outside of the Veil. This doesn't extend to you. What business we have is done. I ask that you never call upon me again, for anything, and that this be our one and only meeting."

She didn't wait for a response but simply turned and walked away from me. It was a nice way of saying "get lost and I never want to see you again." But damn. I kept my feet rooted in place because nothing good could come of me running after her to ask why. But I was curious. Maybe she'd say it was her and not me. No, it was me. It was definitely me. And if it wasn't me, then it was definitely Mephisto.

After leaving the shifters, I didn't return home where I knew people, including Mephisto, were waiting for me. Instead I returned to Elizabeth's. From there I started on a convoluted excursion that I couldn't help but feel embarrassed about twenty-four hours later. I walked from her place to the closest restaurant from where I called a rideshare to take me to a bar where I stayed all night, hoping that by the time I got home at two in the morning, Mephisto would have given up on my return and left. I was right about him leaving. He wasn't waiting for me, but early that morning, after the sun had barely risen, he was at my door. The look of disappointment on his face was etched in my memory. Instead of thinking about his look of displeasure, I clung to the memories of feeling complete. Sated. Whole.

I pressed my lips together, which still seemed to hold the warmth of his lips pressing against them, although that obviously wasn't possible.

"I have to find your box," I said. "Let me help you find it."

He nodded once, his forehead pressed against mine, and I conceded to the knowledge that if it were Pandora's box or released the four horseman or unleashed any number of destructive entities on our world, I would still do it for the benefit of having my own magic. To being complete. It hurt to know that was my truth.

CHAPTER 20

*K*ath appeared to live a rather simple life. She owned a modest ranch home, something she could afford with her three jobs as server and bartender. As long as you ignored the convertible Mercedes she kept in the garage, you wouldn't know she was quietly reaping the benefits of working in an industry where often the staff is ignored.

She heard a lot. Over the years, she had become my most valuable, albeit extremely expensive, source of information. Her calling me to tell me she had a lead on a Xios had me rushing to meet her at her home.

Her fingers scraped her dark-brown hair away from her face. It was much longer than usual and kept forming a straggly curtain that she constantly pushed out of her eyes. But it wasn't only her hair that kept her from making eye contact. She was obviously reluctant to do so.

"Thanks for coming," she said nervously, locking the door behind me. She hadn't done that before. Our visits were typically short, sweet, and direct. She gave me the information; I gave her the cash and added the expense to my client's bill.

Today, her home didn't have its usual calming human

energy, the comfort of a magicless interaction. And her fidgeting was unnerving.

"I heard about what's going on with the shifters," she said. "No one seems to know why they're behaving like that. Is it a spell or something? People are really afraid—especially the humans. You know how we react when we're afraid." She poured herself a drink and took a sip before lifting the glass in my direction to ask if I wanted one.

"Just water," I said, but quickly changed my mind. "Water and a drink, please." She'd probably give me the water in a bottle and the vodka in a glass. I wanted glass. I took a quick inventory of my weapons; a Taser was always with me, but would I be able to get close enough to use it? A knife was sheathed at my lower leg.

When she handed me a tumbler, I held it in my dominant hand: my right. No amount of magic or high tolerance of pain can protect you from having a glass smashed into your face.

Inching closer to the door, I gave myself the vantage to flee if necessary.

"Ian, I know you're here. You can come out," I said.

His airy chuckle eased into the room before he did. Taking slow and measured steps, he entered from a room just to the right of the living room, cradling a small dog to his chest.

"I'd like this to be a civil conversation. Remove your weapons," he demanded.

"I don't have any."

He scowled. "Surely you don't still underestimate me, do you?"

He kept his eyes on me, sliding them over every inch of me, as if trying to see where I'd concealed them.

"Check her," he instructed Kath. He stroked her dog around the neck, and it was hard to miss the threat in it when he did. "Take her glass away, too," he added. He flashed me a cynical grin. "I'd hate for you to get creative with it. I've heard you tend to do that."

Kath took my glass and returned it to the kitchen and, under his scrutiny, she removed the knife and the Taser and put them on the table near me. Responding to his reprimanding look, she moved them all across the room.

"Happy now?" I asked through clenched teeth.

"Very. I would hate to be shot by you again or nicked by those sharp stars you're so fond of."

Once he was satisfied that I had been properly divested of weapons and he was a safe distance away, he released the dog, which ran to Kath who had returned to where he'd sent her, near the door. Untrustworthy people tended not to trust others. The only weapon I had left was the small push dagger on a long chain around my neck. With just a two-inch blade, it wasn't my best weapon, but I still had my most dangerous one: me. If I could get close enough, I could put him in death's sleep.

"You used her dog to get to me? What type of asshole award are you vying for?" I ground out in disgust.

"Apologies for the method I used, but it was important to speak with you and even more important that we do it without violence," he said, looking meek.

If I hadn't seen the look on his face when he had the pack of shifters attack me or the malice that curled his lips at the chaos he'd caused in the park, I might have been fooled by his serene eyes and look of regret.

"What do you want?" I snapped.

"Such rudeness. Are we not capable of having a peaceful dialogue?"

I waited for a smile, a chuckle, something that would indicate he was joking. But nothing came.

"Admittedly, I probably did not make a good first impression," he admitted, the corners of his lips lifted in a coy smile. I wasn't buying that for one moment. There was nothing coy or earnest about this man. It didn't take the perception of a shifter to see the thirst for power, deception, and untrustworthiness behind those dark eyes.

"First, second, third and fourth impression. The first time you met me you had shifters attack me. The second time I watched you use them to wreak havoc in the park while you sat back eating ice cream. You burned the bridge I was on during our third encounter. And the fourth time we met; you were trying to attack my client. And now that you held Kath's dog hostage, I'm going to say you're not doing so well with your fifth impression either."

"My methods might be considered unsavory by some."

Each time I tried to close the distance between us, he made sure it stayed wide. No quick moves would allow me to get close enough. He was cautious and perceptive, two things that didn't work in my favor.

"I ask for your forgiveness, goddess—"

"Don't call me that."

Amusement shone in his eyes. It had been a test and I failed.

"Ah, so you do know who you are?"

My lips pressed firmly together, I refused to give him any more information.

He crossed his arms over his chest and started to walk the length of the room, occasionally glancing at Kath, who was holding her dog in the far corner of the room.

"Perhaps you should take your dog for a walk," he suggested. She didn't move immediately. "Now."

Grabbing her leash and keys, Kath left after giving me another apologetic look.

Once she had gone, he returned his attention to me. It was a performance and he was making sure his audience was paying attention.

"If I had known who you were, I definitely never would have considered using you as an instrument to make my point with Asher. I needed to get his attention, and there wasn't any better way than to let him see I had control of his pack. Adalia and Neri's presence were signs that fate was on my side."

"Was fate on your side when you decided to unleash rabid shifters on people in the park?"

He took a few moments before he replied. "No, it served its purpose. Initially it was to force Asher's hand, but in the end, I got to meet you, and in turn, that led to Olis finding me. He's part of your mother's army," he offered in answer to my blank look.

Remaining impassive, I cringed inwardly at the use of "mother," something he obviously said to get a reaction. I wouldn't give him one.

"They saw me with you. You know your mother's little army has been keeping a close eye on you. But it was my display that day that made them aware of me, and they knew I was from the Veil."

Even with all the effort I was putting into remaining emotionless, hiding my intention of letting him get closer, he remained overly cautious about the distance between us. He'd piqued my curiosity, and I wasn't going to do anything until I got as much information as I could. Once I had it, I'd deliver the kiss, allowing him to slip in and out of the in-between. I would have magic, and it would give us the time we needed to find a way to send him back to the Veil and keep him there.

"You want to know more, don't you?"

He wasn't going to get any points for being perceptive. You don't drop a bomb that one of the Immortalis had approached him, call me a god, and expect me not to be curious.

I waited in silence for him to continue.

"They approached me because they know I want to get back into the Veil. They're quite confident that I will, by the way. And I think I will as well. I've made my desires known." To punctuate the point, he exposed the markings on his arms, his face becoming flushed from a flare of anger. He left his arm turned so I could see the markings. "They want to go back to the Veil too. When you are created for the sole purpose of violence and war, life here is torture. They are without purpose, an army without a commander that could give them the violence they seek. Your mother gave them true purpose. No one has more thirst for control and no one revels in doing it by force more than your mother."

"I wonder if she ever used shifters to attack royals or unleashed animals in a park, putting humans at risk."

"Royals." He spat out the word with contempt. "I'm stronger and more skilled. Far more deserving of their position than they are."

"Fine, then get their position by petitioning for it. Go through the proper channels. Do you believe the others will follow you because you obtained it by force when Adalia and Neri achieved it by campaign? They'll consider your reign illegitimate. Is it arrogance or foolishness that makes you believe the fae would think otherwise? Taking over by coup will only ensure that you will be deposed the same way."

He paused, but I made no effort to find out his angle other than it being his ego. After failing in the Veil, he needed to succeed here. Here, where his magic outmatched others, he felt entitled.

"There are other courts. Why this one?"

"It's the largest with the highest status. The others look up to the royals. I did not make this decision without careful consideration. What I wasn't expecting was their ability to retaliate against me." He extended his arm again to show his mark. He might have done that to make a bold statement, but it made him look like a toddler showing me his ouchie. It was a struggle not to tell him.

"Get on with it. What do you want with me?" Not that it

mattered. I had no intention of brokering any deals with him.

"You're Asher's emissary. Work on their behalf. Tell Asher and Sherrie they have nothing to fear from me. Their only goal is to find a way to remove my marks and all will be forgiven." The aplomb that he displayed made me think he considered himself royalty already. "They found a way once, so they can find it again. No more time spent on trying to take away my control. It will be freely relinquished. They will have my word."

His word meant nothing. He pledged fealty to his queen in the Veil, only to make an attempt for the throne. He made a deal with a demon to remove his aversion to iron, only to kill the demon once he was awarded it. I was positive that no deal he made with the shifters would be honored, and for that reason, I was glad he could no longer control them.

"Convince Neri and Adalia to step down. You've tried to stop me but without success. Stress that they won't win. It's the truth. If they see you as an objective observer and as one who has attempted and failed, they may be convinced, then this can stop. Abdication will ensure an easy transition."

"No, thank you. I appreciate the offer. Are we done?"

"I don't think you want us to be done. The Immortalis fear you as they do your mother. You don't seem to have the same love of violence or thirst for blood"—he glanced at my weapons—"or perhaps you do," he said with a tight smile, "but they fear you all the same. Like your mother, you've surrounded yourself with warriors who will protect you. The only ones capable of injuring and killing them. She created the Immortalis, and until they came across your army, they were indomitable."

I didn't correct him that Mephisto and the Others weren't my army. They weren't even there on my behalf, motivated only by the desire to keep Malific from being released.

"Even gods feared your mother. She did kill one of them,

so I suppose their fear was warranted. She was used to getting away with a great deal. People dislike challenging gods. She probably thought killing the god would go unchallenged as well. It's putative that it led to her being imprisoned. A step too far, I suppose." He shrugged.

"Seems like there's a lesson to be learned from that," I said pointedly.

"Ah, the gods were her equals. Neri and Adalia aren't my equals, nor are any of the fae on this side of the Veil. Your mother killed the god for no other reason than he dared challenge her actions, question her motives, and attempt to stop her. It cost him his life."

Great, my mom is a psychopath.

"I tell you this so you know, because having me on this side of the Veil rather than your mother is the better option. Olis has asked for my help in releasing her. Your blood link to her is the answer. I'm not sure if you are aware of this fact, but the prison is linked to her magic. The Immortalis want to get you into the Veil, use your death to free her."

As he prattled on, we continued our dance of distance. I took a step forward; he took three steps back. It was as if he'd done this before. It made me consider that there might be more in the Veil like me, or rather more Raven Cursed.

"They think they need to get you into the Veil to do it, but I have discovered a way to do it without you going anywhere near the Veil." He smiled cruelly. "Perhaps we can come to some agreement. If not, I'll give that information to the Immortalis and let them use your death to release your mother. She will be rewarded handsomely for it."

A shudder ran through me. I needed more than just the push dagger. Mephisto's suggestion of permanently ending him didn't seem extreme or cruel in any way. He moved slowly toward the door, keeping his distance from me, but I didn't take care to maintain it. I moved closer; he responded with a magical nudge. A warning. Sparks gathered around his finger.

"You have to believe that having me here and meeting my demands is a better alternative than freeing Malific. But if you resist me, then you have no one to blame but yourself for the consequences."

Ian wasn't making a great defense for the case of keeping him alive. I wanted to do the moral thing and the right thing, but he was a threat. He must have seen my intentions on my face or read them in my movements because he took a couple of steps back.

He gave me a half smile. "I have no more desire to release Malific than you do," he admitted. "The witches are responsible for her imprisonment, well, partially responsible. They aided the gods in doing it and Malific is quite upset about that. She's a vengeful woman, and I assure you if she's released she will be unmerciful with all who were involved. I'm confident it wouldn't just extend to the witches within the Veil. She'll ensure that there's never an opportunity to imprison her again."

He regarded me for a long time. I played with the chain at my neck. I might not crave violence or have a bloodlust, but with each passing moment, I was feeling increasingly lust-y and crave-y. I studied him in turn. He hadn't relaxed enough. His stance was cautious and readied.

"You have a fondness for a gentleman who is a witch. Boyfriend? Malific has never been one for subtlety. Her wrath will be a hellstorm that will leave many bodies in its wake. I doubt your friend will survive it. That delightful witch who helped you at the park? She's gone. But if you align yourself with me then nothing happens. All will be as it should. The shifters will be left alone. You will have fulfilled your obligation to them."

"What about my obligation to the fae? You want to overthrow Neri and Adalia. How is that fair?"

"Might is right," he said brazenly. "They're not strong enough to rule the kingdom. Rulers should not be decided based on campaigns and popularity. The shifters are led by the strongest. So are the vampires. Witches and mages by the most skilled. The same should be true of the fae."

I supposed he assumed I didn't know about fae politics. Madison trusted Neri and Adalia as leaders; she revered them, yet she would not follow them blindly. The fae had a democratic process. Their rule could be challenged at any time. I didn't want to get into fae politics, nor did I want to align myself with this cretin.

"So you'll leave the shifters alone, take over the fae courts. What becomes of Neri and Adalia?"

The dark rumble of his laughter filled the room. "It doesn't have to be hostile. I'd prefer that it wasn't. But I have a goal and they are the two people standing between me and achieving it"—a smile flourished over his lips and he gave me a reverent nod—"those two and the goddess."

"Stop calling me that," I demanded.

"Does it change who you are?"

I looked for signs of whether he could hear my heart beating hard in my chest. I assumed the Immortalis hadn't gotten the information from me. As far as they knew, they had to keep me alive and get me into the Veil in order to release Malific. Ian had discovered a way to use me to release her without me even having to go into the Veil. I couldn't let that information get to the Immortalis. They'd track me down for sure. Malific was so infamous, if people knew that I was the key to her being released, my life would be one of the most protected by those who didn't want her released.

"I guess I have not been totally honest with you," he admitted coyly. "There is one more thing I need. It is my understanding that you have access to Obitus blades. Once you have found a way to remove my marks, the Immortalis will eventually become aware. I will need to handle things."

"Don't be modest. You plan to not only betray them but to kill them too." How was he better than Malific?

His head nodded ever so slightly. "It would be best if I had all four blades."

He ushered an innocent smile onto his face and, for a second, he did manage to look innocuous.

"Our alliance will prove to be a great advantage to you."

"Will it?" I asked, incredulous. "Alliance makes what you're offering seem innocent when in fact you're just issuing beautifully worded threats."

"Not at all." His voice was full of innocence. "Just as I was able to walk between here and the Veil, there are others who can do the same. If it were to be disclosed that Malific has a daughter and she's the key to releasing her—I wonder how long you'd live. That, Erin, is a threat."

That was the moment I gave in to the anger flooding me. I yanked the push dagger that I'd been fingering through my shirt. My lunge came in a flash of movement. Faster than I thought I could move I was upon him, going for his neck— the one place that would do the most damage with a blade so small.

The blast of magic hit me so hard in my chest I crashed into the chair behind me, toppling it over.

"Do not disappoint me, goddess, you will live to regret it," he growled. He was out the door by the time I'd come to my feet and grabbed my weapons. Dashing out the door after him, I was just in time to see him fly away. He was close enough for me to see the fiery rage that flushed his face and the daggerlike look that bore into me.

"I'd hoped we would be able to come to terms. I assure you, Erin, you do not want me as an enemy because your allies aren't strong enough to protect you. Must I remind you how you, the Alpha, and your witch fared against me in Dante's Forest?"

With that, he soared into the sky, his midnight wings a small eclipse of darkness in the bright sky.

Assassination is something you can't downplay as anything other than what it is: murder. My job caused me to live in the various shades of gray. I took things that weren't mine, but I always left money. I negotiated with and kept company with my share of miscreants. I had contacts who eavesdropped and gave me information I shouldn't have had. And yes, I'd poached things from other people. But there was no ambiguity about assassination.

Assassinating Ian was something I kept thinking about. He had a way to release Malific without me going to the Veil. The threat was an act of aggression and I had every right to retaliate, right? There wouldn't be any consequences, and I'd be able to keep my magic because I was from the Veil but had been taken from there.

How was he going to do it? Fae couldn't do spells, so it couldn't be a spell. Perhaps a magical object. I'd been vocal about STF policies on illegal magic objects but was starting to rethink my stance on that. There were things out there that shouldn't be accessible.

I examined the shuriken. It was coated with enough blood to make it easy to track Ian. I'd placed the rifle in my bag. Should I take a rifle, a gun, or a sword? Old school. Sir, you have offended me, now it is time to die.

Fuck.

Madison sat across from me, nursing a glass of water but looking in need of something stronger after I told her what I'd learned about myself, Mephisto's suggestion about getting rid of Ian, and me considering doing it myself. Her breathing was slow and measured and she appeared to have given up on blinking. Putting the glass on the table, she dropped her head back and looked at the ceiling.

Calling Madison shouldn't have been my first choice. It should have been Cory. He could do the locating spell, find Ian, and we could be done with things. He would have groused about it, made a half-hearted attempt to dissuade me while walking to the car.

I knew why I called Madison. Part of me didn't want to do it.

She rooted around in her bag for a moment, showed me her badge, and then tossed it aside. We knew that I was talking to Madison my sister rather than Madison the STF agent.

"Do you think he's lying? I still find it hard to believe that a spell protects them against being killed," she asserted. "What if it's not true? That's a hell of an urban legend to propagate."

I was not expecting that line of questioning.

A tight half smile was all I could manage. "I think it's the truth. It rings true. Shifters in the Veil are immune to magic and then there are Mephisto and the Others. They clearly have magic. I'm able to borrow it from Mephisto without consequences, and they can stop me from borrowing their magic. The people from the Veil are different."

"Or it could just be that Mr. Mysterious and his cadre of peculiar friends are different."

"I have to stop Ian. Him being alive will have dire consequences not just for the fae, but the city and me."

Madison stopped mid-transition from standing. I assumed she was on her way to get alcohol. I didn't blame her. She was having her liminal periods, too. Before, I was the woman she considered a sister who she'd risked her career for to clean up a mess. The person she called to bounty hunt and retrieve stolen goods when she wanted to be discreet. And now I was so much more. It had to be hard to process.

"You can't do that. What happened to going with Mephisto to the auction?"

"I went to Dante's Forest with Asher and you saw how that ended."

"Okay, but at least go. You already admitted that he seems to have access to things others don't. Go tomorrow and I'll go through our inventory again."

Concern eclipsed her face, the rigid frown remaining even with the noticeable effort she put into relaxing it. Her expression spoke the words she wouldn't say. If I were Malific's daughter, was there a part of me like her? Could this change me? Would I change? Or maybe I was projecting.

"Go tomorrow and we figure out things from there."

She grabbed her badge and palmed it. I was no longer speaking with Madison my sister but Captain Madison Calloway. "I don't need to confiscate your weapons, do I?"

I shook my head.

"Erin," she entreated.

"No, you don't. I won't do anything reckless."

"Promise?"

I ran my hands over my face. I couldn't break a promise to her. "I promise I'll go to the auction and from there, I'll decide what to do next." That was the best I could give her.

CHAPTER 21

$\mathcal{M}$ephisto stayed at the threshold of the door and looked—no—stared at me. Face indecipherable. His dark gaze traveled from the strappy silver heels to the exposed leg that slipped from the slit of the blush-colored dress. It ran along the planes of the straps of the body-accentuating bodice with the plunging neckline with pleated details along the chest. Roved over the bracelet on my right wrist. Then it breezed up to my neck adorned by a single teardrop diamond necklace. It was one of the few pieces I owned that wasn't an impressive replica of expensive jewelry. He was still staring when I grabbed my purse off the table.

"Ah, so you have been to one of these events before," he said, giving the dress a final look. "I was expecting jeans, or t-shirt and leggings."

The dress looked appropriate, but I was fully aware of where I would be and the type of people who attended these events. The slit in my dress allowed ease of movement and the ability to run freely if necessary. The knotted design of my bracelets were sharp enough that they could be wrapped around my knuckles and used as a weapon. My heels were tall, sharp, and, despite the sorrow it would bring me to do so, could be broken off and used as another weapon.

Mephisto's eyes went to my purse that was larger than appropriate for the dress and had even more weaponry goodness in them. "You know your purse will be searched and all weapons confiscated?"

I didn't know that. In silence, I picked up the smaller purse I had discarded. A smile tugged at my lips as I took the wallet, keys, phone, and a Taser out of the larger purse, which opened too wide, revealing a gun, a dagger, and electric pellets.

"Erin." Mephisto had eased his way in front of me. "What were you thinking? You can't believe they would let you in with all of that?"

I nodded.

"These events are quite exclusive, and I've worked for years to become a regular attendee. I trust you won't do anything to jeopardize that."

Holding his intense gaze was difficult because I knew exactly what he was implying.

He went on. "I have your word that whatever objects are won will stay in the possession of the owner? No reports to Madison."

There was anonymous reporting. I'd prefer that Madison received credit for the retrieval, but an item being confiscated was the most important thing.

"Erin," Mephisto repeated, his tone cool and professional, "I realize that you live in a perpetual state of conflict of interests with you being so close to Madison and her role at STF, but I need your word that what happens at the auction stays there. The magical objects and artifacts of the owners aren't your business to tell."

The set of his jaw made it clear that he was prepared to leave me where I was. He could walk away from this and be just fine.

I nodded. It wasn't enough. "Fine. You have my word that anything that occurs at the auction will remain there."

"Very well. Do you have any weapons in that purse? No matter how small it is, they will search it."

"Um . . ." I gave him a look, hesitated, and said, "No."

I didn't sound convincing and his gaze dropped to my small clutch purse. I opened it and placed the small thin daggers hidden in the lining of it on the table. Then I removed the credit card–shaped blade and the three small shuriken that I kept in the zipped compartment.

Mephisto's lips pursed into a tight line. "Are there more?"

I pulled out the four electric pellets. "These aren't really weapons; they're a distraction device. No more deadly than me pointing my finger and saying, 'Hey, look over there!'"

"Then that's what you'll have to do. Please remove them." He shook his head. "What do you think happens at these events?"

"You had shifter security detail at your last auction." I reminded him of the time I arrived at his home after discovering that he didn't respond to my magic the way others did. It was his duo of shifters that took away my weapons.

His lips lifted into a miscreant smile. "It was necessary for that one. Are there any more weapons?" His gaze dropped to the stash of weapons on the table. "Should I check your person?" he asked in a low drawl, closing some distance between us. Enveloped in his magic, I moved even closer. Another magical seduction I was falling for.

Mephisto stopped a few feet away. He started to push his fingers through his hair but stopped. Probably didn't want to mess it up. Exhaling a slow breath, his gaze lingered on me for a long time.

"We should leave," he said finally, extending his hand to mine. It surprised both of us when I took it. His magic caressed my fingers, a warm tingle flitting over my skin.

"Stop it," I hissed. Mephisto's deep chuckle reverberated off the walls of the apartment. The feeling disappeared.

On the way out we passed Ms. Harp, ignoring Asher's request, holding her cane. Usually she went to great lengths to avoid eye contact, hoping to avoid any conversations with "Chatty Cathys," but this time she didn't. Giving me a cool inquiring look, her eyes dropped to my hand nestled in Mephisto's. Was that a snarl?

Whatever it was, she made a valiant effort to smile and succeeded in creating a rigid line that barely lifted the corners of her lips.

"If you speak with Asher, do you mind asking him to give me a call?" she asked me, her voice dulcet. If it wasn't for the flicker of dark mischief that passed over her face, it would have seemed like an innocent question. "I meant to give him something before he left your home the other morning."

"Of course," I responded in a voice that matched hers.

Touché. I see what you're doing. Bravo, Ms. Harp. Well done. She was the queen of noncompliance, but she was definitely a fan of Asher. She couldn't even give Mephisto a proper glare because her attention kept dropping to our clutched hands.

"He's such a nice man. I can't believe he spent all that time with me when he could have been with you. I hate that I took up so much of his time."

"I'll definitely relay the message." Pulling my hand from Mephisto's, which seemingly was too distracting for her to continue walking, I opened my purse and took out my phone. "I can give you his number again, if you like." I gave her a look that told her I knew exactly what she was doing.

"I have it." The tension that eased out of her was disconcerting. She didn't change like a shifter, but her demeanor toward me with Mephisto was befitting of a pack member. I would have to visit her to explain my relationship with Asher, because clearly she had the wrong idea.

Turning to leave, Ms. Harp's sharp glower landed on Mephisto's hand that was lightly pressed against my back, leading me to the car.

He leaned in, whispering against my ear, "I see you and Asher have made up, Ms. Jensen. He's spending the night now. This explains a few things."

"Ms. Harp is quite the fan of Asher," I explained.

"I can tell. You seem to be a fan as well." His deep voice was professionally neutral but his jaw clenched. It relaxed once he realized I noticed.

Shrugging, I said, "Not really. We just understand each other."

He nodded his head in consideration but said nothing else. Once in the car, he gave me an intense appraising look. "Do we understand each other?" he asked softly, searching my face.

"Sometimes." It was the only answer I could offer. Not to be evasive but because I just didn't know the answer.

Minutes into the drive, Mephisto seemed to be pondering something. My lips curled because I suspected what it was. I sighed and said, "Asher spent the night with me. He stayed on the sofa. He came over the night before I went to the Veil because he was worried about me going into it."

Tension eased from Mephisto's face and he let out a soft breath. "Then I was right. Asher and I tend to have the same interests."

I was surprised to see familiar motorcycles trailing us, occasionally speeding up to the side of the car to give Mephisto an impatient look, obviously not keen on driving at the posted speed limit. After three urges to go faster, they sped past, their bodies bent over the bikes, pushing the machines to speeds that would likely earn them a ticket or worse. Mephisto looked wistful as they zoomed past and disappeared into the night.

"They'll be attending?"

"Not the auction. You're only allowed one guest. They're acting as security detail."

"Another auction with the 'fine people of the city,'" I teased, bringing up the very term he used to describe them when they were targeted by Maddox and his group. "I thought you preferred to work with shifters."

"I do. But I think it is wise to be more cautious. I'm confident Elizabeth's binding worked but not as confident that Ian won't find a way to undo it. He's more tenacious now. Previous failures have led to a desperation that has made him more formidable than in the past."

"You believe he might show up at the auction."

"I don't know, but it's better to be prepared."

That's when I noticed he had his sword on the back seat. Saw the intricate markings of the handle.

I really wished I had my weapons.

Winding up the pathway to the home, I didn't think of an upscale building where I needed to dress up, but more that I was being led to a gothic mansion and that jeans, sneakers, and a taste for horror would be more appropriate. Faint iridescent lights provided an ambient glow to the sparse and neatly aligned trees flanking the road. The road remained poorly lit despite the silvery halo of light from the moon. It wasn't comforting that the road led us to a small parking lot with few cars.

"This feels like the beginning of a story that would make the news."

"Oh, Erin, you do have a vivid imagination." He got out of the car and waited. I thought having Kai and Clay there was a little excessive, but when they pulled up to the side of the car, I did feel more comfortable.

Based on their conversation, I gathered Simeon had plans with Victoria. I suspected he had plans with Pearl, but that just sounded too weird to say. It didn't bother me. It would make Victoria comfortable and decrease the number of disparaging calls and texts I received from her. And keep me from having to come up with creative and kind ways of telling her she was an overdramatic, high-maintenance, self-indulgent, terrible client. There are only so many ways to word that and not sound rude.

Leading to the building, tightly twined vines created a darkened tunnel, with only hints of light from the moon breaking through.

They were going for an image. I'd been to several auctions. The most elaborate was in the living room of a Victorian home. The shadiest, in a warehouse where they hadn't even bothered to turn on the heat. In the middle of a cold room, we bid while competing against the noise of the antiquated space heaters. This auction was a presentation. An artful, dramatic display of magic and menace, and the people approaching the house seemed to be enjoying the pageantry.

Some stopped to take in the graphite-colored bricks, the turret, the similarly styled columns in the front of the home and the gargoyles. I halted too, but to roll my eyes. You don't do something like this and not expect at least one person to be exasperated.

"Sometimes, it's the experience that is the most exciting thing. Presentation is what intrigues." Mephisto was dressed in variations of black except for his watch, which I suspected was platinum. Onyx tailored suit, opened to show a patterned vest. Midnight slacks. Indigo hue of his midnight hair. Glint of his deep-charcoal eyes. Mephisto also was an "experience" and a "presentation" that one or two passersby were enjoying.

Hey, lady, double takes aren't supposed to be obvious. You look while approaching, and when you're next to them, you do another look. Don't do a stop-the-traffic look. It's tacky . . . and very obvious.

Mephisto looked at me, then took a sidelong look at the woman who did the poorly executed double take.

He extended his hand for me to take hold of it. Looking at the woman and back at his extended hand, I gave a second to consider how petty it was to take it. Then I took a step onto the throne of pettiness and took it.

The muted light and rich, dark-blue walls of the interior kept with the outside theme. Breaks in the deep colors were made by light art, sculptures, and vases.

Mephisto released my hand to offer me a glass of champagne as we followed one of the hosts to our seats. The room seemed out of place, although the brightly illuminated space made it easy to see the table of the first group of items for sale.

It didn't take long for the bidding to start, and four items in, I appreciated my policy of not taking people at their word in their name of an object or what it did. Twice, an object was called by a secondary name and given a secondary use. Everything had a secondary use, even regular things in the human world, and usually the secondary use wasn't the most efficient. The same was true of magical objects. I wasn't sure if it was done to entice the audience and garner higher bids or because of a general lack of knowledge. Mephisto won three of the four items he bid for. I couldn't figure out the theme of his acquisitions.

When the next collection of items was brought out, my breath caught. I clenched my hands together, trying not to react. Inconspicuously, I looked around at the other attendees to gauge their interest. Were they simply interested in acquiring exquisite powerful objects or did they know what this item was? There weren't unlimited funds for me to bid with, but for the Xios, the royals and Asher had approved an amount that could run a small town for a couple of months. This wasn't the Xios, however; it was something even better. A Nuli.

When evoked, a Nuli stored magic, and I couldn't think of a more fitting punishment for Ian. It might not remove his mark, but it would render him magicless.

That there were people selling something so dangerous annoyed me. Because of how dangerous Nulis were, the STF had destroyed all five that existed. Was this one that they didn't know about?

I'd mull that over later.

When the auctioneer brought forward the burgundy palm-size teardrop stone with the gold sigils running along the side, he said, "This is a Cante." *Not even close.* "It is used to allow you to travel. Just envision a place of interest and it will take you there. You'll travel like a Master vampire." *No, it won't.*

It did garner some interest. I bid low, giving myself room to increase the bid if necessary. At the half million mark, all but one other bidder remained. The woman who had given Mephisto the second look tossed me a sharp glare, warning me off. I gave it right back to her. The Nuli was mine, but as the bidding inched higher, I wasn't sure. I sent dirty looks in her direction as if the intensity of them would have the power to keep her hand down.

Almost at my limit, I considered the money in my account. Could I go over it? Surely they would reimburse me. This wasn't a "I'll pay you later" situation. Transfers had to be made that night, and if not, the item went to the losing bidder.

Mephisto's admirer finally lost interest. The auctioneer

was making a last call to increase my bid when Mephisto made an offer that I couldn't begin to better.

"Why are you doing this? I had the highest bid," I hissed through clenched teeth.

"And now I have it," he said, his voice just as low as mine but lacking the cold steel and poorly suppressed hostility. His aloof demeanor just added to my anger. Beside shooting glares at Mephisto, I waited for another object that would be as good as the Nuli. Nothing. During the last bid, I leaned over to him.

"Did you purchase that for me?" I asked in a hopeful whisper. I was confident Asher and the royals would buy it from him to get rid of Ian, but would he sell?

His lips brushed against my ear as he whispered back, "Erin Katherine Jensen, how highly do you think of yourself? No, I know what this is. And I want it."

After getting a sharp look from the auctioneer, we both quieted. Humming with frustration, I couldn't wait to get out of there. Mephisto couldn't be the person who stood between me and getting rid of Ian.

He could be reasoned with, I tried to convince myself. *But could he?*

Over seven figures spent and we walked out of the auction carrying a plain black bag. Whether it fit the theme of the house or not, when a person spends that sort of money, they get a tote, a pretty box, or something that can be reused. Not a tacky black sack. I had to fixate on the absurdity of the bag to keep my focus off Mephisto. No emotions were displayed on the defined planes of his jawline, the wings of his cheeks, or the straight line that his full supple lips formed.

The bag in one hand, he kept the one closest to me free, his fingers brushing my hand ever so lightly in a request to hold it. There wasn't an audience to see me ascend my throne of pettiness and I was so livid, I spent the walk trying to crush his fingers with my hold.

Satisfied with our safe return to the car, Kai drove off. Clayton studied my face, frowned, and looked at Mephisto.

"Everything okay, M?"

Mephisto's voice held a note of amusement. "I do believe Erin is upset with me. It will pass."

You want to bet a Nuli on that?

Clayton didn't seem too concerned about me being troubled; I suspected residual displeasure from me attempting to take his magic. I needed to apologize, but he didn't give me the opportunity.

"I'm sure things will work out." Clayton's easy mien was gone. He backed his bike away, turned around, and without another word, he was gone too.

"What the hell was that, M!" I blurted the moment we were in the car.

He leaned toward me, the delectation in his study of me just exasperating my frustration.

"Don't call me that. That was an auction, Ms. Jensen. I'm sure you're familiar with them. It's where people bid on objects they want."

"You knew I wanted it."

"You were there to get the Xios, correct? It wasn't there, and for that, I am regretful."

"The Cante is close to it. It might work." The misdirection was worth a try.

Based on his raised brow and half smile, it didn't.

"You and I both know what it is and how it can be used against Ian. I'm not opposed to you doing that. What I don't want is for Asher, Neri, or Adalia to have it."

"But if we don't destroy it after we take Ian's magic, it will still exist. If he ever gets hold of it, he can have his magic restored. And it's illegal as hell."

"True, to all of it. Are you saying you don't want it?"

"Yes, but—"

"That is the condition of its use. Once used, it will be returned to me. Madison or anyone from the STF will never know I have it. Are these rules you can abide by?" Giving me the full intensity of his gaze, he waited for an answer.

"Asher and the royals won't be happy about you not destroying it."

"Then you're rejecting the offer?"

"No, not at all."

"Good." There was something in his face as he turned from me to start the car. It made me think of his statement about not being wise when it came to me. Was this one of those times? Part of me expected Simeon, Clayton, or Kai to pull up and give him a withering look. To remind him that all decisions regarding me had to be done by committee or something. But it was just the two of us and he was doing me a favor that would end the Ian situation.

He pulled out of the driveway, the only sound in the car soft music on the radio.

"Thank you," I said after moments of silence.

"It's not about cruelty to you, but survival for me."

"That's the problem. If you tell me what you're trying to survive, I can help."

"You will help, Erin Katherine Jensen. I believe you will."

"This is one sided. You have my name and I have the name you have chosen."

"I never asked for your name. You gave it freely. Something you should be more cautious about. Not the name but how it is said. I'm sure Cory has explained to you how important names are."

"I think they're more important to fae than most people. Is that why you protect yours? It's a fae thing?"

From his profile, I could see he was entertained by my line of questioning. "Satan, elf, and now fae. Do you have iron on you? Would you like me to test it?"

"That doesn't mean anything. Ian is immune to iron."

"True, but it isn't a natural immunity. He made a deal with a demon. I assure you that I've never made a deal with a demon."

"Okay, Satan, so a cross is your weakness."

He didn't respond. Maybe he found it too ridiculous to do so, but I added the snippet to the crumbs of information I was gathering about him and the Others.

"I assume you have the other necessary item needed for the spell?" he asked as he pulled up to my apartment.

I nodded. "Can we do it tonight? I'll call Cory."

"No, just the two of us. I can do the spell to invoke the Nuli. Just get Ian's blood. By tomorrow, Ian will be handled."

I couldn't believe that yesterday, I was prepared to kill Ian, and today, I was going to be able to render him magicless. I hadn't realized how heavily this had weighed on me until I felt unburdened.

"Give me a minute to get the shuriken," I said, reaching for the door.

His brow furrowed in dismay.

"It has his blood on it," I explained.

When Mephisto started to get out of the car, I shook my head, stopping him. "It won't take long. I'll be right back."

It was silly, but it would be quicker for me to run into the house, let Ms. Harp see me without Mephisto. I had a feeling she was keeping a close eye on when I returned and whether or not I was alone. Ms. Harp—Asher's unrequested spy.

With my keys in hand, I bounded toward my apartment making a promise to myself to be more careful with my blood. Most of the time I wasn't, although witches, fae, and mages were. Shifters weren't and neither were vampires. There weren't many spells that worked against their magic. But knowing what we were about to do reinforced how important it was.

Wind swooshed against my back and everything was

suddenly obscured by black wings. A shocked gasp escaped me and then a scream when I realized I was nearly thirty feet off the ground. The fabric of my dress bunched under me while Ian held me by the straps of the dress. Fearing they weren't going to hold much longer, or I was going to slip out of the dress and plummet to my death, I yelled.

"I'm going to fall!"

"Perhaps," he offered, releasing one strap.

Fear captured the next scream even after he grabbed hold of my arms. He did it so clumsily, I was sure I was going to slip. He was stronger than he looked but his muscles trembled when he soared even higher and let go of my arms. It's not life that flashes before your eyes when you think you're going to die, it's blinding panic and brief moments of darkness. I fell fast, grabbing for anything but finding nothing.

Arms wrapped around my waist and secured me against his chest.

"Better," he said. It wasn't to comfort me. He just didn't want to lose me before we got to our destination. My heart pounded in my chest and I blinked back tears.

"You betrayed me, emissary," he growled. Terrified that any movement would make him lose his grip, I remained silent. "The shifters are no longer under my control. You had something to do with that." He pushed the words out through clenched teeth, his voice hard and raspy.

"I'll talk to Neri and Adalia. Just give me a chance. I can't do anything here. You said that if I helped you remove your marks and become leader of the fae, they'd be left alone. What does it matter? I'll help you."

"It matters because you're lying," he said, descending so quickly toward a roof I understood why he had been able to catch me after letting go of me. Once we were closer, he dropped me. I hit the ground hard, awkwardly rolling to my feet and taking off my shoes in the process. The spikey three inches were all I had as weapons. When he landed, I charged at him with everything I had. Someone wielding shoes like dual sai made it hard to know how to respond. That was my advantage. The heel of one shoe dug hard into the forearm he put up to ward off the blow. I hit, pounded, and thrashed with the full force of my rage and fear. It was all I had, because if I gave him a chance to retaliate, I was a goner.

Accepting the blow to his left arm, the force of magic burst from him and hit me in my stomach, sending me back to land just a few inches from the edge of the roof. I scanned the area, looking for an exit. I could hear an invocation coming from somewhere on the roof. Moments later I spotted the Immortalis. He eased in my direction, his hands moving fluidly. His fingers twisted and crooked in strange angles, hooks, and shapes. Magic flooded the air. I looked down. There wasn't any way I'd survive the drop.

I got a glimpse of something black in Ian's hands and recalled him saying that he could release Malific without me going into the Veil. Panic made forming a plan harder. Who was the biggest threat, Ian or the Immortalis? I could stop the spell, but Immortalis were immune to the kiss. I wasn't sure about Ian, although his efforts to keep his distance was a good sign.

Rocks, debris, and all the crud on the roof dug into my feet as I sprinted to Ian, crashing into him. He struggled against me. It wasn't about winning pretty; it was about winning. His face reddened and tears formed when I hit him in the groin. I went for the arm where I saw the black object. Taking his magic would make him more amenable and I'd have access to magic. Problem was, the Immortalis were immune to all magic. I wasn't immune to theirs. I hovered over Ian, whispering the words of power. He was frantically turning his head to avoid it, but once the words left me, they ensnared him and his body relaxed, melting against the roof in a state of in-between. His hands relaxed and the object in his hand rolled a few feet away.

I started to move toward it when there was a shift in the atmosphere followed by a dank and toxic feel that overtook the immediate area. I turned to see the Immortalis Wynd in next to me. I also saw the knife he plunged into my side. Choking on my breath, my hand shot out a surge of magic that hit him without any effect. I looked at my hand, which had turned red, and swallowed back the pain. Adrenaline wasn't enough to numb it. Especially when he twisted the knife before yanking it out.

My vision blurring, I fell forward and dragged my body over Ian's stilled body, going for the object that had fallen from Ian's hand, while trying to keep pressure on my side to staunch the bleeding. The Immortalis rushed forward and scooped it up. I clawed at his hand but it wasn't enough. Then I used my right hand, crimson with my blood, and he willingly opened his hand to let me touch it. Satisfaction swept over his face as my blood covered the object. He whispered something. Smoke wisps rose, forming a diaphanous figure I couldn't make out. A bird? Eagle? No. A raven. The raven spread into a vaporous cloud that moved over me, covering me. My breathing slowed to short gasps. I slumped over, trying to suck in breath and push it out.

Breathe. Breathe. Breathe. My body seemed to have forgotten how to perform the most basic function. I blinked once and the Immortalis wasn't there. Maybe I closed my eyes. I wasn't quite sure. It was so hard to keep them open.

"Erin," said a voice as a man slowly descended in front of me, glorious cerulean wings spreading out and commanding the area around him. When he leaned down, I could see the detail of the wings, the many hues of blue. Familiar magic breezed off him, not nearly as frenetic as before but definitely his distinctive brand.

"K . . . K . . ." Darkness dragged me under. The last thing I heard was Kai telling me I couldn't die.

I was really trying not to.

CHAPTER 22

I awoke in a room that definitely wasn't mine. The bed was too large, the mattress too firm, and the space nearly three times the size of my bedroom. I'd stayed there before. Soft-gray walls, textured abstract art on the walls, and carpet that felt just as plush as it looked.

"You're finally up," Cory said, rushing over to me from the seat across the room near the window. His voice was rough and heavy with concern.

"Hi," I whispered.

He hugged me so tight, I let out a small whimper, not having realized how much pain I was still in. When he released me, I lifted my shirt and inspected the scar left by the knife wound.

"I have a scar."

"Yeah, you have a scar," he said softly. His hand caressed the side of my face before he hugged me again, careful to do it more gently.

Scanning the room I saw a Kindle, a phone, and a small overnight bag in the corner.

"How long have I been here?"

"Three days. You woke up for maybe two minutes, two days ago."

"You've been here the whole time?"

"Just two and a half days. You were missing for half a day and when I hadn't heard from you, I asked Ms. Harp if she'd seen you. She told me you were with Mephisto. She definitely isn't Team Mephisto. I was going to try to get in touch with him when he called to tell me you were here. Madison already knows. I've been giving her daily updates and she stops by for a couple of hours."

"That explains a lot." I covered my mouth. "I need a shower and to brush my teeth."

"I was going to suggest that, but it seemed kind of rude."

Laughing made my raw throat sore. I took a long drink from the bottle of water Cory handed me. Assuming the bag placed by the dresser was mine, courtesy of Cory, I hoisted it and went into the bathroom and was reminded that I was stabbed three days ago.

Looking in the mirror, even if I didn't feel like I had been asleep for three days, my reflection certainly showed it. My face was pallid and sallow all at once, there were dark rings around my eyes, my lips were chapped, and my hair was in tangles. I could only look at myself for the few minutes it took to brush my teeth. I stood in the shower, letting the warm water wash over me as I went over the last things I could recall. Kai had wings. Beautiful blue wings. I had Ian's magic—or at least I did have it. I gave an experimental flick of my finger: nothing. I made four more failed attempts. His magic hadn't stayed with me long.

I had been stabbed; the scar on my side attested to that. After showering and washing my hair, I dressed in a shirt and leggings, my body moving better with some of the stiffness gone. The scent of grapefruit from my shampoo and cool melon from my body wash just made me hungrier.

By the time I returned to the room, the bed had been

made, which was a pity because I wanted to crawl back into it and sleep for another day or so. Showering took more out of me than I expected.

"I need to get something to eat."

I started for the door, but Cory stopped me.

"Stay. I'll let the cook know you're hungry. I'm sure he'll prepare something you'll like." He stopped. "I never thought I'd say that seriously." He made an attempt at a smile, but it waned and faltered. "I need to let M know you're awake."

"He doesn't like to be called that. I think only Clayton gets that privilege."

"I'd let him call me C," Cory admitted.

"Oh, stop!" I chided, grabbing the pillow off the bed to toss at him. But that seemed to take more energy than I had. "He's a pretty cool guy."

"Yeah. He is."

My eyes narrowed and I shot him a look.

"I'm agreeing with you."

"Stop agreeing with me."

"Well, at least you're back to normal. So sweet and charming . . . not snarky and feisty for no apparent reason." This time he managed a wide smile.

Cory was hurried when he returned, closing the door behind me and taking a seat on the bed next to me.

"We don't have a lot of time. Tell me what you remember."

Culling through everything that happened before things went bad that night, I told him, ending with, "I thought I was going to die. Oh, and Kai has wings."

"Of course he does. Why not?" Cory waved his hand dismissively as if that information was added to an ongoing list of unusual things. "I think you died," he went on. "I don't mean, your heart stopped for a minute and then it started back up with the miracle of modern medicine type of dead. I think you died and they brought you back."

Automatically my lips lifted into a dismissive smirk. "Okay," I scoffed.

He leaned in closer. "I've been here since he called me and I couldn't stay in the room all day, so I . . ."

"Snooped," I offered when he seemed to be having difficulty finding the right words.

"*Explored.* How can you not? He has a beautiful garden and woods with not only deer but an okapi? Who is this man and why does he have one of those?"

"Simeon gave it to him as a gift."

His eyes squinted. "The one who can speak to animals?"

I nodded.

"Yeah, that's about right. I was . . . exploring and I thought I heard one of them ask 'how long was she' but they never finished. Tall, dark, and fake name came out of the room and asked if I was lost. He was ever so kind to escort me back to this room."

"How do you know they were going to say dead?"

"Because before that I heard them mention a Tactu Mortem that was destroyed. I searched everywhere and there's no information about it. But if that's Latin, it has to do with death."

"I think it means 'touch of death.'" It made me remember the smoke raven that cloaked me, the inability to breathe, and the look of satisfaction that overtook the Immortalis when my blood touched the object.

"Died." I pressed my finger to my neck as if expecting to find a vampire bite or something. There weren't any marks. It wasn't very hard for me to believe that it had happened. It didn't feel like I was going to make it and apparently, I didn't.

I moistened my lips but that wasn't enough. I needed more; my mouth felt like the Sahara. Noticing my searching eyes, Cory got up and retrieved his bottle of water and gave it to me. I drained it.

A light knock at the door had Cory snapping his mouth shut.

The black that Mephisto was wearing seemed ironic. Or maybe appropriate. I had no idea.

"Cory, I'll make sure Erin gets home," Mephisto said, offering Cory a tight smile, his voice professionally neutral and firm and leaving no room for discussion. I could see the challenge rising in Cory. He looked at me, saw my look to let it go, and with obvious reluctance, he conceded.

"Call me if you need anything," he whispered, giving me a gentler hug than the first or second, but he clung to me for longer and I did, too.

After Mephisto escorted Cory out, presumably to prevent any more explorations, he returned to let me know that dinner was ready. He regarded me with concern as I slowly made my way down the stairs. It wasn't surprising to see that we were the only ones in the kitchen.

I was pleasantly surprised to see that the plate he placed in front of me had just a thin slice of chicken breast and a large serving of mac and cheese with crumbles of bacon. I wasn't complaining because no part of that meal didn't appeal to me. It was unexpected. Seeing Mephisto with the same thing is what left me awestruck. "Comfort food," he said.

I had one glass of water, another with juice while he had a glass of white wine. What do you pair with mac and cheese?

"Kai has wings," I announced. The water wasn't enough and I definitely had a feeling I was going to need more than juice based on the air of heaviness that surrounded Mephisto. His magic was subdued, but I wasn't sure if it was because it had been depleted or he was doing it. Bringing someone back to life probably could do that.

"Simeon speaks to animals." I continued on with my list. He nodded once.

"You can Wynd and perform strong defensive magic." Those were things Simeon had said about Mephisto's magic when I asked about the differences. I knew there was more.

He nodded again. "We can all perform magic. A great deal of it. When I loan you magic, I'm significantly weakened."

"Clayton?"

"He has weather and oceanic abilities."

Not used to Mephisto being so forthcoming, I found myself at a loss for the right questions. They turned in my head but there was so much I needed to know, my mind was slow processing it.

Mephisto stood and I gawked after him, wondering if this was how he was going to end the conversation. But he simply went to the cabinet for a wine glass and placed it in front of me. He poured a few ounces and I bent my finger, signaling for him to keep it coming.

Gulping down half of it, I asked the simplest of questions. "What happened to Ian?"

He exhaled a sharp breath and all the emotions on his face melded together into something I couldn't decipher.

"He moved so fast," he whispered, his tone remorseful. As if he'd failed me.

"Ian's very swift and precise in flight," I offered. Skills I'd have lauded if they weren't constantly being used against me.

"Was. He *was* swift and precise in flight. He didn't make it." His dark and baleful look suggested Ian had help being ushered into the afterlife.

Several moments of stiff silence passed before I could ask another question.

"How did you know where to find me?"

"I didn't. Clayton and Kai weren't too far away, so I instructed Kai first to search for you by air. I went into your apartment to find the shuriken to do a locating spell."

Remembering how easily he found blood on a shingle when he'd been robbed by dragons, I didn't have to ask how he found it. Reluctant to do magic in public for fear of leaving a magical fingerprint that could be identified, he probably did the locating spell in my apartment where he couldn't be seen.

Waving my fingers, I gave Ian's magic another try but wasn't surprised when nothing happened this time either.

"I took his magic. Why don't I still have it? I should still have access to it."

"You wouldn't." He took another long draw from his glass. "You lost his magic when you died. It happened moments after Kai retrieved you."

It felt different coming from Mephisto. More real. Scarier. A breath expelled from me in a whoosh.

I definitely expected a different reveal being told something like that. How do you broach the subject? What's the right way to say, "Hey, by the way, you died"?

"And… did you… how long?… was I completely dead?"

"There's no such thing as half dead. You're either dead or you're not. You were dead. By the time we got you to the house, you had been dead for fifteen or twenty minutes."

Cory was right; it wasn't one of those situations where your heart and breathing stop for a few minutes. I was dead for not just a few minutes, but over ten minutes.

Screw it, I didn't care about formalities or rules of etiquette or propriety. I finished my glass. Filled it again and drank the rest. The bottle was finished by the time I thought I was ready to ask more questions. Mephisto left the table and returned with two more bottles. He couldn't possibly think that would be enough.

"I died," I finally said. "And you brought me back."

"Yes, we couldn't let you stay dead. Now more than ever because your death led to Malific's release. Now you're the only one who will be able to stop her."

A cool chill moved through me as I recalled the satisfied

look on the Immortalis's face. It made sense now. When I touched the black object in his hand, it must have linked me to Malific's prison, and when I died, she was released.

Taking a sip from his glass, he placed it back on the table. A dark cast over his face, steely resolve pulled his lips into a tight line. He clasped his hands behind his head and silence stretched thin as he studied me.

"Erin, you are so much more than I expected you to be. Now I think it's time for you to know who we are."

MESSAGE TO THE READER

Thank you for choosing *Silverfall* from the many titles available to you. My goal is to create an engaging world, compelling characters, and an interesting experience for you. I hope I've accomplished that. Reviews are very important to authors and help other readers discover our books. Please take a moment to leave a review. I'd love to know your thoughts about the book.

For notifications about new releases, *exclusive* contests and giveaways, and cover reveals, please sign up for my mailing list at McKenzieHunter.com.

Made in the USA
Columbia, SC
01 May 2024

35148233R00167